# DOCTOR WHO

## GENOCIDE

## PAUL LEONARD

**BBC BOOKS**

Published by BBC Books
an imprint of BBC Worldwide Publishing
BBC Worldwide Ltd, Woodlands, 80 Wood Lane
London W12 0TT

First published 1997
Copyright © Paul Leonard 1997
The moral right of the author has been asserted

Original series broadcast on the BBC
Format © BBC 1963
Doctor Who and TARDIS are trademarks of the BBC

ISBN 0 563 40572 4
Imaging by Black Sheep, copyright © BBC 1997

Printed and bound in Great Britain by Mackays of Chatham
Cover printed by Belmont Press Ltd, Northampton

# ACKNOWLEDGEMENTS

First and foremost I would like to thank the usual crowd who read and made suggestions about this book: Barb Drummond, Mark Leyland, Jim Mortimore, Nick Walters, Simon Lake and George Wills.

Then there are all the people who had to put up with my irritability, writer's panic, and general lack of availability for the last six months or so: my mother, Hazel Bunting, and my stepfather, John; Nadia Lamarra; Barb Drummond (again); Jim Mortimore (again); Damon Burt, Patrick and Martine Walling, Helen Butterworth and Jim Dowsett (good luck at Oxford!). Many thanks to all these, and any I've forgotten to mention. And thanks to Frances Cherry and all the others at Victoria Wine for general niceness, swapped shifts, and a different sort of working environment!

Finally, I must thank Nuala Buffini and Steve Cole at the BBC for their extreme patience and understanding, as well as their many helpful suggestions concerning the plot, the text and continuity matters. Any remaining errors are mine... all mine... ha!

The alien figure on the low bed was little more than a skeleton. The skin was shadowed, pinched – the eyes seemed welded shut. The tan-coloured fur on the alien's head was dull, listless. Its clothes hung loosely: velvet, satin, and a coarser artificial fibre.

Mauvril watched the dying figure for a long time, shivering in the cold air of the cell. Finally she spoke.

'I know that you can't forgive me. I don't expect it. I know that you had a special relationship with humans, and to see them wiped out after all your efforts, and all your love – that must be a tragedy for you.

'And I know, too, that you're right not to forgive me. I haven't cleaned my soul, only made it dirtier. I don't even know whether I've succeeded in saving my people from slavery and extinction. If what you have told me is true, then I have failed.

'But I want you to understand me.

'We're both going to die here, so it really doesn't make any difference now, what we've done, whether we can forgive each other. I just want to know the truth: if you had been me – if you had been in my situation, on my world, and the humans had done to your people what they did to mine – would you have destroyed them? Would you have been without mercy, would you have destroyed all humans, for all time?

'Please tell me. I need to know. I need to know if it was possible to have acted in a different way.

'Doctor? Can you understand me?

'Are you still alive?'

# PROLOGUE

The smell of the wind had changed.

Walking Man knew it as soon as he woke; perhaps even before that. Strangeness had haunted his dreams, lingered into his waking.

He stood, the movement as silent as he could make it. It was still night; no dawn stirred in the east. But something had disturbed him. He sniffed the dark, cold air blowing over the ridge.

An animal... No. It was more like the smell of the air before a thunderstorm. But there was no storm nearby: the steady wind and star-filled sky told him that.

A shuffling sound in the darkness. A faint, uneasy bleating. The sheep could sense it, too.

Walking Man took a cautious step on the soft grass. Whatever it was, this was a *big* thing. Big enough to fill the air with its scent, and far enough away to be silent. As big as a cloud, perhaps.

Walking Man felt a cold, glassy touch of fear at his throat. But there was nothing he could do, nothing he could fight or run away from. In the darkness, he could only wait.

So he wrapped his buckskin cloak around himself tightly, and waited.

When it came, the first light of dawn showed him nothing. The pasture slopes, grey in the dimness, traced with pale silver dew. The sheep, light shadows, dark faces moving, slowly waking. The mountain a hunched back against the sky. Everything was as it should be, but...

The sheep were uneasy.

And the scent in the wind was still there.

Alert, Walking Man stood, peering down into the valley. The wind had stilled, and a thin mist pooled there, its edges dappled with dark beadings of trees. The village…

There was a light in the village. A light that you could see through the mist.

*Fire!*

The shock jolted through his body, set his heart jumping in his chest. He was running before he could even begin to think, running across the cold dewy turf, leaving his sheep, leaving rabbit furs he had prepared while watching his flock in the High Pastures, leaving his pack with his copper axe and his totem. Nothing mattered but getting to the village. Nothing mattered but reaching his wife, her sister, his brother-by-marriage, and their children. He imagined he could hear their screams as he ran, imagined the hut filled with smoke and terror, the wood burning in the wind…

*I have to get there.*

His feet found the stone of the familiar path down, the stone that was smooth because so many Walking Men and their sheep had used the path, season after season, as they moved from pasture to village and back again. The shoulders of the mountain rose around him, hiding the village.

About halfway, at Fern River Gorge, where there was a view of the Low Pastures, he stopped. The sun was clear on the slice of hillside he could see through the end of the gorge. There was no smoke in the air. The village was not burning.

But the smell was there. The hour-before-a-storm smell. The impossible smell, impossibly strong now.

He slowed his steps, slowed his breathing, trying to

think. The boys should be here in the gorge by this time, setting their traps for the water rats and their nets for the fish in the slippery green water. But there was no one. Nothing. Only the river, talking softly to itself in the cold morning air.

Walking Man opened his mouth to call out, then changed his mind.

He advanced along the edges of the gorge, moving slowly, softly, as if he were hunting or tracking a stray sheep from the flock, using the narrow paths weaving between the scrub pines and steep rock walls, the wolf paths that smelled of pine and carnivore dung.

At the end of the gorge, the paths ended in the cleared ground, the goat meadows, the damp earth where the children gathered mushrooms in the mornings, the fields where the old people grew their grain and carrots. He could see the village at last, the low, dark roofs over the dew-silvered swathe of grass.

And he could see the source of the light.

It *was* fire. And yet it wasn't.

It was like a tree, burning. But there was no smoke: only dim, cold flames creeping along the branches, lake-blue and summer-leaf green, moving around huge leaves that were bright orange, as if it were autumn.

But a *tree*?

There had been no tree on the morning he had taken the sheep to the High Pasture, not many days ago. No tree could grow so fast. And no tree he had ever seen before looked anything like this one.

And why were there no children in the fields, gathering the mushrooms?

For a moment, Walking Man wondered if he had

entered the spirit world while he had slept. He looked up, checking the skies for the Eagle, his totem animal.

No. If the Eagle was guiding him, it was from far away. This was still the human world.

Silent as a hunter, he moved across the familiar meadow where he had played as a child, his eyes on the strange tree. As the curve of the land fell away, he could see the village, the rough circle of the lodges, the people kneeling in the open space between them.

He became aware of another smell, a smell like the hay he stored to feed the sheep in winter. And there was something dark beneath the coloured branches of the tree.

Something *alive*.

Walking Man crouched down, then stretched out and lay flat on the grass.

Was it Ox? It was the size of an ordinary ox, such as the hunters might find in the forest, but it was black, and its head was wrong – raised up in front of it, with a long, thin snout like a wolf.

And it had *arms*.

His wife's totem was the Ox. Had *she* died, then? But he could see her kneeling with the other villagers, the distinctive black wool trim on her cloak marking her as Walking Man's Woman.

The Ox, or whatever it was, spoke.

At least, it seemed like speech – it had the air of speech, the density of changing sounds – but it was like the speech of a foreign man, like that of the strangers who came to trade copper and had to speak to the villagers in signs. Walking Man couldn't understand a word of it.

The speech became urgent, angry, like the grunting of a beast. Walking Man saw the gleam of metal in the Ox's hand, felt the danger in the air – too late. Flame exploded around his wife's head. She gave one short gurgling scream, then fell to the ground. Her body thrashed for a moment, then was still.

Her head was black, like burnt meat. Walking Man could smell her flesh burning.

For a second, he remained frozen, then anger and grief got the better of his fear. He rose to a low crouch, darted forward, crossing the meadow, making for the nearest of the lodges.

He was only a dozen strides from the heavy wooden walls when the Ox saw him.

He saw the huge eye in the side of its head open, saw the blood-hatred there. What had his people done to offend the Ox? Had the hunters not killed oxen with proper respect? Had the traps been set wrongly?

There was no point in wondering about that now. The gleaming metal that had killed his wife was still in the spirit-animal's hand, and Walking Man could sense it readying the fire to kill him as it had killed his wife. He ducked, then dodged sideways, knowing he could not avoid a magical fire but not knowing what else to do.

The fire exploded behind him. He felt its breath, heard the curse of the Ox.

He stopped dead for an instant, waited, saw the fire explode ahead where he would have been if he'd kept running.

*Then* he ran, ran as he hadn't run for seasons, ran until he'd put the wood and hides of the lodge between him and the spirit-animal. He lay on the damp leafy earth behind the lodge for a moment, gasping with anger and terror.

There was a flicker of the killing fire, and the short, choked scream of another death.

*I have to do something to prevent this.*

It was madness to fight the Ox, but what else could he do?

He closed his eyes, called out to the spirit of the Eagle, felt the great totem-wings spreading in his soul.

Yes. He could do it.

He crawled along the dark earth to the hunter's door of the lodge, the one that faced out to the forest. Cautiously, he pushed aside the flap of skins and peered inside.

Red lights glittered in the dark interior, and the alien smell, the before-a-storm smell, was strong, too strong, stronger than the human smells of the lodge, the flesh and sweat and leather. Walking Man withdrew slowly, in absolute silence.

The Ox was outside, waiting for him, the metal thing which had brought the spirit-fire in its hand.

With its other hand, it beckoned.

Walking Man looked at the three alien fingers, shook his head, then jumped. Straight up.

His hand found the rough end of a roof-beam; his body fell against the wall of the lodge. He kicked, struggled, heaved himself up. He ran up the sloping roof, the dry turf that insulated the lodge soft under his heels. He crouched down in the hope that the Ox's fire wouldn't be able to reach him.

Then he was at the crown of the lodge, above the open chimney, smelling the faint smoked-flesh aroma of the cooking fire.

He dropped inside.

There was a movement, light at the doorway –

Walking Man could see Ox Hunter's spear, fallen across the floor of the lodge. Ox Hunter must have taken up his spear when the Ox came, and –

Walking Man saw the charcoal form that had once been human, realised it wasn't the cooking fire he'd smelled at the chimney.

His body burning with a rage he hadn't felt since early manhood, he grabbed the spear, charged the door of the lodge.

But when he got outside there was nothing, only deep prints of cloven hooves in the mud.

Walking Man ran, circling the village behind Ox Hunter's lodge and that of his neighbour, Deer Dance Woman, the shaman. Through the gap between the huts, he saw two more of the huge black Oxen standing on either side of the kneeling villagers. He thought he saw Walks-with-Moonlight, his eldest girl, kneeling with the others. But he couldn't stop to be sure.

Behind Deer Dance Woman's lodge, he stopped. The meadows were only paces away. He could run. He might make it. He could hide in the woods. He could go to the people of the Marsh Meadow and ask for their help, perhaps offer them a sheep in return for shelter in one of their lodges, if he could find his flock in High Pasture.

There was another flash of fire, and from beyond the lodge came the sound of people screaming, and high, strange calls, unlike any animal that Walking Man knew. He crept around Deer Dance Woman's lodge until he could see what was happening. Smoke was drifting across the Dancing Place, half obscuring the tree. The bulky black form of one of the Oxen moved in front of him, facing away, towards the alien glow of the tree.

The fire was everywhere. His people were dying.

He couldn't leave them to die. He had to attack now. The Eagle would make him strong.

Walking Man charged, silently, spear in hand, towards the Oxen. The spear glanced uselessly off the black flank of the beast. Walking Man saw the legs kick out, but the spirit of the Eagle protected him: somehow he managed to move aside in time.

He rolled on the hard ground, was brought up against something strange.

Something alien, crawling with glowing light.

The tree.

Yes! The Eagle had guided him! The tree was new, so the Oxen and the tree were linked in spirit. That was obvious. It wasn't possible for one man with a spear to defeat so many of the huge spirit-beasts – but perhaps if he attacked the tree…

It was worth a try.

He crawled under the glowing branches, realising as he did so that this was where the air-before-a-storm smell, the scent he had first sensed in the High Pastures, had its origin. It was all around him here, making his hair move and crackle as if a spirit hand were running fingers through it.

'Spirit of the Eagle…' he muttered. Saying the name of his totem aloud was a last resort: totems didn't like being commanded. If he lived – even if he died – he'd be punished for this later. But he had to do it.

He reached into the tree, found something like a cluster of seeds in his hands. He twisted, pulled down –

And the world changed.

Brilliant sunlight, hotter than summer, was casting

sharp shadows on his skin.

Huge grunts of alarm from the Oxen, screams from the villagers. Through the now-dim branches, Walking Man saw people running, saw fire exploding all around them. Beyond, the world had become a vast white waste, burning in the sun.

Where was the mountain? Where were the High Pastures?

In an effort to see more, Walking Man pulled himself up on to the first branch of the tree, then to the second.

The forest was gone, too. The pale wasteland was everywhere.

Had he already been punished for commanding the Eagle? Was all this a punishment, a spirit-penance for his life? What had he done that was so bad as to deserve this?

Desperately he climbed higher into the strange branches, as if seeing more of the world would better his understanding. His hands closed on another of the seedlike clusters. Almost without intending to, he broke the cluster away from the tree.

The sky became dark, filled with stars and a full moon. Again there was a gust of wind, and the air became cooler. There was a clatter of wings as birds scattered in dark trees.

There was a clatter of rock, a groaning of breaking wood. Rocks were falling! Falling across the village!

People were scattering out of the way, but one of the Oxen was knocked over by a boulder. It screamed, and Walking Man saw the madness of pain in its huge eyes.

It saw him. One arm was still free, and metal gleamed in the hand.

Walking Man dodged aside, but this time the Eagle

could not protect him. Fire exploded everywhere. He clung for a moment to a burning branch, watching gold light spill out of the tree like blood, then the pain hit him and he fell.

When he hit the ground, he felt something break inside him, but he ran anyway, screaming with pain and pent-up terror, ran through the fire and shouting and smoke to where his wife's body should be –

But a sheet of flame wrapped itself around him, and the world faded away.

He woke in agony, pain misting his eyes. He could see tall, golden grass, and rearing above it a strange mountain, not the mountain he knew. It was shaped like a lodge, a lodge of stone, its roof of snow, as tall as the sky.

The lodge of the spirits. Yes.

A rustle in the grass, the heavy beat of wings.

With an effort, Walking Man moved his head.

Yes. The Eagle was here. He saw the dark plumage, a great hooked beak, an eye as black as death, watching him. It was like no living eagle he had seen, but he knew it was the Eagle nonetheless – just as the great black beasts had been Oxen, though they looked like no living ox.

He met the death-black eye and tried to speak, but his mouth opened silently. He reached out for the spirit-bird, though the effort cost him the last strength he had.

Take me, spirit, he thought. Take me within your body, carry me on your great wings, and we will fly in the spirit world together.

As his vision dimmed, Walking Man saw the wings of the spirit-Eagle spread open, huge and dark as the night, ready to carry the burden of his soul into the everlasting sky.

# BOOK ONE

*The figure on the low bed stirred. Its skeletal hands twitched, the eyes opened, focused.*

*'Doctor? Can you understand me now?' Mauvril tried hard to keep the desperation out of her voice, the confusion.*

*The alien's only response was a single nod.*

*'I've kept you alive because I need to know the truth,' Mauvril went on. 'Please tell me whether it would have been different. If it had been you, for example. Back then. If you had lived through that night and that day, and all the days and months and years that followed. If you'd had my perceptions, my limitations.*

*'Tell me whether you would have killed them.'*

*The strange, round, tooth-puckered mouth opened, slowly. 'Then you must tell me something.' A pause. The desiccated throat constricted, managed a swallow. 'You must tell me everything that has happened to you.'*

*Mauvril looked around the tiny dark cell, knew she was looking for escape.*

*Knew that there was none. That she had come here for this, for the fire of absolution.*

*Yet she knew she wasn't ready to begin her story.*

*'Wait,' she said. 'I must think about what has happened to me.'*

*The cracked alien lips twitched in the ghost of a smile. 'I don't think I'll be able to wait long.'*

*Mauvril turned away. 'I will keep you alive,' she said at last. 'I will keep you alive as long as necessary.*

*But no longer.'*

# CHAPTER 1

'I am a tree,' said the man with the brown paper bag over his head. 'I am a holm oak tree and I live by the river. The grass tickles my toes and the ferns whisper against my legs. I have the right to live here by the river, and I have the right not to be chopped down and used by humans for their own purposes. *I have the right!*'

Yeah, thought Jacob Hynes, watching him. Sure you have the right. And when the big fella comes along with the chainsaw, I suppose you're just going to clout him on the head with one of your big tickly branches and tell him to go away?

Jacob looked around the small forest clearing at the other members of the Planet First group. There were four of them, sitting on the pale-brown leaf litter: two women, one about thirty with short bristly hair and baggy clothes, the other with long blonde hair and the bright, naive face of a first-year college student; and two more freshman types, male, with stubble-thick chins and blue baseball caps. One of these watched attentively, as if every word counted; the other had his back against the smooth bole of a beech tree, and his eyes closed. He would probably say he was meditating, but Jacob was fairly sure that he was half asleep.

'I am a Douglas fir,' began the younger of the two women suddenly.

Jacob almost spoke, to tell them that Wray Park was an artificial deciduous plantation no more than fifty years old, and that, given the proximity of LA and its smog, they were probably at least a hundred miles from the nearest halfway healthy Douglas fir. But before he could open his mouth the woman began making a loud, choking, growling sound in her throat, as if she were being strangled.

'Now I'm being cut down!' she yelled. 'And the pain –' more growling, shrieking sounds '– the pain is unbearable!' A prolonged scream. 'I'm dying I'm dying *I'm dying* –' A final scream, and the woman pitched over on her side, twitching.

While Douglas Fir was still lying on the ground, the older woman stood up and spoke.

'A litany for the fallen tree:

> *I grew in the light*
> *But died in the shadows*
> *I grew in a century*
> *But died in a minute*
> *My body was the forest*
> *My corpse is your property.'*

There was a prolonged silence, possibly intended to be respectful.

Jacob felt the blood begin to pulse painfully on the left side of his head. This was useless. Not just useless – ridiculous. Insane. A total waste of time. He'd been sitting here more than a quarter of an hour with these people, and all they'd done was scream, rant, read terrible poetry, and chant a litany of apologies to the damp trees. None of it was going to help the natural world any, and Jacob suspected that it wasn't really intended to. He closed his eyes for a moment, listened to the faint hiss of the wind in the tops of the beeches. *That* was the natural world. This lot, whatever trees they might like to call themselves after, were people.

And people were the problem.

'You're the problem,' Jacob said aloud.

They all turned to look at him, even the guy in the paper bag. The bag, Jacob noticed, was decorated in crayon, wavy green lines around the eye-holes for leaves, brown around the nose and mouth, perhaps for wood, or for the soil. It was quite an artistic achievement – if you were a five-year-old.

'Why do you feel we're the problem, Jacob?' asked Douglas Fir's friend, the poet. There was a slight aggressive edge to her voice that Jacob didn't like. Jacob remembered that she was the one who'd introduced herself as Arc, short for Arcadia.

He knew he should have walked out then. Right away.

But now he was here, he felt he couldn't just leave. He had to show these people what total wasters they were. 'Your Web page said you were "dynamic" and "deeply committed to the planet",' he said. 'That's why I came to this meeting. But "dynamic" – that implies you're moving. Going somewhere. I don't see you going anywhere, except extinct.'

Douglas Fir herself sat up and began brushing pieces of dead leaf out of her hair with her fingers. She looked at him, bright-eyed. 'We're releasing our emotions. Relieving our feelings about the rape of Earth.'

'Relieving your feelings?' snapped Jacob. 'Why do you think that matters? Planet Earth doesn't give two hoots about your feelings. I mean, there are people camped out in woods in England right now, trying to stop them building new highways. Actually *doing* something. All you're doing is sitting in the middle of a recreational forest a half-mile from the picnic site, emoting about dead trees!'

Paper Bag spoke up. 'I don't think it's appropriate for you to get personal, Jacob.' He was taking the bag off now, revealing his face: long, thin, with a short beard and a moustache. His brown eyes focused on Jacob sharply. 'If you don't think our group is right for you, you should leave. It was your choice to come here, after all.'

Jacob stood up, ready to turn and go. These people were a waste of time.

'It's OK, Mike,' said Douglas Fir quickly. 'The guy's got a right to his point of view.' She turned back to face Jacob, pulling her long hair around with her fingers in a nervous, repetitive way. 'I do care. I care so much it makes me hurt, it makes me want to scream.'

'It's a generational thing,' chipped in one of the freshmen. 'Right here, what we're trying to do is change people's attitudes.'

'Yeah, that's what we're trying to do,' said Douglas Fir. 'That matters, right?'

'Wrong!' snapped Jacob. 'What matters is what you do, not what you care about. And screaming is no help at all.'

'OK, smart guy,' said Arc, standing up and facing Jacob, hands bunched against her hips. 'You think it's no help. Let me tell you, Elouise and I do support things. So do the others here. We all pay money to Greenpeace every month. We're on the volunteer rota for the metal recycling collection. And if you want more, I can tell you about the animal liberation raids I did, back in the eighties. We saved about a thousand rabbits in one night and took pictures that got the place closed down. I broke my ankle, spent a night in hospital and another two in jail. How many animals have you saved in your life?'

'I'm not talking about saving a few rabbits,' said Jacob. He was still sweating, but he tried to keep his voice level. 'I'm talking about saving the whole planet. I kind of thought you were doing that too. Obviously I was wrong.'

'And how exactly do you think you're going to "save the whole planet"?'

Jacob looked down at the thin stalks of new green grass that were sprouting through the leaf litter, and took a couple of deep breaths. He *had* to control his anger. Anger wasn't going to be any help here. He needed to show these people that he was the rational one, that he was in control.

'I can't tell you,' he said, trying to sound as calm as possible. 'It's not the sort of plan you can just blab about anywhere.'

Five pairs of eyes swung to look at him. Even the guy leaning against the tree seemed to have woken up.

'You've got a plan.' Arc didn't sound very convinced.

'You bet,' said Jacob. 'Here's a hypothesis, right? Let's just say you could travel in time.'

'We're not here to discuss fantasy –' began Arc.

But Mike held up a hand. 'We can travel in time. OK.'

Arc snapped him a glance.

Before she could say anything, Jacob plunged in.

'What if we went back say two, three million years. Before humans even started out. Back when they were still animals. And then wiped them all out, say with a virus or something. Back then.'

There was a disbelieving silence. Arc had shut her

eyes, and was shaking her head slowly. The guys with the baseball caps looked at each other, then looked at Mike. Elouise frowned at him.

'That seems a bit extreme,' she said. 'I mean...' She hesitated. 'I suppose if I could go back and somehow keep us all in the Stone Age, when we were part of nature, then possibly –'

'Stone Age people wiped out mammoths,' said Jacob. 'They also wiped out Irish elk, giant baboons, megatherium, cave bears, sabre-toothed tigers, mastodons... probably a hundred other species. We even wiped out our own nearest relatives – the australopithecines. We were committing genocide a million years ago.' Jacob paused, swallowed. He felt the heat of blood in his face, the prickle of sweat in his armpits. This was what he should have said to them at the start, he realised. This was the language they understood, the language of emotion. Rationality had been a mistake. 'A disease came out of Africa, a cancer of the earth – and that cancer is us. Humanity. You have to face it, people are a bad idea, period. We replicate out of control. We consume resources needed by other parts of the ecosystem. Eventually we'll destroy it. We shouldn't exist! We should never have existed!'

'No way!' said Mike. 'Sure, we've done terrible things to the planet. But you can't do that. You can't travel back in time and wipe out the human race before it started.' A pause. 'Anyway, it's not possible.'

'But if you could?' Jacob looked into the man's eyes.

'I wouldn't,' said Mike. 'No one would. You wouldn't either, even if it was really possible. You just think you would.'

'I guess he's been watching too many movies,' said Arc. She sounded bored.

Jacob swallowed, bunched his fists, then looked down at Elouise. He had to convince one of these jokers. If only to justify the time, the effort of coming here.

'What about you?' he asked. 'Would you do it?'

'I –' She bit her lip, pulled even harder at her hair. 'No. I wouldn't go that far. But if I could make it so that we kept close to nature –'

'I *told* you!' snapped Jacob. 'It wouldn't do any good!'

Elouise pulled her hair in front of her eyes. Arc squatted down, put a hand on her shoulder, then looked up at Jacob.

'Stop upsetting her!' she snapped. Her voice was edgy, annoyed. 'That's only your opinion. There are Stone Age peoples who did live in balance with the natural world. There are some still around now, like in New Guinea. And you don't know that we wiped out all those species. Some of them might have died out anyway.'

Suddenly Jacob's patience snapped. '"Some of them might have died out anyway"? So what! We killed most of them. So you saved a few rabbits. But millions of living things die every second because of humans. You asked me what I'm going to do? OK, I'll tell you what I'm going to do.' He smiled at them, lowered his voice to a sinister hiss. 'I'm going to kill every last human on Earth. And there's nothing that any of you can do to stop me!'

There was dead silence. Then Arc laughed. 'I think we should just leave this guy to his fantasies and go do something useful.'

The two freshmen stood up, exchanged a glance with Mike.

'You think I'm crazy, don't you?' said Jacob, looking at Elouise.

'Not crazy, just… misinformed,' mumbled the young woman, blushing and looking away.

'OK,' said Jacob. He smiled, and looked around the little group. 'You were telling me what species you'd like to be. Before you go, let me tell you what part of the ecosystem I am.' Elouise was still sitting down, with her hair pulled in front of her face. He leaned forward over her, deliberately intimidating. 'I am the sabre-toothed tiger,' he hissed. 'And I crush human skulls with my teeth.'

Elouise jumped up, took a step backward, then stumbled and fell down again, leaves and twigs crackling beneath her. She gave a little gasp of pain.

Arc was on her feet. 'What the –'

Jacob pulled his knife out, snicked open the blade, whipped it around just an inch short of the woman's belly.

'I am the great cave bear,' he said, 'and I disembowel humans with my claws!'

Jacob heard Mike moving behind him, jumped round, crouched down, made a stabbing motion towards the man, again letting the blow fall just short.

'I am the woolly rhinoceros, and I impale humans on my horn!'

He was beginning to enjoy this now. He swung the knife crudely in the direction of one of the freshmen, saw him jump with fear, then turn tail and run.

'I am the leopard, and I slash open human throats!' he yelled after him.

Mike was shouting, 'Just run! Get the hell out!'

And they were running, all five of them, scampering

away like the upright chimpanzees they were. 'I am the wolf pack!' howled Jacob after them. 'I am the lion! I am –' he began to laugh. '– the anaconda. I am the grizzly bear. I am –' He collapsed on to the leaf litter, giggling helplessly.

After a while the giggles subsided. He got up on to his knees, looked in the direction the Planet Firsters had gone.

Silence. They weren't hanging around; they weren't coming back.

Good.

'I am all your nightmares come true,' he muttered. 'I am Alpha and Omega, Destroyer of Worlds.' Then he started giggling again, rolling around helplessly on the ground until he was covered in the dead leaves.

After a while, a shadow fell over him.

'What happened?' asked a neutral, computer-generated voice.

Jacob looked up, saw the huge, familiar, somehow comforting shape of the alien. It was half-horse, half-ox, with strange, double-jointed, comfortingly non-human arms.

'They weren't suitable. You were right: they haven't got any power.' He giggled again. 'They haven't got any brains either.'

The alien's three-fingered hands clicked on the keyboard it carried around its neck.

'We will have to contact more powerful people, with greater capabilities,' it said after a while. 'We will have to take the risk of contacting your military.' A pause. More rapid clicking of fingers on the keyboard.

Jacob looked up, saw the branches of the beech trees dancing in the sun, far above him.

At last the alien's translator spoke. 'Obtain for me the address of the nearest command station for the organisation United Nations Intelligence Taskforce.'

# CHAPTER 2

'Issues,' said the Doctor suddenly.

Sam looked up from the twenty-third-century sperm-whale songline text that she was reading.

'What issues?' she asked. Save the Whale was the one that immediately sprang to mind, but with the Doctor it was just as likely to be Save the Brontosaurus. Or some obscure political problem on a tiny island on a planet whose galaxy you couldn't even see from Earth.

'Back issues,' said the Doctor, without looking up. '*Strand* magazine. Thirty-five to forty-seven, inclusive. Particularly number forty-two, where they printed the cover illustration in reverse by mistake. But there were only about a thousand of those.'

The Doctor was lying back in what seemed to have become his favourite chair. It was mounted on a swivel base, and its gently curving lines wouldn't have looked out of place in an office in the 1990s. But the pearly, almost organic appearance of the material placed it in a different century altogether. There was a gold-leaf crown embossed at the level of the sitter's head: the Doctor claimed that this meant the chair had been the throne of a pretender to the title of Earth Empress, sometime around the beginning of the fourth millennium. Sam knew nothing about fourth-millennium chairs, but rather suspected it was a fake. She was beginning to know the Doctor, and had worked out that more of his stuff was fake than he was generally prepared to admit. Those clothes, for instance: the nineteenth-century cut jacket, the wing-collared shirt, the tailored trousers. They seemed to be the Doctor's favourite garb: he claimed he'd picked them up on Savile Row in 1892, but Sam had seen the label on the jacket. Party Funtime of San Francisco, California, USA. They were *fancy dress*, if you please. Late twentieth century.

'Why do you need the back issues?' asked Sam at last, when it became obvious that he wasn't going to elaborate on his remark.

The Doctor didn't reply. He appeared to have forgotten what he was talking about, or even that he was talking at all. He was reading: not a *Strand* magazine, which might have adequately explained the mention of back issues, but some kind of computerised book, triangular, propped up on the wooden side table beside his cup of tea rather like a crystal metronome. It bleeped from time to time, and, more bizarrely, whistled, like a steam train. Sometimes one whistle, sometimes two. The many clocks of the console room ticked in the background.

Sam looked around in the scatter of plastic, paper, electronics and old teacups on the floor around the Doctor's chair to see if she could spot the cover. After a moment she saw it discarded by his feet, looking rather like a large, triangular CD case. She walked over and picked it up.

'*Galactic Compendium, YG 7008-7088*', in small, neat lettering, printed over the stylised spiral of a galaxy. Sam wondered which dating system that was.

Then she wondered which galaxy.

The universe! All of time and space! She realised she would never, *never* get used to it. No matter how many places she saw, there were always going to be more to see. And each one was different. You could spend a hundred lifetimes – a thousand –

'*Angelus*,' said the Doctor.

Sam looked at him. He hadn't looked up when he'd spoken. This was a game, right? But she was getting used to it, was beginning to grasp the rules. The thing was, not to *show* that you didn't know what he was talking about.

'Latin for "angel". So?' she tried. It might be the title of an article in one of the magazines he'd mentioned, but on the other hand it might be anything.

'"*Nam et angelicam habent faciem, et tales angelorum in caelis decet esse coheredes*",' commented the Doctor obscurely. 'Gregory was just being funny of course. You see, Augustine fancied almost anything in a skirt.'

Sam looked down at her battered jeans. 'I'm safe then.'

'Not necessarily.' The Doctor looked up at last, seemed to focus on the songlines e-book that Sam was holding. 'Not so good in translation, of course.'

Sam grinned. This was one she could cope with. 'AA//WW-R-o//is()?' she said, careful to get all the clicks and whistles in the right place. 'No, I suppose not. But it's very beautiful.'

'Hmm. Yes. I meant the Venerable Bede. I think there was some kind of editorial problem. I'll have to speak to Oscar about it sometime. He knows everybody.'

Sam's mind raced, making connections. *Strand* magazine had been at its height in the 1890s – so Oscar was probably –

Right.

'At least he dressed better than you,' she said.

'Who?' The Doctor seemed genuinely confused.

'Oscar Wilde,' said Sam drily. 'He wouldn't have been seen dead in fancy dress.'

The Doctor looked down over his clothes and frowned. 'Oh, good. I thought for a moment you meant Bede. Now, these back issues. How would you like a visit to the January sales?'

Sam shrugged, refusing, absolutely *refusing*, to be fazed by the Doctor's constant patter, with its obscure connections and improbable changes of direction.

'Which January?' she asked. As an afterthought, she added, 'Which planet?'

The Doctor got up and headed for the console. When he got there he looked over his shoulder and flashed her a smile. 'Guess.'

No good, thought Sam. I've been out-cooled again.

But I'll get him, one day. If it's the last thing I do.

Silence. Cold, damp air.

High, yellow-green reeds rising in front of her. Muddy water, slopping around her shoes. Cold water.

*Very* cold water.

Sam shivered. 'This is wrong, right?'

'Right.'

'So where are we?'

'No, no, no! I mean this is right. This is London, first of January 2108, the opening day of the winter sales. I've been here before, bought some wings. A long time ago.'

'Doctor, this is a swamp.'

The Doctor wrinkled his nose, looked around once more.

'Well, yes, it is, but –' He broke off, looked down at his

shoes, which had almost disappeared into the grey, sucking mud. 'Oh no! Grace gave me those! I'll have to get some boots in Harrods, and put these in for micromolecular repair.'

Sam looked at her trainers, which were doing a slightly better job of keeping the swamp away from her feet. She wrapped her arms around her body and began shivering in earnest. The Doctor had said January sales, which probably implied winter, so she'd put a coat on, and a thick pullover, but nonetheless she was dressed for shopping, not survival training in the Great Bog of Forever.

She stepped back into the TARDIS. Each foot made a loud popping sound as she removed it from the mud.

The Doctor turned around and grabbed her arm. 'Something's wrong, Sam.'

Sam just looked at him, raised her eyebrows. Something was usually wrong. It was really a matter of scale. Sam had started to rate them in scores out of ten: for instance, (1) the Doctor had misdirected the TARDIS, (5) he'd landed them in the middle of a war zone, or (10) he'd accidentally destroyed the universe.

She looked into the Doctor's blue-green eyes, clocked the degree of worry on his face, and mentally assigned this one about 2.5 on the Jones-Richter scale.

Nothing to be concerned about.

'Get back inside!' ordered the Doctor.

'I am inside,' said Sam simply. 'You're not.'

The Doctor pulled his foot upward violently, left a shoe behind, then knelt down and tried to recover it.

Sam became aware of a buzzing sound. A machine? Probably. She leaned out to have a look; at the same moment the Doctor, still trying to extract his shoe from the mud, glanced up.

'Horses!' he said. 'Well, Tractites at any rate.' He stood up, began shouting out into the misty gloom. 'Hello! Could you possibly help us? We seem to have mislaid our planet.'

The buzzing sound got louder. Sam cautiously stepped out again, saw an illuminated platform approaching, skimming over the tops of the reeds. Two dappled grey-and-white horses stood on the platform.

No. As the Doctor had said, they weren't horses. Horselike beings, then. The heads looked similar, but there were four eyes, a large pair on the sides of the head, and a smaller pair, presently closed, on the snout where you might expect nostrils. The 'ears' weren't ears, but short horns, brightly painted, slightly curved and tapering backward. Their bodies were heavier and squarer than any horse could ever be: more like a cow, or a medieval ox. They wore clothing across their backs and upper flanks: rich, tapestried clothing, in purple and green and saffron yellow. Arms emerged from the torso, improbably close to the head. They were long, strangely jointed, ending in three-fingered hands.

In short, they were thoroughly alien. What had the Doctor called these people? Tractites?

Wonderful!

She didn't think they were the slightest bit dangerous. They didn't have that alert, predatory look that weaponed cultures had. They didn't even seem worried by the fact that two aliens in a blue box had turned up out of the middle of nowhere and were asking for help.

The skimmer was landing now, just a few metres away on a small island. Sam could see that the Tractites were tethered to a central pillar. The pilot was steering with a wooden tiller attached to a post. The second alien just stood and gazed at the Doctor and Sam with its big eyes, its two wormlike tongues darting out to taste the air.

The Doctor was staggering through the mud towards the platform, waving his arms and making snorting noises. Sam followed, more cautiously. Now that she knew what to expect, she managed to find footholds of a sort, places where the mud was a little more solid between the channels.

Sam scrambled up on to the island, which was barely above the water line. The Doctor was now standing in front of the skimmer, balanced on one leg, with one mud-encrusted shoe in his hand. One of the Tractites peered down at him.

'How serious is the damage to your shuttle craft?' the alien was asking the Doctor. 'Can we help you repair it?'

'Oh, it's just a re-entry vehicle, really,' said the Doctor. 'I wouldn't bother with it. But where is this place? I mean, it's an interesting planet, quite beautiful, but I'm afraid it's not where we thought we were going at all.'

Sam looked over her shoulder at the TARDIS. A re-entry vehicle? The Doctor was dissembling, she realised. Prevaricating.

OK. Lying.

Which meant that he didn't trust the Tractites. Sam mentally revised the seriousness level of this situation to 3.5 on the Jones-Richter scale, and rising.

'Paratractis,' the horsy creature was telling the Doctor. It added a string of galactic coordinates.

The Doctor sat down. Suddenly. There was a squelching sound as the seat of his less-than perfectly tailored fancy-dress trousers hit the ground.

Sam looked at the Tractite. It looked back at her. The big eyes were strange: blue-red, filled with slowly moving streaks, like cloud belts on a planet seen from space. As she stared, the large eyes closed, with an audible flapping sound, like a single beat of a bird's wing. The smaller eyes opened. They were different, and, since they were positioned together at the front for binocular vision, they looked disconcertingly human.

'This is Earth, isn't it?' she said, holding the alien's gaze.

'Earth? I don't recall a planet with that name,' said the alien. 'Are you in the wrong sector, perhaps?'

The other Tractite spoke. 'It's cold here. I think you should come to Afarnis with us. It's dry and warm there, and we should be able to find you something to eat and drink. Your vehicle should be safe here, or we can ask someone to recover it later, should you wish.'

Warm, dry air drifted over from the skimmer, smelling of hay. It was tempting, thought Sam, but the Doctor had said they were in trouble.

'Umm – Doctor?' she suggested. 'Hadn't we better get back to the... to our *re-entry vehicle*?'

The Doctor was still sitting on the ground. 'Yes, Sam,' he said. His voice sounded as leaden as the grey light over the swamp. 'We could. But there isn't anywhere to go. Not here.'

Sam decided that this wasn't a time for coolness games. 'So where's here?' she asked simply.

The Doctor didn't reply, just stared at the ground in front of his muddy shoes. Sam noticed that the ground itself wasn't muddy, here on the island, but consisted of a mattress of fallen reeds, pale yellow and quite dry.

She looked up, saw the Tractites talking softly to each other. Then the pilot stepped down from the craft on to the reed matting. It gave under his weight, with a squelching sound from the mud underneath.

Sam swallowed. The alien was big. At least as big as a shire horse, perhaps bigger. The exposed hair on his legs and lower body was short and well groomed, silver-grey and white mixed in large, neat dapples. His legs ended in split hooves, part-shod with what looked like black leather.

He knelt down in front of her, so that their heads were almost level. His clothes shifted on his back with a scrunching sound, like someone turning over in bed.

'My name is Kitig,' he said.

'Sam Jones,' responded Sam automatically.

Rather to her surprise, the huge being extended a three-fingered hand towards her. The arm was thick, well muscled, and covered in short white fur. Tentatively, Sam extended her own hand, wary of making the wrong move and causing offence. But the alien simply grasped her hand: the flesh of the three fingers was dry, rough, hairless, like an elephant's trunk.

The Doctor stood up suddenly and took the Tractite's other hand, his face lighting into an extraordinary smile. 'On the other hand, the Tractites are a very civilised people, one of the nicest in the galaxy. So it isn't all bad news.'

He glanced sidelong at Sam, and his eyes flashed for a moment. She knew the look: do what I say, wait for the explanations when I've worked out what they are myself.

We'll see, she thought. You aren't so infallible.

The Doctor was speaking to the Tractite pilot. 'Thank you very much for your offer of help. We'd love to come along with you. Wouldn't we, Sam?'

'Uhh – yes,' agreed Sam dutifully – not that she had much choice, because the Doctor had already jumped forward on to the platform of the skimmer.

Sam stepped up after him. The warm, dry air enveloped her like a blanket. The flooring was carpeted, with a geometrical pattern in browns and yellows. It had a vaguely Roman look: she wondered for a moment if this was Earth in about 55 BC and the Tractites had been studying the local customs. But if so, where were the locals? She looked down from the skimmer, which was now rising slowly over the swampland, but all she could see were reeds and reeds and more reeds, gradually vanishing into the grey mist.

'I'd sit down if I were you,' said the Doctor. 'I don't think this thing has acceleration buffers.' He was sitting cross-legged, his back against the central pillar. Looking at it, Sam realised that it was a small tree, a black trunk topped by a neat crest of fernlike leaves. Well, fernlike except that they were orange. Sam walked over and grabbed the tree trunk, but remained standing. It couldn't be worse than a bus in the rush hour, and she wanted to see where she was going.

Kitig took the controls and the skimmer began to rise. Sam caught a glimpse of the TARDIS, a little blue box standing in the mud at the edge of the island of reeds. Then it was gone, and there was nothing but the marshland and the dull grey sky. The skimmer appeared to have some kind of force field around it: there was no wind in Sam's face, and the air remained warm, scented softly of hay.

The second Tractite came across and knelt in front of them. This one was actually bigger than Kitig – quite noticeably so – and Sam decided, without really knowing why, that it was female.

The alien shook hands and introduced herself as Narunil.

'I can see you're travellers,' she said. 'Our species doesn't travel much off-planet as a rule. But I went to Tractis with my parents once. Have you been there at all?'

'Oh, yes, many times,' said the Doctor. 'Wonderful place. Top-notch hay – one of the best places in the galaxy for it. There was a restaurant on the Bror coast – Deeg's Place, was it? – Or Keeg's? Can you remember, Sam?'

'Not sure. Teeg's, perhaps?' said Sam. 'Creeg's? Weeg's? Bleeg's?'

She hadn't been to Tractis, and the Doctor knew that perfectly well. But if the Doctor had some reason for portraying her as a seasoned, competent traveller – well, that was OK with her.

As long as he didn't land her in it.

'The Bror coast?' Narunil asked. 'On Tractis? I don't think I've heard of it. Is it in the north somewhere?'

The Doctor frowned. 'Never mind. What's in a name? It was all such a long time ago. I've been to so many places. Ah! Look!' He bounced upright, sprinkling pieces of partly dried mud from his trousers, and pointed out over the marshland. 'Is that Afarnis?'

Sam followed the direction of the Doctor's gaze and saw a blue-grey hillside speckled with lights, bright against the cloud-smothered daylight, slowly emerging from the mist. The skimmer got closer, crossing a wide grey river, and Sam could see buildings: spherical, semitransparent, they seemed to flow into and around each other like a cloud of bubbles in water. Between them, Tractites were moving spots of colour on white stone paths. Some carried lamps, mounted over their backs on delicate wicker holders.

'It's only a small city,' Narunil said. 'Not much more than an observation point. But then, this is only a small, damp island.' This last statement was accompanied by a gentle snort, and Sam realised that it was probably intended to be self-deprecating – but Sam felt a chill despite the warm air inside the skimmer's force field.

*A small, damp island.*

That sounded like Great Britain. And hadn't London once been a swamp? She looked over her shoulder, saw the river receding behind them, broad and peaceful. It was the right size for the Thames.

We *are* on Earth, she thought.

But we're not in time to stop the invasion. The invaders are already here.

The human race is extinct.

The Jones-Richter trouble rating began to climb. Exponentially.

# CHAPTER 3

Rowenna Michaels was talking to a man who had been dead for two and a half million years.

'What was it like back then?' she asked him. 'How did it feel to be you?'

The empty eyes of the skull stared back at her. She waited for them to blink, for the skull to speak, an oracle from the African plains, several orders of magnitude older than Delphi. But there was no movement, no answer to her question.

No answer from a fossil, thought Rowenna. Hardly a big surprise.

She reached out to touch the mottled brown and white surface, and tried to imagine that she could feel through the years and the changes brought about by the process of fossilisation to touch the mind that had worked inside.

Nothing. Only silence. Empty bone.

'Try asking her what she had for breakfast. You might get a reply on that one.'

Rowenna pushed her wheelchair back from the bench, saw her colleague Julie Sands looking in through the open door of the prefabricated hut they were using as a lab, her hands covered in the ochre dirt of the Kilgai Gorge.

'Do you have to bring food into everything?' asked Rowenna, grinning as she noticed the half-eaten Hershey bar stuck into the pocket of Julie's buff-coloured field jacket. 'I mean, don't you ever consider going on a diet?'

Julie stepped up into the lab, patted the flanks of her large, square-built body and gave Rowenna a mock-aggressive glare.

'"Diet" is a medieval term used in reference to a congress of religious and/or secular persons for the purpose of deciding policy, and is also used as the name for some modern parliaments,' she said. 'I'm not aware of any other meaning.'

Rowenna snorted. She gestured at the clutter of papers, fragmentary fossils, plaster casts, cables, lights, computer parts, and minor scientific instruments that occupied Julie's workbench and significant areas of the floor around it. 'Know any good medieval definitions of the word "tidy"?' she hinted.

Julie looked at the chaos around her. 'Umm – no,' she admitted, then gestured vaguely at Rowenna's bench and the assembled skull. 'How's it going?'

'It isn't.' Rowenna gestured at the skull, then at the laptop computer where she was supposed to be making notes on the brain structure of *Homo habilis,* the extinct human ancestor of which the skull was a part. 'He isn't giving me any ideas. I want a talking one.'

Julie laughed. 'Well, I can't do that for you, but I did find something new this morning. Take a look at this.' She crossed the floor, carefully negotiating the clutter, and handed a small fragment of fossil bone to Rowenna.

Rowenna held the fragment, cradling it gently between finger and thumb. It was darker than the skull on the desk, but that meant little. The original bone had been replaced by sediment. The shape of the fragment, however, was true to the smallest visible detail.

It was about five centimetres by three, very slightly

curved, with jagged edges and traces of some ridging on one side. Rowenna turned the fragment over a few times, puzzled. It was too thin, too finely shaped, to belong to *Homo habilis*. It almost looked modern, like a piece of a *Homo sapiens* skull. Of course, that was no reason why it shouldn't be fossilised – skulls of *Homo sap* could date back half a million years – but the sediments where Julie had been looking were supposed to be a lot older than that.

'Where did you find this?'

Julie met her eyes. 'Where do you think?'

'Not in the gorge, I'd say. Too recent.'

'In the gorge,' said Julie quietly. 'About a yard away from where we found your friend on the bench last year.' She gestured at the skull.

Rowenna looked at the fragment again. There were still bits and pieces of brownish dirt clinging to it, and fragments of a harder rock matrix. 'It must be some kind of freak – a *Homo habilis* born with a thin skull.'

'The curvature matches *Homo sap* skulls,' observed Julie. She walked across the lab floor, began washing her hands at the sink. 'I think we've got something new.'

Rowenna felt her heart begin to thump hard in her chest. A new species of hominid. It was more than possible. The entire fossil record for early hominids consisted of two skeletons, a few dozen complete or near-complete skulls, and isolated fragments of teeth and bones, such as the one she was holding in her hand. The things were just so damn *rare*. An entire species, two and a half million years old, missed from the catalogues – yes. It could happen.

And me and Julie have discovered it, she thought. This

could be the biggest thing since Donald Johanson and Lucy. And all discovered by a two-bit reconnaissance expedition with one lab hut and a crippled woman –

Sharp pains shot up Rowenna's back as damaged muscles tried to contract against the bones that had been shattered by an intruder's bullet two years before. She realised that her hands were gripping the frame of her wheelchair. Gripping *too* hard, dammit. She took a deep breath, then another, then another.

*– the kid was turning, turning, the gun in his hand, the gun –*

Too much tension is a killer, she reminded herself. You've got a job to do here, so concentrate on that, not the awards you might win afterwards.

'You OK?'

Rowenna looked up, saw Julie standing over her, watching her carefully, head slightly on one side.

'Fine,' she said. 'Just a bit of back pain.'

Trying to control her excitement, Rowenna rolled her wheelchair back up to the workbench, put the skull fragment down and picked up a brush to clean off some of the remaining dirt. It took a couple of minutes. When she was satisfied that everything remaining was fossil or rock, she carefully prised at the rock matrix with her fingers. A piece fell away, and she saw that there was an indentation in the skull.

She smiled, pleased with her discovery. Marks and indentations on skulls were often important. They gave clues to the lifestyle of the hominid, and often clues to the manner of its death. There might be tooth marks from predators, or perhaps scavengers; cracks and fissures caused by accidental damage; more rarely, blows from stone tools had been found, indicating that humans had practised murder, or at least some kind of killing, for more than a million years. This one was a simple tooth mark, probably a dog or a hyena to judge from the size and shape.

Julie was standing over her again, chewing at the Hershey bar. 'Well, what d'you reckon?' she asked in a muffled voice.

Rowenna looked up at Julie's face, then down at the skull fragment. 'We need to find some more pieces of this,' she said. 'And...' She hesitated, aware of the practical difficulties this would cause her friend, then thought: To hell with that. 'I want to go with you.'

Julie grinned. 'OK, let's get loaded up!'

The Land Rover jolted and jumped along the bed of the dry river, each lurch of the chassis sending waves of pain up Rowenna's spine. She clenched her fists against the rollbar bolted to the roof, trying to ignore the pain and the resentment that it brought back, the anger because *I could have done this on my own before I was shot. Dammit I could have walked down here –*

'Are you OK?' Julie's voice. 'Do you want me to stop?'

Rowenna realised that she'd closed her eyes, and felt her face screw up tight with the pain.

'I'm fine,' she forced herself to say. 'Just hurting a little, that's all.'

'We're nearly there,' said Julie. 'We can stop for a while –'

'Just *get* there,' snapped Rowenna.

Julie glanced across at her. 'Hey, cool it.'

Rowenna took a breath, forced herself to calm down. She was *lucky*, she told herself. Lucky to be alive, after being shot through the spine. Lucky to be fit enough to go on this expedition. Lucky to have friends like Julie who were willing to take her along, despite her disability and the logistical problems it caused.

And she was extremely damn lucky to have made a good find on the third day out. A miraculous find. Maybe the best find for about a decade.

Time to stop bitching.

She let go of the rollbar, touched Julie's arm. 'Sorry.'

Julie nodded abstractedly, the incident already forgotten. She was peering out at the sloping walls of the gorge. 'I think it's about here. These strata are about two and a half million years old, and the fragment was – oh!'

The car gave a particularly violent jolt and stopped suddenly.

Rowenna looked around, saw dust settling, the cracked mud and litter of broken rock that made up the seasonal riverbed, and the familiar eroded bluffs that her experience – and her increased heartbeat – told her were fossil country.

Her eyes scanned the nearest of them, pain forgotten, Julie forgotten, everything forgotten but the possibility of a find.

And then she saw it, and realised why Julie had stopped the car so suddenly.

Less than twenty yards away, embedded into the sloping bank of the riverbed at just above eye level, was a knob of rock that wasn't all rock. The curve of a cranium, the staring socket of an eye. That was all: the rest was still hidden in the sediment, or perhaps eroded away.

But it was enough. Even from this distance, and through the windscreen of the car, Rowenna knew that she was looking at the skull of a hominid very different from any that would normally be present in strata this old. In fact it almost looked like…

'Wow,' said Julie. 'That wasn't there this morning.'

Rowenna glanced at her, frowning, annoyed to have her train of thought interrupted. 'You mean you missed it.'

Julie shook her head. 'Hell, Rowenna, it wasn't there. I walked down this section. I saw that fragment. I'm damn sure I'd've seen a complete skull.' A pause. 'Least, I *think* I would. I'm going to take a look. Want me to load you up into the chair?'

Rowenna looked at the rough ground between the Land Rover and the fossil. 'I don't know whether the chair's motor will take it.'

Julie grinned. 'It will if I push. Hell, all that food energy has to be good for something!' She got out of the car, walked around to the back and opened the door.

A stone bounced off the bonnet, and at the same time Rowenna saw a movement on the rock bluff above the fossil skull.

A man. A man making his way down the bluff. She could see the blue uniform, the shoulder pips.

She heard an intake of breath from Julie, heard her footsteps as she marched round the car to meet the soldier.

'Whoever the hell you are, keep away from that skull!'

Rowenna grinned. Good old Julie, diplomatic as ever. She wound down the window as the soldier trotted across to the car. He was white, tall, with a thin fuzz of blond hair.

Definitely not local: the blue uniform looked like it was a United Nations kit.

'Ignore my friend,' she said. 'Can we help you?'

'I'm sorry, I'm going to have to ask you to leave the

45

area.' The man sounded worried.

Rowenna frowned, but Julie spoke again before she could frame a reply. The big woman had marched around the car and was facing up to the soldier.

'Can I see your authorisation for that?' she said. 'We're here on legitimate –'

'I'm sorry, you've got to leave. Now.'

'And I want to see your authorisation!'

Rowenna reached out through the window and put a hand on Julie's arm. 'Hold it –'

But the man had produced an ID. Julie studied it. 'Intelligence Taskforce?'

The man nodded. 'This entire area is a restricted zone at present.'

'Why?'

'I'm afraid I can't say why.' The ghost of a smile. 'That's why it's restricted. Now, can I ask you to leave, please?'

Rowenna decided to try again. Whatever military nonsense was going on here, the fossil was too delicate, too rare to be exposed to it. 'We're palaeontologists,' she said. 'We only want to have a look at the fossil – that one, there. We aren't interested in any military stuff. You can stay and watch us if you want.'

'Sorry, ma'am, I have my orders. You have to leave now.'

'Can we check that with your senior officer?' asked Julie.

That ghost-smile again. 'I am in charge, here, now.'

'I want the name of your senior officer!'

'I'm not at liberty to tell you that.'

Again, Rowenna touched Julie's arm. There was a look in the officer's eyes that she didn't like, a coldness that reminded her –

*– turning, the gun in his hand, the gun –*

'Let's go,' she said.

Julie glanced at her. 'Are you crazy? That skull's got to be –'

'Please.' Rowenna could feel the panic growing, like an animal in her chest struggling to get out.

Julie glowered at the soldier, then walked slowly around to the driver's door. 'We'll be back, just as soon as your military nonsense is over,' she said. She started the engine, reversed the Land Rover. Rowenna caught a last glimpse of the skull, staring at her one-eyed, like a warning.

Then Julie turned the Land Rover around.

'I didn't like that man,' said Rowenna quietly.

'Neither did I,' said Julie. 'I'm going to make an official complaint.'

'I mean, I was afraid of him.'

Julie glanced across at her. 'Yeah, I know. Don't worry, I got his name. Captain Jacob Hynes.'

Jacob watched the two women driving away.

*Damn*, he thought. Damn it all to hell. We don't need fossil-hunters. I knew I should have closed off the gorge this morning.

He lifted the satphone to his lips, muttered the voice ID that opened the local uplink. After a few seconds, the UNIT logo and a security code appeared on the machine's small screen, together with the words BUSY – LEAVE MESSAGE.

'Brigadier General? Hynes here, at Kilgai. I need the back-up platoon down here. We have several new anomalies, and there are civilians around, palaeontologists. They might blow the whole thing open. I need an ETA –' He paused, deliberately theatrical. 'I need those people, sir.'

He cut the connection, put the radio away in his pocket.

Then he waited for a while, looking at the fossil skull in the bluff, until he was sure that the Land Rover had gone, that the fossil-hunters weren't going to try to sneak back. Finally he scrambled up the bluff to his makeshift camp in a narrow cave at the bottom of the cliffs.

Inside, behind the UNIT standard-issue portable stove, the folded canvas awning, the rolled-up sleeping bag, the time tree glittered, its branches snaking with light, the seed clusters ripe.

*Pick one and you go back a thousand years. Or ten thousand years. Pick a hundred and –*

Jacob smiled to himself.

He reached under the sleeping bag, pulled out the *other* radio. It was a sleek, strange, organic-looking machine with a surface like polished agate. It moulded to his hand. There were no buttons, no controls, no screen. Once he was touching the machine, he needed only to speak.

'Gavril?'

The response was immediate, the familiar synthesised voice. 'I am here.'

'I think –' This time the pause was not deliberate. 'I'm almost ready to go. I've sent for the UNIT people to seal off the gorge.'

'And the tree?'

'It's OK,' he said. 'Ready to go.'

'Good. You have chosen the correct moral path, Jacob Hynes. You will be honoured for all time by my people.'

Jacob nodded, but he wasn't interested in honour, nor in Gavril's people.

*Alpha and Omega.* A dream come true.

# CHAPTER 4

The Tractite city was even more beautiful from directly above: the buildings were like misted glass eggs, illuminated from within, and there were amorphous coloured forms inside the walls, like embryos with green and amber and blood-coloured flesh. The paths between the buildings glittered, showing tiny fragments of colours: pale blue, lavender, silver, and gold.

Four Tractites drifted below, standing in a bright-green field in what must be artificial light, throwing a small, glittering object between them; every time one of them caught it, it chimed. Even the mist seemed beautified by the city, transformed into a slightly coloured haze. Gauzy clouds formed around the lights as they approached, dissipated as they passed by.

Sam heard the Doctor's voice, talking to the Tractites, the faint snorts and whinnies of their responses.

She focused on the conversation, realised that the Doctor was talking to Narunil about spaceships. The Tractite was sounding puzzled: every type of ship the Doctor mentioned seemed to be something she hadn't heard of. Sam was sure that the Doctor was nosing around for information, and equally sure that what he was trying to find out didn't have anything directly to do with hyperspace or warp drives.

Well, she would work it out. And one thing was sure: she wasn't going to ask, not unless she absolutely had to.

Cold, damp air hit Sam in the face as the force field around the skimmer was powered down. They had landed. The city looked less ethereal, now that she was on a level with it. Bubbles had become domes, some of them several storeys high. Paths had become streets, lamps had become brilliant streetlights. Tractites were clopping about in the white glare of the lights, their breath pluming in the air, and there was a bustle of carts being loaded and unloaded, of coloured fabric rolls and wicker baskets and food bubbling in metal pots. Despite the cold, the air smelled like a summer garden, sweet grass and soil and flowers.

Kitig had parked the skimmer in the middle of a large circular intersection. Several paths looped around them, and there were even flyovers – though they could hardly be further from the concrete monstrosities of human make. They looked as if someone had thrown an arc of water through the air and frozen it to pastel-coloured, glinting ice. Connections flowed from the bridges to the ground, and into adjacent buildings.

As they followed a path towards one of the bridges, Sam noticed that there were flowers growing from narrow beds of soil around the supporting pillars. They looked as if they were cast from wax in the pale light, but when she knelt to touch them they were soft, real flowers, and unmistakably terrestrial: daffodils. Looking around, she saw winter jasmine, wallflowers, crocuses. But there were subtle oddities about them: the crocuses came in bright red, as well as the usual purple and yellow. And almost all of the daffodils were pure white.

Sam stopped, took a closer look. Surely they *were* daffodils? Everything else was right: the shape of the flowers and of the leaves, the length and colour of the stalks.

'I see you've noticed too.'

Sam jumped. The Doctor was crouching beside her, his breath frosting the air. Sam nearly said, 'Noticed what?' but stopped herself just in time.

The Doctor gently touched the petals of the flowers. 'Almost the same. And everything else is so different. It's as if there's some fundamental instability –' He stood up. 'Never mind. Even simplicity itself is never as simple as it seems.' He started after Narunil and Kitig on a curving path that led under the bridge and into a small, bright street lined with beds of the white daffodils.

Sam followed him. Two huge Tractites cantered past her on the path and began ascending the gentle incline of the bridge. Sam felt their eyes on her, but tried to ignore the feeling. It was too much to expect that these people wouldn't be curious. There didn't seem to be many other aliens around.

Sam realised what she'd been thinking and stopped suddenly, staring at the flower-lined street in front of her.

*Aliens.*

And this is Earth. These are daffodils, and I'm an alien. Sam frowned, then remembered something about the Doctor's conversation with Narunil on the skimmer. He'd mentioned the Bror coast on Tractis. True, he'd pretended to be confused and absent-minded, but Sam was pretty sure that he'd been faking that. So presumably the Bror coast was a real place, and very well-known – and Narunil hadn't heard of it. So either she'd been lying about having visited Tractis – which seemed pointless – or the Tractis she knew wasn't the same as the Tractis the Doctor knew.

Just like this Earth isn't the same as the Earth I come

from. Different flowers. A different intelligent species.

She tried to remember what the Doctor had told her about the nature of time, and quickly realised that it wasn't much. But she'd always had the impression that time was relatively constant – that the TARDIS was a sort of shuttle craft moving from one century to another or one planet to another, using pretty much the same mechanism for both sorts of transition. Yes, they could make small changes, like saving a child's life. But what if they could make larger changes? Changing the outcome of a major war, for instance.

Yes! That was it! She felt a weight lifting from her shoulders. Earth hadn't been invaded at all!

'Doctor! I've got it!' she shouted, racing along the street after him.

The Doctor turned from where he was walking between the two carthorse-sized Tractites.

'We're in an alternative universe!'

The Doctor frowned and shook his head, glanced at Narunil and muttered something. Then he walked back to Sam and grabbed her by the arms.

'Sam, Sam, Sam, *Sam*,' he said, speaking in a low voice. 'Do *please* be careful what you say. Yes, we are in an "alternative universe", but the trouble is, it's inherently unstable for a reason I haven't yet understood. And if it collapses, it won't just disappear, it's far too big for that – it will create a rift in the vortex so huge that the whole fabric of reality will collapse.'

Sam opened her mouth to object, but the Doctor wasn't stopping.

'And before you ask, no, we can't just go away and pretend it isn't happening. I have to fix this, and the only way of doing that is if I can somehow find out when things changed, and how, and change them back – but given how far back that's likely to be, and how much is likely to have changed, there may well be nothing I can do, and even if we do try anything, our kind hosts will probably try to defend their own existence, which means stopping us from doing it, perhaps by killing us. So it really would be a good idea if you didn't tell them about it in advance. Because if I can't fix it then neither you nor I will ever meet another living human being again, and we, and the Tractites, and everything else, will probably cease to exist by about next Tuesday. Now do you understand how serious this situation is?'

Sam hesitated. Then she looked the Doctor in the eye, and said, 'Eight-point-five.'

The Doctor jumped back as if she'd hit him. 'What?'

Sam broke away from him and hurried along the street after Kitig and Narunil. She wanted to explain about the Jones-Richter scale, but she was trying to hold in a fit of giggles. She knew the situation was serious, but then, it always was. And she was sure the Doctor was overreacting. This place was so peaceful, so *good*. It might not be the world they'd left behind, but it could hardly be a threat to the existence of everything.

And anyway, Sam didn't like being told off for no good reason.

After a moment the Doctor came up behind her and put a hand on her shoulder. 'I'm sorry, Sam.'

She finally had to let the giggles go. 'And so you should be,' she spluttered. 'Browbeating me like that. The Tractites are hardly Zygons, are they? Or those stupid Daleks you go on about.'

The Doctor stared at her in amazement. 'But I didn't know what you were going to say next! I had to make you realise –'

'Realise what? That we're stranded in a dodgy situation again? Come on, Doctor! I can work that out for myself, can't I? Do you have to tell me everything? I'm not stupid, you know!'

The Doctor turned away without a word and began staring into one of the buildings. The window showed that it was full of water inside, blue water with bright corals and thousands of small, brilliantly coloured fish.

Sam stepped towards it, saw the Doctor's face reflected in the dark water. It seemed disembodied, timeless – no, not timeless. Old. Sam remembered his jokes about the centuries, his nine-hundred-year diary, and realised that it wasn't all a joke, not always. Inside the youthful energy, the brilliance, was someone who had seen perhaps too many things.

'We all have to be Daleks sometimes,' he muttered, looking down at his mud-caked shoes. 'It's just a matter of knowing when you really don't have any choice.'

Before Sam could even begin to work out what this meant, he looked up again and smiled brilliantly at her, all traces of age and weariness gone. 'Come on, there's a whole world to explore!'

Sam looked ahead and saw that Narunil and Kitig were standing under a glass archway that crossed the street, their heads on each other's shoulder, their arms entwined.

Tractite love.

Not just a world to explore, thought Sam. A universe. A whole *other* universe.

Suddenly something that the Doctor had said while he was telling her off came back to her mind.

– *find out when things changed, and how, and change them back* –

Which means that we have to change something in the past so that this universe ceases to exist –

Oh.

Sam closed her eyes. Suddenly she couldn't look at the Tractite city, couldn't look at the Tractites who had welcomed them so kindly, so calmly, the Tractites who seemed so totally devoid of suspicion or malice.

No wonder the Doctor had been angry with her for telling them about the alternative universe. Effectively, she'd been telling them, *We're going to have to destroy you.*

She could only hope that they hadn't understood the implications.

She made herself open her eyes, found herself looking at the aquarium. She remembered Narunil saying that this was only a small city – which meant that there were many more. She imagined them, growing everywhere on Earth, illuminated in their soft colours like the fish in their tank.

She imagined chucking a brick through the glass wall in front of her. All the water pouring out, all the bright fish stranded and flopping on the stone path. Struggling. Asphyxiating.

OK, dying.

We're going to have to *kill* the Tractites, she thought. Me and the Doctor.

Kill all of them.

She looked for the Doctor, saw him with Kitig and

Narunil, talking. She opened her mouth to call him, but then thought better of it.

Because he was right. There really wasn't anything you could say.

# CHAPTER 5

'Wine's bad for your liver, you know.'

Rowenna grinned at Julie. 'So are candy bars.'

'I ate a slice of pizza first!'

'Case proven.'

The two women were sitting on the floor in their room, ignoring the ancient, uncomfortable beds and the even more ancient and uncomfortable chairs. Above them, insects crawled over the dirty plastic surface of the roof light. Stray bugs flew around the room, occasionally settling on their arms and faces. Propped up against a suitcase, free of her wheelchair, Rowenna felt almost normal, almost as if she could just get up and walk around the room. A few months ago, when she'd been particularly drunk and angry and bitter, she'd actually tried something like that, and paid for the experiment with a night of agonising pain and three days in bed.

Tonight, she wasn't particularly angry and bitter, but she was planning to get drunk.

'That skull,' said Julie suddenly, 'd'you reckon it was a *Homo sap*? I mean, it *looked* like a *Homo sap* – there wasn't a trace of any occipital ridge. But it doesn't make sense.'

Rowenna took a sip of her pink wine and thought about it. The skull had definitely seemed too big for any known early hominid. But according to existing theory *Homo sapiens*, modern humans, hadn't evolved until half a million years ago. Julie was right: it didn't make sense.

'Are we sure about the stratigraphy here?' she asked Julie. 'I mean, the sediments are two million years old, right? No one's made some kind of error here?'

Julie shrugged. 'Maybe. But it's unlikely.' She took a bite of her Snickers Giant Size, went on in a muffled tone, 'Hell, Rowenna, people have been digging in the Kilgai for thirty years. Any anomalous strata would have shown up by now.'

'Perhaps it eroded out,' Rowenna suggested. 'Or fell down from a higher level. Or got washed down when the river flooded in season.' But even as she said it, Rowenna knew that it was unlikely anything so delicate as the skull they'd seen would survive such a process even partially intact. Even the fragment Julie had found would probably have been ground into smaller, more eroded pieces by processes like that.

Julie reached across for the wine, took a swig straight from the bottle. 'If that goddamn soldier boy had let us near the skull we wouldn't have to guess at it like this. We'd be looking at it now.'

'I know,' said Rowenna quietly. 'If I could walk I reckon I'd go out there first thing in the morning, military restrictions or no, and just hope that Captain Jacob Hynes and his friends didn't see us.'

'Well, I reckon I'm going to make that complaint. Perhaps if we put a rocket under his ass he'll let us in.' Julie stood up, wavered across the room towards a cluttered table, in the middle of which sat a palmtop computer. '"A murder of crows, a military of idiots",' she muttered, tapping away at the keys. LEDs winked on the external modem linking it to the satphone they'd set up outside. 'What's the goddamn e-mail address for this

United Nations Intelligence force?' she asked after a while. 'I can't find it anywhere on the net.'

'How would I know a thing like that?'

'Didn't you know someone in England who worked for UN Intelligence?'

It took a moment for Rowenna's alcohol-fuzzed brain to work out who Julie was talking about. When she did, memories flooded back: the cottage on the green hillside in Wales, the protest marches with Cliff and Jo, the older woman's hair flying like a banner in the sun. It had felt wonderful then, it had felt like the world was going to change.

Well, it had, but not in the way she'd expected.

Hell, she'd been so *young* then.

And so dumb.

'You know, the one who reckoned she could "time travel".' Julie fluttered her fingers at the end of the sentence as she adopted what she felt to be a suitably spooky tone.

Her voice brought Rowenna back to the present. She looked into her wineglass, hesitated. 'I never really believed that stuff.'

'Still, it's a lead. I think we should try it.'

'Get my organiser out of my bag, then. I'll have a look for her number.'

Rowenna looked out of the dirty plastic window of the lab at the dusty, lamplit forecourt. Moths and beetles flickered around the lights, and the ghostly smudge of the moon was visible above the rocks. Julie was out for a walk, too restless to sleep. She'd taken the satphone handset, said something about calling Jo, trying to get an authorisation through before morning.

Rowenna knew how she felt. She couldn't stop thinking about their find.

The impossible skull fragment. The impossibly ancient 'modern' human.

The faint rattle of the disk drive operating on Julie's computer made Rowenna look up. She rolled the wheelchair the short distance from the window to the desk. As she approached, the computer's small screen was filling with the ghostly shape of a fossil skull.

For a moment it was superimposed on the faint reflection of Rowenna's own face, caught in the glare from the overhead light. Her eyes stared back from the empty sockets, her short, neat blonde hair obscured the cranium, and, more bizarrely, the bright-red collar of her sweatshirt was visible around the jaw bone.

Then the colours came up, and the measurements, and a message:

ANIMATRIX: Kilgai fragment 1c/45, 6.5.97. Modeling now complete.

A toolbar offered various options for further work.

Rowenna looked at the image of the skull critically. The program she was using took the measurements of the fragment and built up an image of the most likely complete skull. The computer's guesswork wasn't inherently any more reliable than hers or Julie's, but its results were easier to see.

The complete skull was undoubtedly human. There were no eyebrow ridges, no occipital crest. The jaw was modern, lightweight, and did not protrude. On the other hand, these features were the sorts of assumptions the machine was told to make if the skull was thin, and had a certain curvature. It didn't necessarily rule out the possibility that the fragment was part of the skull of some variant of *Homo habilis* which just happened to have a thin skull with an odd curvature.

Rowenna told the computer to add the rest of the guesswork: musculature, cartilage, skin. The process was faster than generating the initial skull map: within a minute, a sketch of a human face was looking out at her.

A completely *modern* human face.

She shivered. To hell with odd curvature. There was something *wrong* about this.

She found her wineglass on the desk, took a last gulp of the now-warm liquid. Time for bed: perhaps in the morning she'd be able to work out some kind of answer. She rolled the chair away from the desk, towards the door that led to the tiny bathroom. The facilities inside were cramped, and weren't exactly set up for wheelchair users, but Julie had rigged up a rope handle so that Rowenna could manage. She didn't bother with the effort of washing and changing in the cramped space: that could wait until morning.

Afterwards she hauled herself back into the chair, rolled it forward. But at the door she stopped, with her hand on the cold metal of the handle.

She could hear footsteps, moving away.

Very soft, but definitely footsteps. A rattling sound, like leaves, and a faint click. Off to the left? It was difficult to tell, through the door.

Silence. Gone now.

Rowenna hadn't heard the person approach. He or she must have been standing there, must have heard her moving around, heard the faint whine of the chair's motor, and crept away, quietly. Hoping Rowenna wouldn't hear.

She felt her heart freeze for a second, a cold, hard, absolute terror, because *all this had happened before.*

The board creaking outside the door. The bedroom door, and getting up, half asleep. It must be the neighbour's cat got in again, but no, the intruder in the corridor, *no this can't be happening*, a man, a man *turning, turning, the gun in his hand, the gun –*

Rowenna clenched her right hand into a fist, hard, until the nails bit painfully into her palm.

'Julie?' she called, softly.

There was no response.

Probably some small-time local crook, she thought. Perhaps they think there's something worth stealing here.

'Whoever you are just get out,' she said, trying to hide the panic in her voice. 'Just go. There's no money here.'

A scrabbling, the sound of something being dropped on the floor.

The laptop. Of course. *Damn.* Computers were worth money anywhere.

She took a breath. 'Look, I'm not going to hurt you, but I need that computer. If you leave it here I'll –' She stopped, aware that her voice was shaking. 'We'll get some money and pay you to leave us alone.'

Silence.

More scrabbling sounds. Hell, the guy was just carrying right on with looking for things to steal. Did he know she was in a wheelchair? Did he think he could just ignore her?

A muttered curse from the other room. More things clattered to the floor.

Hell, if he broke that skull fragment –

*The skull fragment.*

There was no way she was losing that. She opened the door, and even as part of her mind was shouting, *this is insane, this is just what you did last time and got yourself in a wheelchair for life*, she was rolling the chair into the room, into the bright light where a man was sorting through a pile of stuff on the floor.

Not a local. A man in a *uniform*.

Jacob Hynes.

'What the hell –' she began.

Then she saw what was outside the window.

A horse with arms.

A horse with arms and huge eyes.

The eyes stared at her, the arms moved and touched a keyboard slung around the huge thing's neck.

A voice spoke.

'I'm sorry, but you must come with us. You are a sample.'

From the corner of her eye, Rowenna saw that Hynes had aimed a gun at her.

*– turning, turning, the gun in his hand, the gun –*

Rowenna did the only thing she could. The only thing left to her right now.

She screamed.

# BOOK TWO

When Mauvril returned to the cell it was dark. The lights in
the cell had been dimmed, too, but she knew that the alien
could see her. He didn't need night eyes.

She opened her own night eyes, watched his breathing
for a while.

'You can hear me, can't you, Doctor?' she asked.

There was no reply.

If he had replied, maybe she wouldn't have been able to
start telling her story.

Maybe he knew that. Maybe that was why he stayed
silent.

Anyway, she began.

'I'm not pretending that everything before the invasion was
perfect, that ours was an ideal world. You know as well as
I do that there isn't such a thing. For instance, in the place
where I lived, children were regarded as property. You were
owned by your parents, and if they died before you came
of age, you were put up on the open market just like their
house, their land and their clothing. It wasn't a nice custom.

'When my parents died, my elder brother Pakip bought
me to work on his farm. It nearly bankrupted him, but he
was the sort of person who thought of it as a family duty.
The good sort, you know. He didn't treat me badly, but of
course he had to make me work, to justify his investment.
I hated it. I was only a kid – soft-skinned, my hooves only
half formed – and I still had the silly romanticism of
childhood: I yearned for the city, Tafalis, or better still our
distant capital, Noctutis. I had the idea that my life would
have been better if an offworlder had bought me, instead
of sensible old Pakip. I imagined dancing for some two-
eyed, pink-skinned alien, imagined waiting on her table,

*imagined being given plastic and gold and glittering electronics. I imagined being taken into space, seeing the world from above, travelling between the stars.*

*'I think I knew better, really. I knew in my heart that my brother had done the best thing, buying me before the offworlders could do it. I was just old enough to know that if my dreams came true, they might turn out to be nightmares in disguise, and then there would be no going back.*

*'I didn't know that the nightmares were going to come visiting.*

*'Still, I didn't like that farm. Grass, grass, and more grass, fields and fields and fields of the tall wavy green stuff. Pakip grew it fresh for the restaurants in Tafalis. I had to get up before sunrise, so that I could harvest the grass in the old way, soft, cold, with the dew on it. Pakip even made me use the old ivory scythes: they crushed where they cut, he said, and the grass grew back in a better way. But they were hard work! I would bale the grass at first light, roll it in the canvas, damp and cool to keep it fresh, and load it on the cart. Then Pakip would yoke himself to the cart and trot off to the market at Tafalis, his hooves clopping on the road, while I watched the farm, drove the insects and flying lizards from the grass, mended gates, planted where Pakip had ploughed the previous day. Sometimes, if it rained, or if there was an evening dew, we would do a second harvest just after sunset, and I would go to the night market with Pakip. We got better prices then. And I met the offworlders. All shapes, all colours. They seemed extraordinary: it must be hard for you to understand, with all your experience of the alien, what it was like for a little quadruped from a little grassy place on a big grassy planet*

to go to the city and see people with two legs, or six, or external skeletons. Even more seductive was the babble of alien sound and flicker of alien light, the powerful, glittering technology of the offworlders. It blinded me. It blinded most of us, I think.

'There was an Earth Reptile called Morkal, or Menarc, or something like that. I remember being particularly impressed by him, his solemn bearing, his strange, lizard-like skin, the glowing third eye in his forehead. He used to talk to my brother at a red plastic table in the open-air restaurant by the market. I would listen, not understanding very much of it. The alien was sophisticated, some kind of diplomat I think; he tended to talk in abstractions, in abbreviations, in evasions.

'But I remember the last time we saw him. He had a glass full of that black, fizzy stuff that Earth people called cola, but he wasn't drinking it: he was looking down at the flat red surface of the table, almost as if he was ashamed.

'"They are serious, Pakip," he said. "Deadly serious. You should leave, if you can."

'I remember being afraid.

'But Pakip didn't leave, couldn't leave. He had his wife, Larnaj, and their new child, who was still in her pouch. And he had the farm. Or perhaps he didn't quite believe the Earth Reptile's melodramatic warning, didn't quite think that things like that could be part of the real world. I don't know.

'But I know he screamed when we saw the lights.'

'I was with Pakip one evening, taking our harvest to Tafalis, when they appeared above the city, drowning its glitter in a cold blue-white glare. All the roofs and streets became visible, and I could even see tiny figures staring upward, Tractite and alien alike frozen in that strange, shadowless, illumination. Sometimes I catch myself thinking that the city is still there, Tafalis, the Tafalis I knew, fossilised in time like a tiny animal caught in the sap of a tree – don't tell me, I know. It's another romantic dream. The lure of the alien, the lure of the past that never was – perhaps we don't grow up, after all.

'Pakip, of course – practical Pakip – I think he knew in that instant, on the night road to Tafalis among the usual smell of grass, that his world had ended. But he was trying to kid himself that his little piece of the world would somehow survive. People always do, don't they? Even the most practical ones.

'I didn't know anything, of course. I didn't think about the Earth Reptile's warning at that moment. I remember thinking – you'll laugh at this – I remember thinking how silly my brother was being, because the lights were obviously only some big alien spaceship. I looked at the huge, square, moon-bright thing, almost as big as the city itself. I saw the clouds boiling away around it, and I thought of all the aliens on the ship, and how they'd probably want to eat our grass, and the price would go up. I thought my brother should be dancing for joy. Instead, he kneeled on his forelegs, shrugging off the yoke. As I stared at him in confusion, he wrenched the tack free from both of us, breaking the precious leather, and pushed me down on my knees, so that the yoke fell away. The cart tipped sideways with a groan of wood, spilling some of its load. The long bundles of grass rattled as they rolled across the stone.

'Automatically, I turned to pick them up, but Pakip kicked my flank with his foreleg.

'"Mauvril!" he shouted at me. "Run!"'

'"But the cart –" I began. I could scarcely believe the damage my brother had done to the leather tack. It would take days to repair, and it would never be as good again.

'But Pakip wasn't listening to my objections. He just grabbed my shoulder and pulled me around, forcing me into a trot. Our hooves clattered on the road. Behind us, the lights grew brighter. There was a tension in the air, like the feeling before a thunderstorm. I could even hear a distant booming, not unlike thunder.

'Displaced air, I thought. The ship materialised in the upper atmosphere. The Earth Reptile had talked about things like that.

'There was a flicker of light behind us, and Pakip broke into a canter, then a gallop. I stared after him for a moment, still confused.

'"Run!" he shouted again.

'Pakip was well ahead of me now, moving at full gallop across the fields, head down, careless of the damage to the precious crops. I started after him, infected by his panic, lowering my own head into the green-smelling swathe he had made through the eating-grass. Cold drops of dew spattered my legs and flanks. The black mass of the forest rose to my left as I galloped, cutting off my view of the alien ship. I could hear Larnaj shouting from the farmhouse. I imagined her big white cloak flapping in panic in the strange light, the copper thread on her old coat glittering, the baby wriggling in its pouch, infected by its mother's fear.

'"The cellar!" Pakip's voice, clear and authoritative. "Get in the cellar! Now!"

'I could see him ahead, galloping across the courtyard of the farmhouse, his hide shiny with sweat, his tail high, his

71

*hooves raising the dust. The light was brighter still, almost as bright as day, and, although it was hard to tell with my night eyes, it seemed to have gained a blue quality. The sky itself was brightening, as if dawn were coming. The stones of the courtyard glowed as if they were burning. I slowed to a canter, shutting my night eyes and opening my colour eyes, so that I could see more clearly.*

*'The light was blue: an eerie, unnatural blue.*

*'In the doorway of the house, Pakip looked over his shoulder, nostrils flaring with panic, and screamed back to me, "Mauvril! Get under cover!"*

*'I hesitated, motionless in the blurry edge of the forest's shadow, not sure what to do.*

*'My indecision saved my life. Suddenly the farmhouse burnt white, blinding me for a moment. I could feel the reflected heat on my skin, hotter than sunlight. I looked behind me, was dazzled by the sky behind the thick overhang of the forest. An instinct older than civilisation took over, and I dived for the cover of the trees.*

*'Behind me, I heard Pakip screaming as he burnt in the light, but I knew there was nothing I could do.'*

Mauvril hesitated, realised that the Doctor's eyes were closed again.

'Do you know what it's like, Doctor? To watch them die, to hear them die, and know that there's nothing you can do to stop it?'

For a long time the Doctor said nothing. Then his mouth opened slowly and a hiss of breath came out.

'Yes,' he said. 'I know what it's like.'

His eyes opened. A tear spilled out on to one of his cheeks, and slowly trickled across the desiccated skin.

# CHAPTER 6

Jo Grant woke up with the feeling that something was wrong. She lay in the darkness for a moment, listening, hearing nothing but her own breathing and the faint pulse of blood in her ears.

'You'll have to help me, Jo,' the Doctor had said.

Yes. That was it. The Doctor had been talking in her dreams again. The same old, familiar, fatherly voice. The same old, familiar, fatherly demands.

'You'll have to help me.' And the TARDIS in the background, and some sort of mist.

Go away, Doctor. It was all a long time ago. Another Jo. Another universe.

*Beep.*

Jo jumped, sat up in the bed.

For a moment, nothing. Then the sound was repeated: a faint, unmistakably electronic beeping. She sighed. Matthew was still awake in his room, playing computer games. *Again.* She opened her eyes, glanced at the brass alarm clock on the bedside table by the lamp. It was ten past one in the morning.

He shouldn't, thought Jo. He really shouldn't. He's got school tomorrow.

She reached out for the bedside lamp, leaning across the cold sheets that she'd probably always think of as Cliff's side of the bed. She fumbled for the switch, awkwardly positioned underneath the old-fashioned cloth shade. It clunked across and a warm brown light filled the room, illuminating the familiar stained-oak panelling of the wardrobe opposite the end of the bed, the white wicker laundry basket, the *Treasure Island* clothes chest with its brass decorations and huge fake lock.

'Your room looks like a throwback to the seventies, Mum,' Matthew had said to her the other week. A new sophisticated phrase from his new sophisticated school, she supposed. But he was right. Purple carpet. Sea-blue walls. Grapefruit-yellow ceiling. She really ought to redecorate it. She'd done the rest of the house not long after Cliff had left, but she hadn't been able to bear the thought of changing this room too much. There was even a pair of white moon boots, thick with dust, stuffed into the narrow gap between the wardrobe and the wall. She hadn't worn them for perhaps twenty years.

Jo lay back, propping herself up against the headboard. She closed her eyes, felt herself drifting back to sleep.

'You'll have to help me –'

*Beep. Bip-bip-bip-beeeep.*

Reluctantly, Jo opened her eyes again; then, even more reluctantly, she got out of the bed. She padded across the room, pulled an old pink dressing gown off its hook on the door, stuffed her feet into some slippers. In the corridor, she could see a faint, changing glow of coloured light under Matthew's door. She heard a click, a loud whisper, then silence.

She tapped gently on the door.

No reply.

'Matthew! I know you're playing with that machine again. I want you to go to bed. Now.'

'Sorry, Mum.'

He didn't sound sorry, and Jo could still see the coloured light.

She opened the door, saw her son in his dressing gown, sitting cross-legged in front of the computer. On the screen, huge, grey, saucer-shaped spaceships floated over a stylised burning city. The words GAME ON HOLD flickered in red in the middle of the screen.

'Off,' she said firmly. 'Now.'

'But I've nearly reached the highest kill rate ever!' Matthew looked up at her, bright-eyed. His hair was golden blond, just the colour hers had been at that age. 'Please! Just five minutes!'

Jo looked at the screen again. She was reluctant to turn the machine off herself: an eleven-year-old was entitled to a certain amount of dignity. And she also knew how addictive computer games were. If she turned it off, and Matthew lost his chance at the highest kill rate, it was quite possible he'd start all over again as soon as she was gone.

'It's ten past one,' she said gently. 'Please, Matthew. You're going to be so tired in the morning. Save the game and finish it tomorrow.'

Matthew hesitated, then reached out and fiddled with a mouse on its mat on the floor. The screen blanked, and the words GAME SAVED appeared in green. Slowly, reluctantly, his hand reached out and turned the machine off.

Jo reached down and ruffled Matthew's hair. 'If you had real space invaders to deal with, you'd have a lot more than a kill rate to worry about,' she said.

Matthew looked up, grinned at her. 'So you keep telling me, Mum.' A pause. 'How many invaders did you stop, really?'

Jo smiled. 'Don't start that again! Half of it's classified –'

'– and the other half I wouldn't believe. I know, I know.' Matthew stood up. 'You know, sometimes I wish I had a normal mum.'

He was still smiling, but Jo could sense the serious undertone in his words. A normal mum wouldn't wake up in the middle of the night with her heart beating double time because she'd been dreaming of a time-travelling alien who needed her help. A normal mum wouldn't think that the best part of her life, the only important part of her life, had happened more than twenty years ago, and that everything that had happened since was a sort of afterthought. First she'd saved the universe with the Doctor; then she'd saved the world with Cliff; now she was raising her son on her own in a two-bedroom house in Hackney with two jobs and a bedroom that needed decorating and a roof that needed retiling and hadn't life been supposed to get *better*?

Jo became aware that Matthew was still looking at her, a solemn expression on his small, round face.

'Sometimes I wish you had a normal mum, too,' she said. Then she bent down and kissed him. 'You be up on time in the morning, OK?'

Matthew nodded.

Jo retreated to the landing, waited until she heard the sound of Matthew getting into the bed, until she saw the remaining light under his door go dark. She thought about going back to bed, but she was thoroughly awake now, and really felt like a cup of tea. She shuffled downstairs, her fluffy slippers flopping on the beige carpet.

In the kitchen, the neon strip light flickered into life, dazzling her. When it had settled down, Jo saw that the blinds were still up over the double windows, revealing black squares of night. Irritably, she pulled them down, trying to remember whether she'd told Matthew to do it, and he'd forgotten, or whether she'd just forgotten about it altogether.

She put the kettle on and found a brown box of tea bags. She smiled to herself, remembering the Doctor and his Assam and Darjeeling. Then Cliff: rosehip, camomile, nettle, maté. Now, on her own, she bought Sainsbury's own in tea-bags, like everyone else. The latest bags were triangular, for some reason. She put one in a chipped and none-too-clean blue mug labelled SAVE THE WHALE, and wondered if the entire course of her life was reflected by the tea she drank. The Doctor would have been amused by that theory, she decided. He would have given her one of his I-know-better grins and told her it was interesting. Cliff would have smiled vaguely and started talking about something more important. But it was true, nonetheless. Both of them had told Jo what tea she had to drink. Now she had a free choice, and she bought the cheapest, the first off the shelf.

'The story of my life,' she muttered, but she was smiling again. This was freedom, she supposed: to sit in your own kitchen, making a cup of your own cheap nasty tea.

The kettle boiled, and she poured water on to the alien-looking triangular bag. She prodded the sacklike body a few times with a teaspoon, then fished it out, added a drop of milk and took a cautious sip.

Too hot.

She slopped a little of the tea out into the sink, to make it easier to carry, then left the kitchen holding the mug in one hand. She'd got as far as the corridor when the phone rang.

Jo jumped. Automatically, she started towards the lounge where the phone was, but was halted when the ringing stopped and her ancient answering machine spluttered into life.

'Hi, I'm not able to answer the phone –'

Quite, thought Jo. It's one o'clock in the morning, thank you very much.

She started towards the stairs.

The answering machine's speaker crackled. 'Is that Jo Jones?'

The voice was American, female.

Whispering.

*Afraid*.

Jo froze.

The line fuzzed for a moment, then, 'My name is Julie Sands, and I'm calling from a satphone in Kilgai, Tanzania, and I'm calling because we really need your help. I sent you an e-mail. I don't know whether you've got that – but it's got worse. This Captain Hynes has got – Jesus, you're not going to believe me – he's got an *alien* with him.'

*What*?

'Look, Rowenna's inside. I can't get to her and there aren't any police for miles. Oh, God –'

A pause. Slowly, tea in hand, Jo started towards the phone.

'Jesus Christ he's dragging her out – I think he's shot her.'

Jo almost dropped her tea on the carpet. She jumped for the phone, scrabbled the handset off its rest.

'What's happening there?'

Clattering sounds. Something which sounded like it might be a gunshot. The line fuzzed.

A mechanical voice. Faint, artificial, alien.

'– get this one too –'

'Jo, are you there? We need your help.'

A roar of static, then silence.

After a while, there was a click, and a dialling tone.

Jo stared at the handset for a while, her heart thumping.

Then she pulled the telephone notepad, the stupid one bordered with kittens playing in roses that Cliff had bought her on their first wedding anniversary after he'd left her, and scribbled:

> Kilgai, Tanzania
> Two women. One shot?
> Alien, artificial voice. Not Dalek.
> UNIT connection?
> —
> 1. Contact UNIT.
> 2. Get Matthew OUT OF THIS.
> 3.

She hesitated. She remembered the Doctor's voice in her dream.

*You'll have to help me, Jo.*

OK, Doctor. You win.

She underlined the words 'OUT OF THIS' on the notepad, then lifted the phone and dialled a number she'd never thought she'd need again, but had somehow never forgotten.

Rather to her own surprise, she was smiling.

Regimental Sergeant Major John Benton looked at the screen and frowned. 'There's certainly something going on out there, Jo,' he said. 'We've got a team in Kilgai now.'

'Doing what?'

Benton sighed. 'You know I can't tell you that.' He nearly added, 'You shouldn't even be here', but thought better of it. He and Jo had been through too much to allow a remark like that, even after all these years. He glanced at the decanters of whisky and gin on the polished wooden sideboard, and wondered if he should offer her a drink.

'Just give me some idea,' she was saying. 'Does it involve any of the known alien races?'

Benton shook his head. 'Come on, Jo. I don't make the rules.'

As Benton had half expected, Jo simply got up, walked round the desk, and looked at the screen for herself. 'You haven't changed, Jo,' he commented. 'Always ready to cross the front line.'

' "Kilgai, Tanzania. Incident class N",' she read. 'What's class N?'

'They divide incidents up into Y for "Yes, it does immediately threaten the existence of the human race" and N for "No, it doesn't".'

Jo laughed. 'You haven't changed, either. Or you wouldn't be able to say that with a straight face. Come on, what does it really mean?'

Benton felt himself blushing. For a moment he'd

thought he'd managed to fool her. Suddenly he was twenty years old again, outclassed and outwitted by all the smart university people, the captains, the scientists, the brigadiers. 'I don't know what it means,' he snapped. 'They're always changing the categories. It's not my job to keep up with them.' He waved around the huge office with its regimental and UN flags, its silver swords and polished wood. 'All this is just a show, you know. I file reports, keep an eye on the paperclips, and tell the wives and kiddies when one of the lads cops it.'

Jo was silent for a moment. 'Do you really have to do that?' she asked.

'Twice in the last week. The captain couldn't do it himself: he's still out there.'

'Out where?'

'You know I can't –'

'It's Kilgai, isn't it? And who's the captain? Jacob Hynes?'

Benton looked helplessly at the desk. 'You seem to know all about it already,' he said at last.

'The e-mail they were talking about mentioned Jacob Hynes by name. Julie said he warned them away from the area. Look, that woman was afraid when she rang me. And she was *afraid* of Jacob Hynes. A UNIT officer. You should at least look into it.'

Benton picked up a paperclip that was lying on the desk and began bending it back and forth with his fingers.

'Jo, do you know how many hysterical reports of aliens we get at the front desk? Two hundred a day. I'm sure your friend met Captain Hynes at the gorge; I'm sure they found something strange – that's probably why the team are there. But I don't believe that a UNIT captain –'

'Do you know Hynes personally?'

Benton sighed. Jo was relentless, he thought. It was worse than dealing with the press.

'Not personally. But all UNIT officers are thoroughly vetted. You know that.'

Jo thought for a moment. 'Then it's probably mind control. It has to be mind control.'

The paperclip broke in Benton's hand. He stared at it for a moment, then said, 'Look, I'll contact Captain Hynes today –'

'If he's just killed two women, he's not very likely to tell you the truth, is he?' A pause. She looked at the computer screen again. 'Can you check his personnel record?'

Benton shook his head. 'That's confidential, and you know it.'

The desk thumped, shook. After an instant Benton realised that this was because Jo had hit it. Hard. He looked up, amazed.

'What's happened to you, John?'

Benton wanted to say, 'I grew up. I got married, I have a wife and three kids and a job to hold down.'

But there were tears in Jo's eyes, and that stopped him from speaking.

'Listen,' she said. 'Those women could be dead. There's something going on out there. I need to find out what it is, and to do that I need you to make the arrangements. I know you can do it.' The big, brown, caring eyes fixed on his. 'Please, John.'

Benton looked away, not sure whether he was amused, embarrassed, or just plain irritated. This was getting ridiculous. Jo had always been an impulsive person, but flying four thousand miles on the strength of a phone call struck him as taking impulsiveness to new dimensions.

'It's not on, Jo,' he said at last. 'If you're so sure there's something wrong, I'll contact Hynes's CO in Nairobi, ask him to look into the situation. That's all I can do.'

Jo got up, swallowed, looked at the floor.

'The Doctor asked me to help,' she said suddenly. 'He wouldn't have done that without a reason.'

'The *Doctor*?' It occurred to Benton that Jo might simply be lying, in order to get what she wanted. But if not –

'Don't worry. I suppose I can pay my own air fare.' Jo turned, started across the plush Whitehall carpet towards the heavy wooden door.

Benton looked at his hands. If the Doctor was really involved –

'All right, Jo,' he said. 'You win. You'll have to get to Kenya on your own, but I'll lay on a chopper from Nairobi to Kilgai. You'll be a guest of the regiment, out there to do your scientific research. But just remember, if you get it wrong – if you put one foot out of place and start babbling about aliens that aren't there – my career's on the line.'

Jo opened the door, then turned and said quietly, 'There's a lot more on the line than your career, John. I wouldn't be here otherwise.'

She went out, and closed the door behind her.

Benton stared at the cracked leather of his desk for a while, then picked up the phone.

# CHAPTER 7

The Tractite library was a greenhouse.

Sam stared at it in astonishment. She couldn't even see any books. The place was crammed with plants, and the air was warm and damp. It smelled of sweet perfumes, spices, and fresh flowers. But this was certainly the right building: the Doctor and Kitig were walking ahead along the stone path, chatting amiably. And she was sure the Doctor had said they were going to the library. They'd even discussed which books he was going to need to look at to establish where Tractite history had diverged from their own.

She peered ahead to see if there was any kind of inner building where the books were housed. But all she could see were the plants, some growing in huge, brightly coloured china pots, others from long beds of black soil dotted with leafy clusters. There were even full-grown trees, reaching all the way to the dark, translucent dome above. Plume-leafed species, pastel-coloured and clearly alien, were mixed with the deep-green tropical succulents of Earth. Fine sprays of warm water jetted down from the dark glass dome above, beading the leaves. There were flowers everywhere, creamy, sensual blossoms, long ropes of red and violet, a lemon-coloured tassel as big as Sam's head. A green, glittering movement caught Sam's eye, then turned into a butterfly with wings almost as big as her hands.

As they moved further into the building Sam at last saw books, but there was no sign of any shelving or organisation. The books were scattered around in piles, some on stone tables under the dripping greenery, some on the paths, others on low, padded couches. Most of them were large and flat, like children's colouring books. Some, confusingly, were shaped like the leaves of plants. Tractites knelt at the tables or on the couches, chatting, reading the books, drinking what she guessed was green tea from large, brightly coloured china bowls.

'Lavender, you said?' the Doctor was saying to Kitig.

'Lavender with a hint of musk. I'm sure of it.'

They both sniffed the air, Doctor and alien, then moved suddenly up a flight of steps. Sam followed, but paused when she saw a book apparently discarded on the black soil under the roots of a pineapple plant. She picked it up, but the pages were glued together with damp, and the spine was rotting.

She hurried after the others. They were sniffing at a pile of books stacked by a fountain.

'Kitig,' she said. 'Where's the librarian?'

He glanced up at her. 'In the white robes, over there.'

Sam looked, saw a Tractite standing at a high stone table decorated with lilies and moss. He seemed to be reading two books, turning the pages quickly as if looking for something, and tasting the air with his tongue.

'Why do you need a librarian?' Kitig was asking 'Hasn't that book been marked?'

'Marked?'

Kitig took the book from Sam, brushed the mould away from part of the cover, then pointed at a heart-shaped mark in the top left corner. He showed it to Sam. 'That means the book's finished with. We usually just put it back on the soil – it's quicker.'

Sam grinned at the alien. She looked around, and saw that there were large numbers of books scattered around on the soil under the plants, and that most of the things she'd put down as dead leaves were in fact stray pages.

'Recycling!' she said. The more she learned about these people, the more she liked them. But then she thought for a moment and frowned. 'What happens if you want to keep something, though? I mean, everything must go mouldy pretty soon in here. Do you reprint it?'

Kitig gestured at the librarian. 'They make a new copy, changing anything that needs to be changed. We do use printing, sometimes, if a large number of copies are needed. There's a press over by the high table.' He gestured beyond the fountain, to a tall stand of trees. Sam could see glimpses of bright stonework between the trunks.

But she was still confused. The Tractites seemed too advanced for this. Where were their computer systems?

'Haven't you got a permanent store of information?' she asked.

'How can information be permanent?' Kitig seemed genuinely puzzled. He shut his eyes and made a slight tossing motion with his head, very horselike, then said, 'Information is what people need in order to know about the world. The world is always changing, therefore the information has to change as well, or it's no longer information. The books are copied for as long as they're needed. When they're not needed any longer – when they're no use to anyone – what's the point in keeping them?'

Sam thought about it. 'OK, not permanent. Long-term. Like physics and stuff.'

Kitig's eyes clouded for a moment, and his tongue tasted the air. 'Honeysuckle, I think,' he said. 'I can taste some here. Did you want to look at them?'

'Judging by their antiquity,' the Doctor broke in, 'I should think that the Tractites have forgotten more about physics than the human race ever knew.' He was lying on the floor, sniffing at a small, diamond-shaped book with pages stained purple and pale yellow. Sam couldn't see any writing, as such, and eventually decided that the colour patterns must constitute words.

Or – maybe it was the smell.

She looked around again, observed the librarian more carefully.

Yes. He was tasting the book, his tongue flicking out to touch it, then moving to the new book and – presumably – copying the information. The process was quite rapid, perhaps ten pages a minute. Sam wondered how much information was on a single page.

'Colours set the framework, taste is used to convey specific events,' commented the Doctor after a while. 'Apparently they've been doing it for over two million years.'

'Must be a pretty good system then,' said Sam, as usual refusing to be fazed.

But *two million years*? How long had the Tractites been here? It was beginning to look as if, in this universe, the human race had simply never existed.

She glanced at the Doctor, hoping he would say something more about the Tractites' apparent antiquity, but he was still sniffing the book and talking about language. 'Well, it's better than a limited set of shapes, a bizarre set of combinatory rules and a syntax where you can't do more than two clauses before – Hello, this is interesting. Who's the Uncreator?'

'The mythical entity who brings about the End of Time,' said Kitig, before Sam had even managed to pick up the broken pieces of the Doctor's own syntax and work out that the final question had been addressed to the alien.

'Ah,' said the Doctor. 'Hmm.' He sprang up and beamed at Sam. 'Time for that tea that Narunil promised us, don't you think?'

Not a very adroit change of subject, thought Sam. Obviously there's something in that book that the Doctor doesn't want Kitig to know he's especially interested in. Something that gives a clue to how we're going to have to change the past and –

*Destroy this universe.*

Sam suddenly felt cold in the warm, humid air. Her interest in the alien library and its books had made her forget all about the fact that the Doctor was going to destroy this entire world if he got the chance.

It's like knowing you're going to die, she thought. You don't think about it most of the time, then suddenly you remember, and your heart starts thumping, and you feel sick. Except that death is something that happens to everyone, and I can't do anything about it, so I can just tell myself not to think about it. But this is only happening to me, and I have to think about it.

*We're going to kill the Tractites. All of them.*

The Doctor was looking at her curiously. Sam realised

that her emotion must be showing on her face.

'Just homesick,' she said quickly.

'Homesick? You?' He took her arms, looked into her eyes, his gaze earnest and reassuring. 'Oh, Sam, Sam, Sam. It'll be all right. I'll find a way.'

Sam nodded, bit her lip, broke away.

Kitig gave her a sympathetic glance. 'I'm sure you'll be able to go home,' he said. 'We do have spaceships, though not at Afarnis; I'm sure our people can lend you passage on one, if yours can't be repaired.'

Kitig, of course, thought 'home' was another planet, because that was what the Doctor had let him assume.

More lies. And I'm helping him, just by keeping quiet.

Kitig touched her arm with his big, three-fingered hand. It almost broke her heart.

She glanced at the book that the Doctor had been reading, now discarded in the pile on top of the table. She wondered what was in there that was so important.

'And you're sure there's never been a species that looked like us on this planet?' the Doctor was saying. 'Not even in the fossil record?'

'There were some bipeds,' Kitig replied thoughtfully. 'On one of the equatorial continents, I think. They'd have been about your size. But as far as I know, they're extinct. And they weren't intelligent.'

'Obviously I must have got it wrong again,' muttered the Doctor.

'Not necessarily,' said Kitig politely. 'The fossil record is patchy; there may well have been a small alien colony here. But it would have to have been a long time ago.'

'When did you come here, then? You're not natives, I take it.'

Sam could sense the sharpness behind the apparently casual question. She opened her mouth to interrupt, then thought better of it, and looked away into the dripping foliage.

'That's a bit of a puzzle,' Kitig said. 'We have records going back thousands of generations, you understand. There are even Tractite fossils here on Paratractis. But the strange thing is, Tractites definitely evolved on Tractis, not here. There are genetic differences between us and most other Paratractian species that can't be explained any other way. There are a lot of theories about it – our civilisation on Tractis may have been overrun, after seeding the Earth colony, and later rebuilt itself. There's even a theory involving time travel –'

Sam glanced at the Doctor again, but his face gave nothing away.

'– though that's always seemed paradoxical to me. "I'm my own grandpa." You know.'

'Yes, we have that saying on our planet as well,' said the Doctor. His voice was distant, as if he were thinking of something else. Sam watched his face, looking for clues.

Suddenly he seemed to come to a decision. He set off along the path, obviously expecting Sam and Kitig to follow. Kitig did, but Sam didn't. She walked a little way, waited until the Doctor was out of sight, then dropped back and scooped the mysterious book up from the table where the Doctor had left it. She opened it, looked at the meaningless patterns on the pages for a moment, then cautiously put it to her mouth and licked the soft material. It wasn't papery: more spongelike in texture, and it had a faintly metallic taste.

No – something more than metal.

Meat.

*Cooked meat – no, cooked flesh.* Burnt *flesh. Corpses rotting, orange worms burrowing in it, bodies piled high against a wall –*

Sam recoiled, feeling sick. She could see why the Doctor hadn't wanted her to know about this. It wasn't going to be pleasant. The worst aspect was that she seemed to be actually experiencing what she tasted, rather than simply reading words.

But she had to find out.

She screwed up her courage, took another taste –

*A city, drowned in a cold blue-white glare. All the roofs and streets visible. Tiny figures staring upward, Tractites, caught in the shadowless illumination like insects in amber –*

*And then the light. Light burning her eyes, burning her flesh, her bones, searing, destroying –*

Sam turned a page. She was feeling dizzy, and her throat was hurting, but she had to know more. She took another taste –

*A black-carapaced alien walking towards me, the band of plastic over its eyes glowing an uneven red. Fire leaps towards me and the searing light, the pain–*

*The humans are coming! The humans! They're going to kill us all!*

'Sam!'

Sam felt the blow on her face, and for a moment she almost tried to kick out with forelegs she didn't have. Then she became aware of the library around her, of the Doctor's anxious face, of Kitig staring at her.

'I – I was a Tractite,' she said. 'Several Tractites.'

The Doctor was shaking his head, putting a finger to

his lips.

*No*, thought Sam. You need to know this.

Then it occurred to her that the Doctor already did know. It was the Tractites she was supposed to be keeping the secret from.

She was getting tired of this.

'I don't know what was happening,' she said. 'There was just a lot of pain –'

The Doctor nodded vigorously, as if encouraging a toddler to walk. 'It's all right,' he said. 'You don't need to worry about it now.' He turned to Kitig. 'She'll be fine, I think,' he said airily. 'But some of your fiction is a bit gruesome, isn't it?' He tossed the book down on the ground and trotted off along the path.

Sam hesitated, then followed him. They passed the high table in its tamarind grove. The printing press, a big, wooden-framed machine with metal springs and coils and cogs and levers, seemed to grow out of one of the trees. Glass retorts hung suspended from the framework, stained with various coloured fluids.

For putting smells on to paper. Of course.

Another machine, smaller, was set in a niche, like a classical statue. It looked a bit like a large vice: perhaps it was for binding the books. The Doctor paused to look at it; Kitig went ahead.

Sam caught the Doctor's arm. 'Was it fiction?' she asked.

The Doctor turned and looked at her glumly. 'No. That's the problem.'

Then he marched on after Kitig.

Sam stared after him for a moment.

If it's not fiction then there must have been humans

in the past of this universe, or maybe that record is from our universe, in which case –

In which case she hadn't the faintest idea what was happening. Thinking about it made her head spin.

There was an exit behind the high table; a librarian sat there, copying a book. Sam noticed that her fur was patchy, dry, like that of an old cat or dog. And she *looked* old, bones protruding from wasted flesh under her white robe.

She looked up suddenly and glared at Sam. 'The scents have changed,' she said. 'It's all your fault.'

Kitig laughed, the sound booming around the chamber like thunder. 'Oh, Partil, the scents are always changing for you!'

The librarian shifted her glare to Kitig. 'That's just the problem,' she said. 'They didn't always change.'

'Don't take any notice of her,' muttered Kitig when they were outside. 'Her sense of taste is gone – has been for years. They only keep her on because her daughter's on the library council.'

Sam bit her lip. Even in their weaknesses, these people were more human than humans.

She thought about the book again. If it wasn't fiction then humans had already destroyed the Tractites once – or tried to. But if this was 2108 that would have to have been in the twentieth century – too early in human history for interstellar travel, let alone conquering alien planets..

Unless the humans came from somewhere else. Unless the Tractites came from somewhere else.

And there were two universes to consider.

Sam shook her head. It was no use: she wasn't going

to be able to make sense of this without drawing a diagram. Probably not even then.

She followed the others outside and took a deep breath of the damp, marshy air. She looked at the beautiful city that the Tractites had built here in the middle of a wasteland. The Tractites were good people – better, probably, than humans. However they had arrived here, they showed every sign of being good managers of Earth and its resources. Did she and the Doctor have the right to destroy them? What right did either of them have to start unpicking the threads of the new history that had formed around them?

She looked at the Doctor. He was still talking to the aliens, but, watching closely, she thought she could see it now: a crafty expression on his face, underneath that charming smile.

He was going to do it. If he could, he was going to change history. Of course he was. And she was going to help him. She was going to have to; she didn't have any choice.

According to the Doctor.

Perhaps if I don't think about it, she thought, it will all go away. The Doctor will have put it all right and I won't have to do anything.

But she knew there wasn't much chance of that.

# CHAPTER 8

The fax machine started just as the helicopter was coming in to land. Jo stared at the curl of paper, watched as the words TOP SECRET rose slowly over the tiny plastic horizon of the portable machine, followed by a string of security codes.

She glanced out through the small porthole of the military helicopter, saw low concrete buildings, a woman in shirtsleeves waving the aircraft down in the middle of a storm of dust. She looked over the roofs of the buildings for the hills that surrounded the famous gorge, but saw only a featureless red plain dotted with thorn trees.

The machine in her lap beeped. Jo looked down. The body of the fax was in John Benton's neat handwriting: *'Jo – Computer record of Captain Jacob Hynes back to June '81 – but no record on microfilm. You were right. It sounds dodgy to me. I'll take it up with Brigadier Bambera ASAP. Take care – John'*

Jo shook her head slowly. Once, you'd have come out after me yourself, she thought. But that was a different world. A galaxy long, long ago and far, far away.

The helicopter was down now, the dust settling. The door clattered open and the shirtsleeved woman peered inside. 'Welcome to Kilgai! You Ms Grant?'

Jo nodded, stood up, picked up her luggage and went to the door.

'Do you know where Rowenna Michaels and Julie Sands were staying?' Jo asked.

'I don't know much about it, I'm afraid. But don't worry. Captain Hynes is here to meet you. He'll take you wherever you need to go.'

Jo felt a jolt of panic, but quickly controlled it. This was a UNIT flight. Hynes was bound to know about it.

She peered out into the hot sunshine, saw a man in a blue UN uniform walking out from the shade of one of the buildings. She clambered down to the ground and called hello. They exchanged introductions, and Jo found herself hustled into a dusty green Land Rover which looked as though it had been around since the days when the British army ran this part of Africa.

'You don't know where my colleagues Rowenna Michaels and Julie Sands have got to?' Jo asked, as they drove through the dusty streets. 'I've been trying to get in touch –'

'I warned them to stay out of the gorge area yesterday,' said Captain Hynes. His accent was American West Coast, almost a caricature: Jo found herself wondering if it was a fake. 'I have no information about them after that time.'

They were out of the town now, and she could see the hills ahead, a gentle russet colour in the low sunlight. A solitary man, wearing a checked shirt and jeans, herded a few goats across a field of yellow grass by the road.

'It seems like a peaceful enough place. What's the problem here?'

'Temporal anomaly,' said Hynes. 'We've got our science people on to it now.'

'What kind of temporal anomaly? You can tell me. I used to help the chief scientific adviser to UNIT.'

'Sergeant Benton informed me about your status. But

I can't reveal anything about current operations.'

He's like a machine, thought Jo. She felt a chill inside her despite the dry African heat. She wondered if she was walking into a trap. She'd always been good at that.

What if I don't come back?

She thought of Matthew for a moment, his bewildered, sleepy face as she'd dropped him off at Cliff's. His eyes looking at Cliff, then at her. She knew he'd heard their hasty, whispered conversation, knew he'd worked out that this was some big, terrifying adult thing that he couldn't be told about.

Her heart clenched, and she turned to Hynes, ready to tell him to turn the Land Rover around and take her back to the town.

But he spoke first. 'There's a barracks hut outside the restricted area. You can sleep there.'

The hills were rising around them now, dark shoulders of rock blotting out the sun. Peaceful russet had turned to dark, shadowed red, the colour of old blood. The sky was darkening as she watched, blue leaching away. A star appeared.

The Land Rover jolted, turned off the road. Jo looked ahead, saw a couple of prefabricated buildings resting on wooden supports. There was a truck parked between them: it reminded Jo of the UNIT of her day, big, with round headlights and a canvas covering. They even had the old dull-green paint. Jo supposed that, like Hynes's Land Rover, they were on hire from the Tanzanian army.

'Looks like you're planning to be here for a while,' she commented.

To her surprise, Hynes laughed. 'You sure you're not a news reporter?' He pulled up the Land Rover by the nearest of the huts. Then he took hold of her arm and squeezed it, hard.

Startled, Jo turned, met his eyes.

'Don't even think about going into the restricted area, right?' he said. 'I know why you're here. We don't need any trouble right now. So just do the job you came to do, and make a good report to Geneva, right?'

Jo stared back at him, trying to hide her relief. It was obvious that Jacob thought she was checking up on him. A Command Office spy, sent to check that he wasn't stealing UN-issue toilet paper.

'I'll stay out of the restricted area,' she said, trying to sound cool and authoritative, the bureaucrat abroad. 'But I'll report what I like. Clear?'

Hynes let go of her arm. He laughed again. 'OK,' he said. 'Report what you like then.' He got out of the Land Rover.

Jo suddenly felt cold in the hot, stuffy cab. Hynes didn't seem to think that it mattered what she reported.

And if it didn't matter, then probably –

The Land Rover door opened.

'I'll show you to your room.'

Fossils.

Rowenna Michaels was staring at hundreds of fossils. Skulls, ribcages, hips, femurs, jawbones. Many of them seemed almost complete.

I must be dreaming, she thought, but she knew she wasn't.

She began to feel afraid.

'Rowenna?' Julie's voice. 'Rowenna are you OK?'

Rowenna tried to move, felt a stab of pain from her back.

*- turning, the gun in his hand, the gun -*

'I'm -' Rowenna struggled with a dry throat, dry tongue, dry lips. 'I was shot. I was shot again -'

She couldn't believe it, couldn't believe she'd been so dumb as to put herself in the way of a bullet again. And all for a piece of skull.

Skull. Fossil. Fossil skull.

She stared at the fossils, found her voice again. 'What the hell are those?'

'Dead humans.'

The voice wasn't Julie's. It was oddly inflected, neutral, strange. The voice of -

*- the alien oh God the alien where am I what's happening to me -*

'You will join them soon.'

'Ignore him.' Julie's voice. 'He's just trying to scare us.'

But Julie sounded scared herself. *Very* scared.

Rowenna took a deep breath, then slowly, painfully, pushed herself upright with her arms.

She was in a cave. Low, badly lit, damp, smelly. Turning her head, she could see the end of Julie's legs, with black restraining straps around them. She couldn't turn far enough to see her friend's face. Looking forward, she saw straps around her own legs. She couldn't see a bullet wound, couldn't feel any wound. Had Hynes really shot her? Perhaps it had been some kind of tranquilliser...

She couldn't *remember*.

With an effort, she levered herself around so that she could face the alien. He was lying on a wooden pallet, his legs folded beneath him. He looked less horselike now, more like a folded dragon in his black body armour with its glittering constellations of lights. Rowenna could see a keyboard unit around his neck: more primitive technology, almost certainly human in origin. There was a speaker attached, and a voice processor. She'd seen similar units in the hospital when she'd been recovering from her injuries; they were used by people who had lost the power of speech.

'What's going to happen to us?' she asked the alien.

The three-fingered hand moved over the keys. 'You will die painfully, as many of my people will die painfully at the hands of your descendants.'

'Why?'

'My life began in your future. Humans invaded my planet. This is my response.'

A whisper from Julie. 'Jesus, Rowenna, this can't be happening.'

Rowenna remembered Jo, the stories of Autons and Axons and Daleks. 'It's happening,' she said. Then to the alien: 'Look, *I* haven't done anything to your people. Julie hasn't either. Perhaps if you talk to our government now, we could find some way to prevent –'

'I tried all that,' interrupted Julie. Her voice was raw with fear.

'You are already dying,' said the alien. 'You will be dead soon.'

Rowenna closed her eyes. What did the alien mean? Poison? Virus? She could hear Julie's breathing, fast and hoarse.

A faint moan of pain.

Suddenly Rowenna realised why Julie was so afraid. It had already started: she was sick, in pain.

'No.' Rowenna's own voice surprised her. 'This is

crazy. You have to stop it, whatever it is. There's got to be a way we can live with your people.'

The fingers moved on the keyboard. Julie moaned again, a stifled, terrified, sound.

'*No*,' came the reply at last. 'There is only a way you can die with us. All of you, with all of us. The entire world we have both known. And that will happen very soon.'


There was a guard, a single, tall, dark-skinned man pacing up and down in the weak moonlight.

Jo watched him for a while with some annoyance. Then she stepped down from the doorway of the hut, gave him a wave and a grin, and set off towards the trucks.

He didn't challenge her.

Hynes's Land Rover was gone. She followed the tyre tracks as far as the road, then walked a little way up the road towards the gorge. The night was hot: insects whined in the darkness, and there was a faint chatter of cicadas from the long grass on the hillside.

'Hey! Miss!'

The guard. Jo sighed.

'Miss! You can't go that way – captain's orders!'

Jo turned, saw the man dimly silhouetted against the lights of the barrack huts. 'I'm just getting a breath of air,' she explained. 'Should I go the other way? Where does this restricted area start?'

'Here, really,' said the guard. 'But I guess as long as you stay away from the cave, there won't be a problem. Go up to the top of the gorge – there's a path.' He pointed, and Jo saw a crude flight of steps leading up from the road.

Jo thanked him and started up the steps.

*The cave*.

Right.

Only about three kilometres of cliff face to look at. In the dark. Where the hell was she going to start?

A sharp click ahead of her answered her question.

'Ms Grant.' Jacob Hynes's voice. 'It's clear that you want to see your friends real bad.'

Jo could see him now, crouching in the shadows, the gun aimed directly at her. 'I –' she began.

'It's your lucky day,' said Hynes. He stood up, aimed the gun carefully at Jo's chest. 'I'm able to reveal their location now. Just come along with me, and you'll get to join them right away.'

# CHAPTER 9

Kitig stood at the window of his bedroom, looking down at the garden where the Doctor and Sam were playing tag with his children.

They're *happy*, he thought. They're *laughing*. Surely the Destroyer of Worlds would be a sour-faced fellow, full of the plasma and brimstone of his calling.

But the facts remained. The Doctor might be the Destroyer of Worlds, the Uncreator. He had given several signs, not the least of which was his interest in the *Book of Keeping*.

Kitig studied the aliens, knowing that the existence of his entire world might depend on his observation, on his judgement.

Sam was just small enough to ride on the back of Critil, Kitig's eldest: they were cantering round the garden, leaping over the low walls, twisting between the frosted junipers, barrelling down the bright-yellow arch of the trellis, which was thick with winter jasmine. The Doctor, was with the twin foals Jontil and Mritig, chasing them – or, rather, Jontil and Mritig were doing the chasing, while the Doctor did clownish things, running on the spot, making wild leaps into the air that just failed to connect with the target, instead landing him in the junipers, or ending in a long skid across the frozen pond, with his light-brown mane flying in the air.

It all might be misdirection, of course. In fact, it was *obviously* misdirection, of a sort. The Doctor was happy because he was happy: but perhaps he was also be pretending to be happy because he was hiding something.

The question was: what? Was he merely a spy, a petty thief on the run? Or was he truly the Destroyer of Worlds, the legendary nemesis of the Tractite species?

The *Book of Keeping* was vague on the subject of the Uncreator: he will be a biped, with pale skin, and he will know our language and our ways. He will arrive unexpectedly. That was all that it said *about* him. But it also said that he must be destroyed, at once and without mercy, 'or everything that the Tractites have built, on all of the worlds, will cease to exist'.

Kitig looked away from the window, at the translucent walls of the bedroom, the ancient crystal furniture, at his wife, Narunil, lying on the hay bed, her eyes closed, her legs and arms crossed, the fear and tension apparent in every line of her body.

He swallowed. It can't be true, he thought. This can't be real. Not now, when I have my house to grow, my family to care for. This alien can't be the Uncreator. There is no Uncreator: it's just an old legend from the times when our people were weak and our cultures steeped in xenophobia. This is all just a horrible coincidence...

He turned back to the window. The Doctor was now lying on his back in the freezing grass, laughing at Sam ,who was trying – and failing – to stand up on Critil's back.

There was a rustle of cloth behind him, and the heavy clopping of Narunil crossing the floor. She slipped in by his side, her body against his, her breath against the side of his neck.

'What do you think?' she asked after a while.

'I don't believe it,' said Kitig. 'I never did believe it. Evil without purpose doesn't make sense – and I can't believe that the Doctor is so deranged that he would deliberately destroy us. Look at him!'

'Why did you choose to be a Watcher of the Keeping, then?'

Kitig shrugged. 'I don't know. My father did it.'

Narunil moved away from him, gave a derisive snort.

Kitig turned to face her. 'How often do you think someone who might be the Uncreator comes along? About once every thousand years! It was just a sinecure. A guaranteed income for life, a ridiculous title from the Primitive Ages, and no work. If I'd even thought it possible that it would really happen, I wouldn't have taken it on.'

'It *has* happened,' said Narunil. 'And you have a duty.' She tossed her head, went to the jade wardrobe at the far wall, found some leather shoes and began pulling them on over her hooves.

Kitig took a breath. 'Narunil. My father told me that the Watchers aren't just there to guard us against the Uncreator. They're also there to make sure we don't go killing every biped who arrives here in unexplained circumstances. There have been irrational reactions in the past, unnecessary killings –'

'I don't think I'm being irrational. I'm just trying to protect my family, and everybody else's family. Which is *your* job, I think.'

'Narunil –'

Narunil walked across to him, three shoes on, the fourth in her hand. She opened her night eyes and Kitig saw the angry clouds there, flushed amber with blood.

'He was interested in our history – our *evolutionary* history. He asked about the Uncreator. He has the right physical shape, and he lied about the spaceship – a "re-entry vehicle"? It obviously came out of nowhere. It obviously travelled through time.'

'Not obviously –' began Kitig.

'How else could it have got there?' snapped Narunil. 'What more does he have to do, Kitig? Wave a banner in the air saying "I have come to destroy you all"?'

Kitig turned his head to hers, so that their cheeks touched, and put an arm around her shoulders.

'I've contacted Berulil, the Watcher in Defiris. He'll be here in a couple of hours.'

Narunil pulled away from him, went to the pool near the bed and splashed her head and neck with the scented water. 'You don't need anyone else's opinion! It's *obvious*!'

Kitig turned back to the window, saw the Doctor looking up at him from the garden. The strange, round face was still smiling, the golden mane still bright in the sun, but –

*The Doctor was watching him.*

He felt a prickling of fear along his spine. The Doctor couldn't possibly have heard anything that he and Narunil had said.

But – those eyes...

Suddenly, the Doctor frowned, then put a hand on his chest and fell over backward. Kitig saw Sam laughing down at him from Critil's back.

Then the Doctor's face began to turn blue.

Sam looked around in consternation, said something to Critil and slid down off her back. She bent over the

Doctor for a moment, then set off for the house at a dead run.

Narunil trotted to the window. 'What's happening?'

'I don't know. I think the Doctor is ill.'

The garden door slammed, and Sam's rapid, uneven, bipedal footsteps echoed in the lower parts of the house. Kitig went out to the inner gallery, a helical chamber in pale-green crystal. Roughened steps led down the helix to the ground level, and Sam was bounding up them.

'Kitig!' There were still pieces of ice and soil on her clothing from the game, but her expression was tense and frightened. 'We need to get back to the TARDIS straight away!'

'Your ship?' asked Kitig.

'Yes – the TARDIS – please, the Doctor's ill.'

Kitig and Narunil glanced at each other, a flicker of night eyes. Kitig could see his wife's suspicion, could almost feel it, like a breath against his skin.

And she was right. He knew that. This 'illness' was very convenient. And the way the Doctor had looked up at him –

Kitig could feel the evidence closing in, like a wire noose.

*I don't want to kill anyone.*

'He says he needs some medicine we have in the TARDIS,' Sam was saying.

'Let me see him,' said Kitig. He could feel Narunil's gaze following him as he went after Sam down the stairs.

In the garden, the Doctor was lying quite still on the cold ground. Sam leaned over him. Kitig looked around, saw Critil and the younger children standing by the winter jasmine, nuzzling one another's neck and snorting nervously.

Abruptly, Sam jolted upright, her face creased with emotion.

'He's - umm -' She broke off, stamped a foot on the ground in an almost Tractite gesture. 'I don't know.'

Kitig knelt down over the Doctor, put his head to the alien's chest, listened.

'He still has a heartbeat,' he said. 'Two, I think. Is that normal?'

Sam swallowed, looked at the ground, said nothing. The exposed skin of her face was pale. From what he knew of species of her type, Kitig guessed that she was in shock.

He came to a decision.

'Jontil, Mritig, find my saddle baskets. I'll carry him. Critil, call a skimmer from the park.'

He saw Narunil in the shadow of the house, her day eyes wide with astonishment.

He walked over to her slowly.

'What are you doing?' she asked in a low voice. 'There's no way we should take them back to their ship. We can't wait for any more consultations. We should kill them ourselves. Now.'

Kitig put an arm on hers. 'I've told you. I can't take the risk of killing an intelligent being - or letting one die - for the sake of an ancient story that might not even be true.'

Narunil glared at him, her night eyes open again, dark with blood. 'If you won't do it now,' she hissed, 'then at least let me come with you. I will kill them, if it becomes necessary.'

Kitig looked down at his hooves planted in the cold soil. He knew she was right. The Doctor and Sam might be innocent – but they might not be. There was always the possibility that the *Book of Keeping* was telling the truth.

In which case, the stakes were too high to take any chances.

'Very well,' he said. 'Come with me. Kill them yourself if you have to. But wait until I have made the decision. Until we have no choice. Will you promise me that?'

Narunil's night eyes closed. 'I promise.'

But Kitig wasn't sure he believed her.

# CHAPTER 10

The alien had been gone for some time when Rowenna heard the voices. They echoed in the cave, and for one disorientating moment they seemed to be coming from the fossil skulls embedded in the walls.

'What's that?' whispered Julie. She'd calmed down a bit, but her voice still shook. She claimed she was feverish, but Rowenna was beginning to wonder if it was shock: she felt no symptoms herself.

She shushed Julie, listened. She couldn't yet make out any words, but the tone of the discussion was clear. The voice was earnest, aggressive, demanding. Some accomplice of Jacob Hynes who was quarrelling with him, perhaps? Rowenna put her mind on full alert, looking for any clue that might help her argue her way out of this.

Then she heard footsteps, and suddenly could make out the words. 'Look, for the last time, I'm *Jo Grant*. I've been on the UNIT books since 1971. I'm a personal friend of RSM Benton in London. If I go missing, believe me, they're going to notice, and they won't just think I wandered off into the sunset. You won't get away with –' A pause. 'Rowenna!'

Rowenna licked her lips, tried to kick-start her dry throat into life. After a couple of coughs she made it. 'Hello, Jo. Looks like I've messed up your life again.' It was an old joke between them: back in the cottage, Jo had always complained that Rowenna was untidy.

Jo's face appeared. It was older, and sadder, but it was

Jo. 'Hello, Rowenna. I suppose you know what it feels like to have an adventure now.'

Rowenna couldn't stop herself from smiling. 'It's crazy,' she said, 'but I'm certain, absolutely certain, that you're going to get us out of this.'

'Just tell me what's –'

'Lie down, please.' Jacob Hynes's voice. Bizarrely, he sounded more anxious than Jo.

Jo turned round, said calmly, 'Shut up, I'm talking to my friend,' then turned back to Rowenna. 'Don't worry about him, he's nobody. Have you seen the aliens yet?'

Rowenna nodded, trying to repress hysterical laughter. 'I've seen one. He's trying to poison us, claims we're going to die soon.' She swallowed, the humour suddenly leaching out of the situation. 'Julie says she's ill.'

'I'm running a fever,' said Julie.

Jo moved, knelt down between Rowenna and Julie.

'Gavril is testing a virus,' said Hynes. 'We're going to destroy the human race with it.'

'Mm-hmm,' said Jo. 'Let's check your pulse, Julie.'

'Are you listening to me?' bawled Hynes. He moved inside Rowenna's field of vision. She could see the redness of his cheeks, the insanity in his eyes.

But she knew the game Jo was playing, or at least had a pretty good idea. She kept quiet.

'I'm Alpha and Omega. The Beginning and the End. I'm better than God. You understand that?'

'Have you got a glass of water for Julie?' asked Jo.

Hynes was practically drooling now. 'I could kill you right now!' he bawled. 'It won't make any difference!'

Jo stood up and faced him, hands on hips. 'Look, I'm not interested in your loony plans. I want a glass of water for Julie. If you don't get it I'm going to tell your alien friends that you're really working for us.'

Hynes began to laugh: helpless, insane laughter. He collapsed against the wooden platform giggling. 'Working for you? Working for UNIT? You think that Gavril's going to believe that after all I've done for him?'

'And what exactly have you done?'

Hynes's expression became sly. 'I'm afraid I can't reveal that information.' He began giggling again.

'Jo? Where are we?' whispered Rowenna.

'Kilgai,' said Jo. 'In one of the caves. Here, let me just look at your leg, it seems to be –'

There was a snapping sound, and Rowenna realised that the leg restraint was gone. She was being lifted up, and Julie had jumped up, her face flushed, her body swaying.

'Follow me!' yelled Jo, right in Rowenna's ear. She saw Hynes aiming the gun –

'Jo!'

But Julie had collided with Hynes, knocked him back against the wooden pallet. The gun spun out of his hand.

Rowenna saw shadowy movement at the back of the skull-walled chamber. 'The alien!'

Jo was running, clumsily, Rowenna in her arms. Ahead was a glowing tree, clearly alien, clearly –

A gunshot. Sharp, loud, followed by the whistle and echo of the bullet. Rowenna flinched inwardly, but tried not to move for fear of unbalancing Jo.

*If it hits me let it be in the head this time, or the heart, let it be instantly fatal; please, God, I don't want to suffer like that again.*

Rowenna could sense fresh air around her now, the

grass and dung smell of the outside. The tree was directly ahead, its branches seeming to writhe with light. For a moment Rowenna wondered if it was something other than a tree, if it would move to block their progress, but it remained still. They passed it and Rowenna caught a glimpse of infinite detail, light in motion. Beauty.

'Stop right there!'

*He was ahead of them, how had he got ahead of them?*

She was sliding sideways, into the branches of the tree, she was going to fall and –

*A gunshot* –

The tree flared with light, and she was falling –

# CHAPTER 11

It had been the wink that had finally done it. Sam had been fairly sure that the Doctor was acting, before that, despite the alarming symptoms. But that wink, when she'd leaned over him in the garden. So playful, so let's-fool-the-baddies, as if they were still fighting Zygons. She'd almost said it then, she'd actually started to say it: '*He's just pretending. He's got a reason for going back to the ship that he's not telling you about.*' But she hadn't quite dared. It would feel too much like betrayal. More importantly, she hadn't known how the Tractites would react. They might kill the Doctor. They might kill her – or worse, not kill her, and leave her on her own in an alien universe for the rest of her life.

But, even so, it had to be wrong to let the Doctor destroy this world. There had to be another way, an easy alternative that wouldn't mean anyone getting hurt.

She just couldn't think of one.

Kitig been had carrying the Doctor across his back in a large wicker pannier; for the journey, he'd put it down on the deck of the skimmer. The basket had a padded lining, smelled faintly of citrus fruits, and looked more comfortable than most beds. The Doctor appeared to be, quite simply, asleep. His hair fell around his head, shining in the sun like the halo of a saint in a medieval painting. Kitig and Narunil stood at the tiller of the skimmer, their cheeks touching. They seemed tense – but then they thought the Doctor was ill, possibly dying. Maybe they thought they were to blame for it.

And I can't explain, thought Sam. That's the worst thing. If only there was someone to talk with. Someone who would understand.

The skimmer was flying over marshland now, the Tractite city of Afarnis invisible in the glare of sunlight on water behind them. In this light, the marshland was a different world: the dull reeds now glowed in startling greens and yellows; the water was bright blue; even the mud banks that formed the sides of the islands seemed clear, alive with shades of sandy brown and dark shadow. Wading birds stood in the water, waiting for passing fish. A solitary willow tree stood on a small, hunchbacked island, and a pair of falcons were perched on a dead branch, watching the landscape.

This was Earth as it was meant to be, thought Sam. Clean, wild, almost infinite in its variety; and, yes, a few cities spotted here and there, what was wrong with that? The difference was, the Tractites had it under control. No drugs, no wars, no starving millions, no smoggy monoculture destined to get slowly worse and worse for the next thousand or two years and then – if the Doctor was to be believed – simply cease to exist. Instead harmony, balance, perfection. And it had gone on for millions of years.

How could the world be so beautiful and so difficult to handle at the same time?

Suddenly Sam thought of something. A way of hinting at the truth – but something that she could retract if it looked as if the Doctor was in serious danger.

'Kitig,' she said slowly. 'You said that you thought the Tractites might have got to Earth – that is, here, to Paratractis – by time travel.'

Both Kitig and Narunil looked round sharply.

'I've been thinking about that,' Sam went on, 'and I don't think it makes any sense. Time travel isn't possible. If you could have time travel then – well – for example, the Doctor and I could just go back in time and stop the Tractites from ever coming here. Then the place might fill up with – oh, I don't know. Talking giraffes. Insectoids. Perhaps even bipeds, like us.'

She said the last words slowly, holding Kitig's humanlike day eyes with her own.

Kitig looked down. 'Yes,' he said. 'I see that it's possible.' He was silent for a moment. 'It's also possible that Tractites could do the same to the bipeds. The cycle could go on for ever.'

Sam fancied that she could hear a sharp intake of breath from the Doctor, behind her. Was that what he was afraid of, then? An infinitely repeating loop of mutual genocide?

The skimmer swayed slightly, and Sam realised that Narunil had taken a step towards her. The Tractite stretched out her arms so that they almost touched Sam's body, lowered her huge head as if she were about to charge. Sam could feel her breath, warm, scented of musk and grass.

Suddenly Sam felt afraid. She realised that if Narunil wanted to kill her, she could very easily do it. One kick would be enough.

'Narunil,' said Kitig. 'We're almost there. Could you help me lift the Doctor's basket on to my back?'

For a moment, Narunil didn't move, then she slowly stepped backward, one leg at a time, her eyes still on Sam.

'Narunil,' repeated Kitig.

Sam swallowed. 'I'm sorry,' she said. 'I didn't mean to frighten you. Time travel's impossible, of course.'

'Of course,' said Kitig quietly.

Sam sat down at the edge of the skimmer, watched as Narunil lifted the Doctor in his basket up on to Kitig's back.

Had Narunil been going to hurt her? It seemed an overreaction to what she'd said. Even if the Tractite had guessed that it was a warning, then surely it would have been more sensible to ask her some questions.

But they weren't asking anything. The skimmer was landing, and there was the TARDIS still parked on its mud bank, with a small brown wading bird perched on top. The bird flew away in alarm as the skimmer crunched into the reeds.

Then the skimmer's force field went down, and cold damp air hit Sam's face. There was a wind on the marshes: the reeds were stirring, rattling. The bird was calling out, a steady, piping note. Other birds joined in.

Alarm calls. Warnings.

*The humans are coming*.

Sam remembered the Tractite book: the starship, the burning light. Perhaps the Tractites didn't need to ask any questions. Perhaps they already knew.

Had Narunil been going to kill her?

Kitig stepped down from the skimmer, balancing the basket with the Doctor in it carefully on his back; Narunil stayed by the tiller. Sam walked past, her steps unsteady.

But Narunil did nothing, said nothing.

Sam followed Kitig, keeping a safe distance from his powerful rear legs.

The TARDIS door opened. Kitig paused outside. 'Just keep walking,' said Sam. 'It'll let you in, if you've got the Doctor.'

Kitig took another step, another, then seemed to vanish through the door, even though it was far too small for him to pass through. There was an intake of breath from Narunil behind her; Sam hastily followed Kitig. She heard the familiar low hum of the console room around her and heard the ticking of the clocks.

The Doctor was sitting up in his basket, smiling. 'Wonderful!' he said. 'I feel much better already! Now if I can find the myalgesic medication –' He sprang over the side of the basket, rushed across to the console.

No medication there, thought Sam. More lies.

Kitig was looking up, his eyes wide with wonder. Sam followed his gaze, saw the vast blue-bronze height of the console room. It somehow seemed to merge with infinity, the heavy substance of the console arms and distant walls gradually becoming pure light. The Doctor had never explained adequately whether it actually had a roof or not. 'It used to,' was all he would say. 'Can't think where it's got to.'

There were clicks and thumps from the console. Sam sat up, saw the Doctor fiddling with controls. He looked up, saw her watching, popped a jelly baby into his mouth.

'Medication,' he explained. 'I feel fine now, but it's best not to take any chances. Would you like one?' He advanced towards her, holding a bright-red jelly baby.

Sam screwed up her face. She didn't like the sickly things at the best of times, and the red ones were her least favourite. She shook her head.

The Doctor's eyes met hers.

'They're good for you,' he said.

Reluctantly, Sam took the sweet and put it in her mouth.

'An infinitely repeating loop of mutual genocide,' said the Doctor, speaking very quietly.

Sam felt her stomach turn over.

*He knows everything – of course. He wasn't asleep on the skimmer. He overheard what I said. He overheard what I thought.*

*Well, that's not really a surprise. But I'm still going to find another way. There must be some other way, whatever he says.*

'The effects of the medication can be a bit alarming,' the Doctor said suddenly. 'Kitig, I wonder if you would be so kind as to leave Sam and me for a few minutes.'

'Of course. I hope that you recover soon, Doctor.' He trotted slowly towards the doors. 'Remind me to ask you about this dimensional displacement effect at some time,' he commented over his shoulder, waving an arm around him at the vast dimensions of the console room.

Sam stared after him, bewildered. He seemed almost ludicrously unsuspicious. Did no one on this planet ever pull a fast one?

As the doors closed behind Kitig, the Doctor remarked, 'That was a bit of a chance you took, on the skimmer.'

'I know,' said Sam simply. She looked at the floor. 'I just wanted to find out how much they knew.'

'Yes. And did you?'

Sam shook her head.

To her relief the Doctor didn't say any more, but returned his attention to the screens above the console.

They had lit up, become windows to a world of animated mathematics: scrolling lines of equations, three-dimensional helices with bar graphs inside them, moving bubbles whose surfaces were whirling drifts of symbols. The Doctor pulled on a chain that brought one of the displays to eye level, watched it for perhaps half a minute, then nodded.

'We're in trouble, Sam.' He gestured at the display, which had now settled down to show a succession of blobs and bars. They meant nothing to Sam, but the Doctor had evidently forgotten that, because he went on, 'You can see the problem. The quasi-stable flux interference – the blue stuff – is the original universe, that's the one we came from. It's stable enough, but shrinking. The rest is just a series of interference patterns.'

Sam looked at the screen, then at the Doctor. 'Which means?' she prompted.

'I don't know...' The Doctor pushed a few more switches on the console. 'I daren't take off. We might never land again. The whole multiverse could fall into the vortex, Sam, just dissolve as if it had never been there.'

Sam thought through what the Doctor had said, unravelling every word, as if it was some particularly difficult concept in GCSE maths. Finally she said, 'Interference patterns between what and what?'

'I don't know. Kitig's listening at the door. Possibly there are several alternative universes, just as you said at the beginning – but that isn't supposed to happen, it can't possibly stabilise, ever. Unless...' He paused, put a finger to his mouth. 'It has to be something to do with us.' He jumped up suddenly, grabbed Sam's arms and swung her round like a child. 'Yes! That's it! *We're* doing it!'

Feeling slightly dizzy, and with her mouth still tasting of sickly jelly baby, Sam tried to collect her thoughts. 'So what are we doing that's making –' she began.

'I don't *know*,' said the Doctor. 'There has to be something else going on.'

It's at least the third time he's said that since this thing began, thought Sam. A strange feeling came over her, as if she were watching herself on video, or perhaps watching her own thoughts, ticking like the TARDIS clocks, lots of different ticks all mixed up together.

Perhaps I'm going to faint, she thought.

Then suddenly the console room came back into focus, and she remembered something. 'Did you say Kitig was listening to us?'

The Doctor grinned. 'Don't worry, he can't hear anything.' He looked at the screen again, frowned. 'It's shrinking.' His voice had changed again: solemn, almost afraid.

'What's shrinking?' asked Sam, although she was fairly sure that she knew.

'The original universe. The stable part of the vortex. Let me see, I might be able to get us back to –' He pounced on the console, attacked switches and levers. 'Oh, *no*. No, no, no, no, *no*!'

Sam looked at him, feeling that strange sense of displacement again. She couldn't destroy Kitig's world, but she had to if she wanted to go home – but she couldn't but she had to but she *couldn't* it was so *right* it was so *beautiful*…

'We're losing the eighties,' the Doctor was saying. 'And

everything back to 2002 – in Earth terms, that is – has already gone. What's left is shrinking fast. But wait a minute – no, that's not right. That *can't* be!' He was shouting. Sam heard the deep rumble of the TARDIS powering up.

'Doctor, we've got to let Kitig back on board.'

'*What?*'

'It's his world too. He has to be here. He has to help us decide.'

The Doctor was just staring at her. She jumped forward and hit the door control with her palm. Kitig was kneeling outside in the bright sunlight, his shoes and legs covered with mud. He sprang back as the doors opened.

'I'm sorry, I thought –' he began.

'*Get in!*' shrieked Sam.

'Sam, what are you doing? You can't possibly save him, you can't save any of them and anyway what would be the *use*? He'd be just as stranded as we are! Sam, please, you've got to –' His hand was trying to push hers off the door control. The TARDIS was screaming, a noise Sam had never heard before, and if only she knew what was happening, if only she knew what to do –

'Get *in*!' she bawled at Kitig.

And suddenly he jumped, a great showjumper's leap through the strange geometry of the door.

The Doctor knocked Sam's hand away from the control, hard, and the TARDIS jolted, rolled like a ship at sea, roared. Sheets of light fell around the console, controls sparked, screens flashed warnings.

'Oh, Sam,' said the Doctor, bowed over the console. 'Sam, Sam, Sam, Sam. What have you done?'

Sam stared at him for a moment, glanced at Kitig, who was looking wildly around the console room with his smaller, human-style eyes. And suddenly she knew. She knew what she'd done, she knew what to say.

And she knew she was right.

'I've saved Kitig's life,' she said. 'Did you want me to leave him behind to die?'

For a moment the Doctor said nothing. Sam felt her muscles bunch with unexpected anger. Of course he couldn't say anything. She was right.

Kitig was still staring around him. The TARDIS was still pitching like a ship at sea.

The Doctor said, 'Sam, listen to me very carefully, because the future of the entire multiverse may depend on whether you understand what I'm going to tell you.'

Sam drew a breath, ready to argue, then took a look at the Doctor's face and thought better of it.

'Time itself is losing cohesion. If complete instability occurs everything goes into the vortex: your Earth, Kitig's Earth, every star and galaxy and quasar and black hole and everything that ever was or will be or might be. The entire multiverse will collapse like a sand castle in front of the tide.'

Distantly, Sam became aware of a bell chiming.

The cloister bell.

That's all I need, she thought.

'I wasn't going to leave Kitig to die,' she said stubbornly. 'It was the only moral choice to make.'

But the Doctor wasn't listening. He was staring at the console. The time rotor had stopped moving, and one by one the screens were going blank.

'We're too late,' he muttered. 'The tide's come in.'

# BOOK THREE

*The alien seemed less like a corpse now. His figure was
still skeletal, but the glucose solution had brought a
faint echo of colour to his skin, and the semblance of
life to his eyes. Mauvril wondered if this was going to
make it harder after she had finished her confession;
because she knew that she was still going to have to
kill him.*

*She met his eyes, knew he saw the truth in her gaze.*

*Her future. His future. All of the futures, or lack of
them.*

*The lack of choices.*

*'You've got to understand,' she muttered.*

*He nodded. 'Go on with your story.'*

*She looked away, marshalled her thoughts for a
moment, then went on.*

*'I don't know how long I hid in the forest. The sounds
of explosions almost deafened me. The ground shook.
There was a terrible, hot, metal-scented wind, and the
trees thrashed about like demons. One nearly fell on
me. After that, it was dark, and almost silent, apart
from distant rumblings echoing from the hills. The air
smelled of burning, and gradually filled with ash and
dust, until I found it hard to breathe.*

*'At last, a weak, grey dawn light began to show
through the damaged tree tops. I found my way back
to the farm, staying away from the paths, wading
instead through crumpled brush grass thick with grey
dust. My eyes watered, my lungs wheezed: by the time
I reached the edge of the forest I was dizzy and
exhausted, and confused enough to carry on walking,
out into the ashen ground, until the heat began to*

burn the skin above my hooves.

'Then I realised. The farm wasn't there any more.

'In fact, I wasn't even at the edge of the forest. The black, smouldering stumps of trees told me that, and the slope of the land was wrong, rising instead of falling. The air was blurred with smoke and dust and it wavered in the heat, making grey illusions jump in the distance. I began to think that it wasn't just the farm, that the whole world was gone, replaced by this burning plain.

'I staggered back into the forest. This time I didn't stop walking until I dropped.

'When I woke up I was cold and thirsty. I found a stream, and drank, though the water tasted of ash. Then I walked through the dense trees, following the stream up, with some idea that it might be better in the hills. Eventually I came to a path, and started to recognise the country. I realised that I was near Daranos, the next village along the white road from Tafalis.

'There wasn't much ash now, though I could still smell burning. The patches of sky that I could see through the trees were strange - grey and hazy with smoke. But there was some - weak - sunlight, and it was getting warmer. I began to feel some kind of hope. Perhaps there was a limit to the disaster. When I saw the village, glimpses of sunlit stone through the trees, I felt a surge of joy.

'But Daranos was dead, of course. You know the story, I expect, without my telling it: the melted stone of the houses, the potholed roads, the chemical reek of alien explosives. You've seen it so many times. But it *was new to me then, and these were my people. You have to remember, too, that we were a peaceful race, for the most part. Physical conflict was rare, murder was unheard of. I almost died there in Daranos, from the sheer agony of what I saw. Orange insects crawled over dead eyes of the villagers, in and out of dead mouths. Charred bones projected from the remnants of flesh. There wasn't much blood: most alien weapons burn rather than cut. But there were some who seemed to have been beaten to death, in what I now realise, looking back, can only have been the exercise of gratuitous cruelty.*

*'I wandered from house to house, saw the burnt heap of rubble that had been the temple. I thought of Pakip, of Larnaj and their baby, and I knew for certain then that they, too, were dead. I didn't know why it had happened. I didn't even really know that there had been an invasion – I simply didn't think of it that way, you see. Everything since I had seen the vast alien ship appear over Tafalis was confused in my mind: if someone had asked me whether there was one kind of alien, or two, or whether they were attacking us, or helping us against some great natural disaster, I couldn't have answered. My mind was paralysed, unable to reach even the most elementary conclusions about what had happened to my world.*

*'Eventually I found myself walking towards the village well, drawn by the smell of fresh water. I heard a movement, turned, and saw a black-carapaced alien walking towards me, the band of plastic that augmented its eyes glowing an uneven red. It was clearly hurt: its gait was unsteady on its two legs; its breath*

rattled in its throat. It must have been injured in the attack on the village; why it had been left behind by the others I don't know.

'My first instinct was to help. As I've said, I really didn't understand what was happening. Even if I had, I don't think I'd have thought any differently. There hadn't yet been time for the outer shock to work its way inside me and change the habits of a lifetime.

'So I stepped forward and offered to fetch water from the well. I remember thinking that if I helped the alien perhaps it would be grateful. Perhaps we could talk. Perhaps I could find some way of understanding why the people in Daranos were dead, and what had happened to Tafalis, and to my farm and my family.

'The black-carapaced beast raised a glittering object in its hand and spoke, its voice little more than an animal growl. I couldn't understand the words – it wasn't until much later, when I found out about the combat drugs that the aliens used, that I realised they probably hadn't made sense anyway.

'Anyway, the alien shot me, but because it was dying, or perhaps because the targeting systems fitted to its eyes were damaged, it missed, burning my legs instead of killing me.

'Instinctively, I jumped clear. The alien turned the gun round for another shot, and this time the movement was more definite, more controlled. Dying or not, I think it would have killed me the second time. Fortunately I didn't give it the chance: I jumped forward, kicked out.

'I only meant to knock the gun out of its hand, but my aim wasn't too good either: in my panic I killed it.

'You have to understand how terrible this was for me, then. I had killed a living being, terminated the development of a mind; in our culture, nothing justified such a sin. I remember watching the blood leaking from the alien's mouth. I took the eye-shield away, saw the dead eyes behind it, with their strange gossamer attachments. For a moment the light moving along those optic fibres gave me hope: then I realised they were only machines.

'All my strength went then. The body chemicals, the natural drugs that had kept me going, desperate to survive in the chaos of the invasion, suddenly deserted me. I had killed. I deserved to die.

'So I collapsed in the soil and waited to die, shivering, the body of my enemy cooling beside me.'

Mauvril had to stop then. The story was choking her throat, choking her brain. The dark walls of the cell were pressing in on her, as if she were the prisoner, and the Doctor her captor.

She looked at the Doctor, who nodded.

'I understand,' he said gently. 'I know why you killed that one. But why did you kill all of them? After killing one had felt like that?'

Mauvril closed her eyes – all four of them – and looked away. She couldn't answer.

Not yet.

# CHAPTER 12

Jo was falling.

The light of the tree was flowing around her, and Rowenna was slipping away, out of her grasp, her limbs flailing, her mouth open in what might have been a cry of pain.

Jo reached out for her friend, saw Hynes, gun in hand, silhouetted against –

*Against blue sky* –

She landed awkwardly on hard brown earth, found herself surrounded by crushed dry stalks of grass. She sat up quickly, rubbing her eyes against the dazzling sunlight. As her sight adjusted to the glare, she saw a sea of yellow grass around her, shimmering in the heat of a noonday sun. A shambling, dry, purple-black mountain of rough cuboid blocks rose from the plain in front of her, capped with a thin crown of trees.

*This is clearly a displacement in space*, said a small cool voice inside her. *Possibly also a displacement in time. Question is, by how much?*

Something growled.

A woman screamed: Julie.

Jo stood up. She saw Julie standing, red-faced, pointing at something moving in the grass.

The something that had growled, roared. A fully grown lioness reared up out of the grass only yards away, jaws wide, snarling. It started to run straight at Jo.

Before she could think about reacting, Jo was aware of the impact of the hard earth against her back, the kick of a paw which felt as hard as a bone against her leg. Then the lion was gone. There was the sound of another growl, and –

Another lion, leaping right over her.

A chorus of hoots and grunts and bird screams joined the growls, and Jo heard the clatter of wings and hooves thudding on the hard ground. She stood up, ignoring pain from her leg and back, saw lions of all sizes running away in several directions. As she watched, they seemed to disappear, blending into the golden grass. Beyond them, antelope stampeded, and a cloud of birds rose from a patch of thorn scrub.

She saw a nearer movement, jumped, then realised it was Rowenna. Her friend was sprawled in the grass, one leg bent under her body. Their eyes met, and Rowenna nodded slightly.

'I think I'm OK,' she whispered, as if she wasn't quite sure that she believed it herself. As Jo watched, she pushed herself half upright with her arms, and tried to look around.

'I think they've all gone,' said Jo. 'They'd be afraid of us. Appearing suddenly like that.'

'Never mind that. Where's Julie?'

Jo looked around, and saw the big woman kneeling in the grass. Praying?

Then she heard the woman's voice. 'OK, Mr Jacob Hynes. You've killed us, so now we're going to kill you, right?'

Rowenna and Jo exchanged a brief glance, then Jo set off at a run.

There was a metallic click and Jo realised that the gleaming thing in Julie's hand was the barrel of a gun.

'No!' called Rowenna. 'Julie! Don't do it!'

'We need him!' yelled Jo at the same time. She reached Julie's side, saw her finger pulling the trigger –

Nothing happened.

Julie looked up, then sagged like a deflating balloon. 'Hell, can't even work this thing.' She held the gun out to Jo, holding it by the barrel. 'You want to shoot him?'

Jo cautiously took hold of the gun. Only when she'd done that did she take in Julie's knees pressing down on the man's stomach, his terrified face, the drool coming from his mouth, the pieces of dry grass on his cheeks and forehead.

There was an unnatural sheen on Julie's skin, a sweat that wasn't just due to the heat.

Jo turned the gun round, got a proper grip on it. 'You need two trigger pressures to fire this type,' she commented absently, then levelled the gun at Hynes's head. 'What I need to know, Mr Hynes, is where we are, how we got here, exactly which aliens you've contacted and what they said to you. And also –' She gestured around her at the mountain, the sea of grass, the vast, distant horizon – 'I'd like to know how I'm going to get home to my son.'

Hynes's eyes rolled in their sockets for a moment, then focused on Jo. 'The last one's easy,' he said. 'You can't go home.' He began to giggle, and odd, choking sound. 'Home doesn't exist any more.'

A thin layer of smoke drifted within the console room, just above the level of Sam's head. The time rotor had stopped, the screens were dead. A single light flickered on the console, and the Doctor was staring at it, arms folded, an expression of acute concentration on his face.

Most frightening was the ceiling of the console room. The blue-and-gold infinity had been replaced by a grey void. This was infinite too – or at least there was nothing to say it wasn't – but it was insidious, frightening. It seemed to suck at Sam's vision, holding her gaze and drawing away her thoughts like a vast predatory insect. She remembered something that her maths teacher had once said, about there being several kinds of infinity. He'd been talking about algebra, but Sam knew that what she was seeing now was that algebra made real. It was all she could do to look down.

Kitig was also watching the void above, with all four of his eyes open. He tilted his head from one side to the other in a slow, regular motion. After thinking about this for a moment, Sam realised that the night eyes, mounted on the sides of his head, didn't have an overlapping field of vision, and the rocking motion gave Kitig the nearest thing he could get to binocular vision with the bigger, more sensitive eyes. He was simply trying to get a good view.

'We're here,' said the Doctor suddenly.

Sam glanced at him. 'Where?'

The Doctor glanced up at her. 'Stability point. The only part of the multiverse that currently exists. But it's only stable because it's the fulcrum. Whatever is happening is happening here.'

'The scents are changing,' said Kitig.

Sam jumped. It was the first time the Tractite had spoken since he'd leapt aboard the TARDIS.

'I should have listened to Partil. She wasn't raving.' He gestured upward, and Sam saw that the grey mist had receded, become no more than a patchy shadow on the familiar blue-and-gold infinity.

'It's just the TARDIS,' said Sam. 'It does funny things sometimes. You get used to it.'

The TARDIS lurched, and the time rotor made a single, spasmodic movement. There was a choked-off fragment of the usual materialisation noises, then silence.

'You know, I always did want to visit the Rift Valley area of Africa around this time,' said the Doctor. 'Fascinating period. Absolutely crucial in human evolution. Sam, can I have a word with you for a moment?' He grabbed her arm, not giving her much choice in the matter.

Kitig stepped away, towards the doors that led from the console room to the library.

'He's got to stay inside the TARDIS. Is that clear? You can tell him what you like, debate with him as much as you want, but he's *got to stay in the TARDIS*. Otherwise there aren't going to be any choices at all.'

'Why not?' asked Sam patiently.

The Doctor glanced at Kitig, but the Tractite had picked up a book and was glancing through it. Sam wondered if the TARDIS was translating it for him, or whether he was just trying to work out how mere ink on paper could actually communicate anything.

The Doctor put his lips very close to Sam's ear.

'The trouble is,' he whispered. 'I'm the Uncreator.'

'I know,' said Sam simply.

There was a pause. The sound of the Doctor swallowing. Then: 'You don't want me to do it, do you?'

Sam shook her head.

Another swallow. 'I don't want me to do it either. But

you have to believe me, there just isn't any choice. This point won't remain stable for ever. And then –'

'I think you ought to tell Kitig about this, not me,' interrupted Sam. 'It's his universe. His family.'

'And yours, Sam. And yours. I've told you. It's not a choice between one and the other: it's a choice between everything and nothing.'

'Maybe. But I've made my decision.'

'No you haven't,' said the Doctor softly. 'And, you know, I think that's part of the problem.'

He stood up, then turned and walked swiftly out of the console room. The doors opened for him, revealing rocks, a patch of brown grass, and dry earth, all of it shining in the brilliant tropical sunlight.

'Put my dinner in the oven if I'm not back by five,' said the Doctor over his shoulder. He pulled a white cloth sun-hat out of a pocket, like a magician producing a handkerchief, and put it on his head.

Then the doors closed behind him.

'I can't even see a water hole,' said Jo. 'There should be one around here somewhere. There's plenty of game.'

Rowenna glanced up, saw her friend standing on an outcrop of rock in a classic explorer pose, gazing into the distance, her eyes shielded by a hand. From her own position propped up against the dead trunk of a thorn tree she could see several large, golden antelope warily nibbling at bushes no more than a hundred yards away, and a few dark shapes that might be jackals squatting in the grass.

The alien tree towered over the plain, its colours still flowing in the sunlight. Rowenna wished they could get further away from it.

In the distance, a lion roared. The antelope looked up, their bodies visibly quivering.

Although she knew there was no immediate danger, Rowenna felt her own body tense, felt the sweat trickling down her back. The whole of her back hurt, as far down as it could hurt, as far as the nerves still worked. She wanted to reach around and massage it, but she knew that it was futile. She would just fall over.

'You need to get up higher,' she said to Jo. 'The water hole could be ten miles away.'

Jo stepped down from the rock, sat down in the short grass at its base. Her face was flushed, and there were sweat patches on her shirt. 'I hope it's nearer than that,' she said seriously. 'Julie needs water soon.'

They both glanced over to the long grass near the stark form of the strange tree, where Julie sat with the gun, on guard over Jacob Hynes.

'How sick is she?' asked Rowenna.

Jo shrugged. 'I don't know. She thinks she's dying, but that's just what Hynes says. She's certainly got a fever. Are you OK?'

Rowenna hesitated, then decided on the truth. Lying in this situation wasn't brave: it was just stupid. 'I think I'm a bit feverish. My throat's dry. But my back's hurting a lot, so it's hard to tell. I might just be shaken up.' She hesitated. 'What did Hynes say?'

'Just some demented apocalyptic nonsense. He's going to cleanse the earth of humans, that kind of thing. I don't think he knows where or when we are any more than I do. Though he did admit that the tree is capable of time travel.'

'Time travel?' asked Rowenna. Rowenna looked at the

alien thing. 'Are you sure? I mean, I know... I assume that "horse" wasn't from Earth, but –'

Jo cut her off. 'It was night when we left the cave, it was midday when we got here. I only noticed a few seconds passing. So we moved half a day, at least. Probably much further – there don't seem to be many signs of civilisation around.' She stood up again. 'Look, I'm going to have to try to find some water. Or a village, or something. And –' She broke off, staring over Rowenna's shoulder.

Rowenna turned awkwardly to follow her gaze, keeping her balance with one hand planted firmly in the hot dry earth. For a moment she saw nothing.

Then she realised that there was someone standing in the grass.

Several someones. With rough brown hair, shaggy manes, and angry brown eyes.

All of the animals were male. And all of them were about five feet tall and built like all-in wrestlers. One of them grunted, and began to beat his fists against his chest, tossing his head from side to side so that the rust-coloured mane flew in the wind.

Rowenna swallowed. *This was impossible.* 'Did you say time travel?'

Jo nodded. 'Let me guess. This lot have been extinct quite a while.'

Rowenna looked at the apelike faces, the almost human posture of the animals. 'If I'm right, they're australopithecines,' she said. 'I don't think you'll find that village, Jo.'

Jo turned to her. 'How long have they been extinct?'

Rowenna swallowed again still struggling to come to terms with the implications of what she was about to say. 'Two and a half million years.'

# CHAPTER 13

Sam punched the TARDIS door control furiously, but nothing happened. She hadn't expected it to.

After a moment she heard Kitig's heavy footsteps approaching. 'This is a time machine, isn't it?' asked the Tractite.

Sam nodded miserably.

'And the Doctor is going to change the history of our world, so that the Tractites don't exist, just as you "hypothesised" on the skimmer?'

Sam nodded again. She felt like crying.

She felt a three-fingered hand touch her arm gently. 'You are not responsible,' said Kitig. 'The Doctor is. And I am.'

Sam turned round, found herself looking right into Kitig's eyes: the Tractite had knelt down so as to be level with her.

'You're responsible?'

She listened as Kitig explained the role of the Keeper in the Tractite world: to watch for the coming of someone who might never come, who might be no more than legend – but who might destroy everything.

'And there's one in every city on Earth?' she asked when he'd finished.

'Every city in the galaxy,' said Kitig quietly. 'But you must understand, our role has changed over the centuries. The main threat is that innocent travellers who merely happened to resemble the description in the book would be destroyed by other Tractites, in case

143

they were the Uncreator. I was given the job of Keeper by my father because I showed qualities such as calm judgement, rationality under pressure, and mercy towards others. He - and I - never really believed that there was an Uncreator.'

'And now?'

Kitig let go of her arm, sat down on the floor, folding his legs beneath him. 'It seems that we were wrong,' he said after a while.

Sam took a breath. 'Look, Kitig, you've got to *fight*. You've got to do something. You can't just give in like this.'

'I'm not giving in,' said Kitig. 'But there's nothing I can do, is there?'

Sam thought about it. There had to be a way. She couldn't let Kitig out of the TARDIS, but she was pretty sure there would be a way that she could get out. She knew the Doctor. He always left a back door open.

She looked towards the carved entrance to the cloister room. 'I might be able to help you,' she said slowly. 'I could go after the Doctor - I could at least talk to him, try to find some other way.'

'I can't ask for your help, Sam. Your loyalty must lie with your own people.'

Sam swallowed. 'I think your people are better. I saw what our people did to them, when - in the other universe, or wherever it was.'

'I know. That story may or may not be true. Your people may or may not be "worse" than mine, if you can make such comparisons about an entire species. But if you helped to destroy humanity - or prevent their creation - you would be betraying all your life up to the present time. Your parents, your siblings and friends, your children –'

Sam had to laugh. 'I haven't got any children! I'm only seventeen!'

Kitig snorted softly. 'That may explain it. Imagine, then, how your parents would feel, if they were in your position and were asked to betray you to save another species.'

Sam thought about it.

Her mother. Her father. Would they think the Tractites were better than humans?

Yes. Almost certainly.

Would they abandon her in order to save the Tractites?

Well, they'd abandoned her to save the whale. They'd gone on marches, weekend protests, left her with Gran or with friends. Or made her march with them – back when she hadn't wanted to, hadn't really understood what it was all about.

But would they leave her to die?

She thought of her mother's earnest face, her father's grey beard and old blue rollneck sweater.

No. They'd marched as an investment in the future. Her future. For her. And they were trying to save, not destroy things. Nonetheless, they would be on the Doctor's side, if they were here instead of her.

And they would be doing it *because* of her.

Sam shook her head, reminded herself to make sure that the Doctor dropped her off soon at some point in time not too long after she'd vanished, so that she could tell them she was OK, and not to worry. Or at least send them a postcard.

Except that –

Unless the Doctor succeeded, they'd already ceased to exist.

'Oh,' she said aloud, and sat down rather suddenly.

Kitig looked at her.

'My parents don't exist any more - unless I -' She broke off.

'You see?' said Kitig gently. 'It's not so easy, making choices.'

Sam stared up for a long time at the brass infinity of the console-room sky. Finally, she stood up.

'Kitig,' she said. 'If I go after the Doctor, will you promise me something? Will you promise me that you won't try to come after me - that you'll stay here?'

Kitig looked at the ground for a moment, then met her eyes. 'I promise.'

Sam was certain, absolutely *certain*, that she could trust him. It was the only thing she was certain about at the moment.

She walked around the console, towards the huge, dark, door that led to the cloister room.


'So you're saying this is two million years ago?' Julie was shivering despite the heat: she was very obviously feverish, her skin pale, sweat dripping off her face. She'd given the gun to Jo while she worked on tying Hynes's hands together with shredded pieces of his shirt.

Jo shrugged. 'Time travel isn't all that rare. The Doctor's lot try to keep it to themselves, but you can't really stop a technology from spreading. I've never seen a tree do it, but I dare say the Doctor could explain it.'

'Who's the Doctor?' asked Hynes suddenly. His voice was thick with spit and fear, but Jo had no sympathy for him. Julie was ill. Rowenna was ill. Probably they were dying. If Captain Hynes was telling the truth about infecting them with a virus, he was a murderer.

'But how are we going to get back?'

Jo knew that Julie was still thinking about a hospital, about treatment for whatever nightmare disease Hynes's alien friends had given her. But Jo had seen too often what happened to people infected by alien viruses: she didn't have much confidence in the ability of twentieth-century hospitals to save Julie's life.

'If only the Doctor would turn up,' she muttered aloud. 'But then, timely rescues never were his strongest point.'

Julie's eyes fixed on hers. 'D'you reckon he might turn up, then? This friend of yours? Could he have an antidote for this – this thing?' Her voice was cracked, desperate.

'I've no real reason to believe he's anywhere near this place,' said Jo carefully. 'But…' She shrugged again. 'Call it a hunch.'

Julie sat back suddenly, swaying on her knees.

Jo stepped forward, and saw Hynes move at the same time. 'You keep still,' she cautioned him. 'Julie?'

Julie had put both hands on the ground to steady herself. She looked at Jo with terrified eyes. 'You'd better give Rowenna the gun,' she whispered. 'I'm losing it.'

Jo nodded. She checked the knots holding Hynes, and decided that he was reasonably secure. Jo closed her eyes for a moment, suddenly aware that she was thirsty. Very, *very* thirsty. Had she been infected too?

She walked slowly over to the thorn tree where Rowenna was sitting.

'I guess I'm pretty nearly useless here,' said her friend as Jo approached. Her voice was distinctly strained: Jo supposed that she was in more pain than she was owning up to.

Jo squatted down next to her under the tree and put an arm round her shoulders. 'I feel pretty useless myself,' she confessed. 'We'll just have to do what we can. Hope that the Doctor can find us. Or that we can somehow make the time tree go back.'

Rowenna's shoulders hunched under Jo's arm, hard bone and muscles shivering with tension. 'I don't think we should rely on either of those things. I mean, if the time tree dumped us here, it could dump us anywhere next time. We don't even know how to work it. And as for your friend, you haven't actually seen him for twenty years, have you?'

Jo shook her head. 'I just don't know what else we can do,' she admitted.

'Find our ancestors,' said Rowenna quietly after a moment.

Jo frowned. 'I thought we'd found them.'

Rowenna shook her head. 'No, no. Not the australos. *Homo habilis*. Our ancestors in the direct line. They'll be a lot smarter. They'll have access to water. Maybe they'll look after us if we get sick, I don't know. We'll survive longer if we can get them to help us.'

Jo stared at her.

'It's not impossible,' said Rowenna. 'Anthropologists have often made good relationships with ape communities. These people are a lot closer to us than apes.'

Jo looked down at her friend, listened to her shallow, unhealthy breathing. She had seen too many deaths, knew too well just how easily a living, thinking being could be turned into a body, a nothing, an empty bag of chemicals.

'We've got to do *something*.'

Jo felt the blood flow to her face. That had been her line, once, many years ago.

'Rowenna's right, Jo.' Julie, standing over them, still visibly shivering in the tropical heat.

Jo came to a decision. 'OK. Have you any idea where I might find these *habilis* things?'

'Habilines? Try by the mountain. They might use caves for shelter, especially in the heat of the day. And there might be a spring, a pool, something.' With a shock, Jo realised that Rowenna too was visibly shivering.

Jo took a step forward, looked around at the heat-rippled plain, at the rough, dark rocks around the base of the mountain. Anything could be hiding there: leopards, lions – or perhaps unknown aliens here to make sure that Hynes's mission was a success.

This was *dangerous*. She might not get back.

But on the other hand, if she didn't do it, she wasn't going to live until morning, and neither were the others.

She made herself remember the jungles of Spiridon, the Daleks cruising through the mist. Autons, faceless faces turning the corner – Sea Devils, Xarax, deadly parasitic Axons. If she could cope with that, she could cope with a leopard or two.

She noticed that there was a backpack on the ground.

'I don't suppose you've got anything as old-fashioned as a mirror in there?'

'You mean you want to look your best to meet your great-great-great-great grandpa?' said Rowenna.

Jo had to smile. 'No. Signalling. Anything that will reflect sunlight will do.'

Julie unlaced the bag, scrabbled around inside it. 'Will this do?' she asked weakly holding out an electronic personal organiser. 'The screen's reflective.'

Jo tried it out: the screen caught the sunlight well enough. Angling the machine carefully, she could see the pale reflection from it on Rowenna's face in the shade of the thorn tree stump.

The woman squinted, looked around, then realised what was happening and waved at Jo.

'One flash – everything's OK,' said Jo. 'Two – I've found water. Or habilines, or something useful anyway. Three, I'm coming back. OK?'

'How many for "I'm being eaten by a lion"?' asked Rowenna, deadpan.

Jo didn't reply, just started walking.


The floor of the corridor sloped downward so steeply that Sam needed to keep a hand on the wall to maintain her balance. It was made from stone, great grey flags glittering with tiny crystals. There was a constant breeze blowing up the slope: it seemed to promise a door, an outside, a vast fresh field full of poppies and daisies.

But Sam knew it wasn't true. This was the TARDIS. There was no outside, just the wind, coming from nowhere and going nowhere.

She looked over her shoulder, to check that Kitig wasn't following her. She'd asked him not to; he'd promised that he wouldn't; and she was sure he'd keep his promise. But she still felt guilty. The Doctor had told her to stay put. He'd told her that the existence of the universe was at stake.

I'm only seventeen, thought Sam angrily. How does

the Doctor expect me to cope with making decisions about the fate of entire universes?

The answer was, of course, that he didn't. He hadn't. He'd told her not to. And she was still doing it, because she was certain that he was wrong.

Had she stopped trusting the Doctor?

It seemed like it.

I just have to give Kitig's people a chance, she told herself. I took him on board. I couldn't just let him sit there, paralysed, and watch while the Doctor destroys everything in his life.

The passageway began to level out, and the breeze declined. The stone walls began to change, becoming whiter, smoother, the material changing without a clear break from stone to a substance that resembled plastic. Round depressions appeared in them – she remembered that the Doctor had called them 'roundels'. Ahead there was a bright, even light.

She walked on, saw the angular white shape of the secondary TARDIS console. A clean white floor. The smell of plastic.

Sam walked to the console, looked around until she found a likely door control. A red lever almost begging to be pulled. She pulled it.

The roundelled doors opened. Africa was outside.

In the main console room, Kitig watched the screen as Sam stepped through the doors. It hadn't been difficult to work out how to operate the alien machinery: the scanner control was a simple knob – push in for outside view, pull out for inside view. No keypads here, no microcalipers. Kitig wondered how something so apparently simple could control the massive forces needed to travel through time.

He watched as the doors closed behind Sam, then changed to an outside view. He hadn't followed her, he told himself. He'd just watched her go. And he wasn't going to follow her now: he was just going to use the same route.

Even so, he knew he was breaking the spirit of his promise to her.

But she had been right. He had a greater loyalty.

Kitig thought about Narunil, about Critil, Jontil, and Mritig playing in the garden, about the vast, quiet city around them, about the vast, quiet, *civilised* world he had left behind.

'I will save you,' he murmured aloud. 'I will save you all somehow. And then I will come home.'

# CHAPTER 14

'You really ought to think about letting me go.'

Hynes's smile was almost more terrible than the fact that Julie was dying, thought Rowenna. His *confidence*.

'Why?' asked Rowenna, her speech thick in her dry throat. 'In case Jo doesn't come back and we die and leave you tied up to die from dehydration? I'd say that was fair, wouldn't you?' She gestured down at Julie, curled up asleep in the patchy shade of the alien tree, breathing heavily, her skin a blotchy red and crawling with flies.

Rowenna's own skin was beginning to darken, and her head felt like it was on fire. She wondered how much longer she could hold the gun, let alone stay upright in this awkward position. Her back hurt like hell.

How long had Jo been gone? A half-hour? An hour? It seemed like forever.

Suddenly she became aware of a movement behind Jacob.

A figure, walking through the grass.

'Jo?' she called.

Not Jo.

A man.

A young man wearing an extraordinary costume, as if he were at a party: a long, bronzy-green velvet jacket, light-grey cotton trousers, and a white shirt with a wing-tipped collar. On top of it all was a folding sun-hat, like something from *South Pacific*, from which fell light-brown, shoulder-length hair. He was strolling along with his hands in his pockets, admiring the scenery, as if he was taking an afternoon constitutional.

He saw her, and he smiled. 'I should be careful with that thing if I were you.'

After a moment Rowenna realised he meant the gun. She was pointing it straight at him.

She lowered it, slowly. 'Sorry, but I have to keep an eye on him,' she explained, indicating Hynes. 'Now perhaps you could oblige me by explaining who you are and how you got here?' But she was already feeling a curious sense of relief, a sense that everything would be all right now.

The man repeated his charming smile. 'I should be asking you that,' he said. 'But I think I won't, at least not straight away. Your friend needs help first, don't you agree?'

Rowenna shut her eyes for a second, opened them again.

The guy was still there. Not a fever dream then.

He bent down over Julie, then reached into his pocket and produced a hypodermic syringe. Rowenna opened her mouth to object, and though the guy didn't look round, he must have heard her indrawn breath, because he said, 'Trust me. I'm a doctor.' He was fitting a white plastic cuff around Julie's arm.

'*The* Doctor? Jo's friend?'

He didn't look up. 'Yes. I used to be Jo's friend. You're Rowenna, aren't you?'

Rowenna nodded, wondering how he knew her name. She looked over her shoulder to check on Hynes. He was staring at the Doctor, his eyes almost popping out of their sockets, his face twisted into a grotesque expression of anger or fear or both.

If Hynes didn't like this guy, then chances were she should be liking him.

The Doctor was drawing blood from Julie's arm into the hypodermic. Lights flickered in the air in front of it, and Rowenna heard an inanimate but somehow soothing voice speaking. She made out the words 'virus' and 'fatal' but everything else was a chatter of incomprehensible medical-speak.

Advanced technology, thought Rowenna blearily. Jo had said he was from the future, or something.

'Can you save her?'

'I can hold off the virus,' muttered the Doctor. 'Standard antiviral. But no, it won't save her. The virus contains prions – five different kinds. They're virtually indestructible, once they're in your system.'

Rowenna felt a wave of dizziness run over her as hope drained out of her system. 'You mean we're gonna die anyway?'

The Doctor didn't reply immediately. He stood up and began pacing around the trunk of the alien tree, glancing at it curiously. 'Chronon-wave asynchronous transmission. Didn't think anybody was still using that,' he muttered. 'Trouble is –' Suddenly his face brightened. 'Yes! That's it! Because to feed its organic nature it draws from the energy in our universe, it can only force a divergence in time, not rewrite it from the start. Therefore when it tries to force a new universe into creation it's borrowing energy from ours – and that will create a rift! No wonder the vortex is unstable!'

'Doctor,' Rowena interjected, more concerned for herself and Julie than for the vortex at this precise moment, 'how long are we gonna live?'

The Doctor glanced at her. 'Oh, don't worry. Prions take a long time to kill. They have to change your brain chemistry. Whoever designed this thing intended it to spread through the food chain. Anything that dies of this and gets eaten will pass the prions on to the scavenger. If *that* gets eaten when it dies –' He stopped pacing, stared at the horizon, transfixed with anger. 'This could wipe out the whole mammalian population of the planet! Whoever did this didn't care about *anything* –'

Rowenna swallowed, felt her body shaking.

For the first time the Doctor seemed to notice her distress. He walked over, crouched down, put his hands on her shoulders, gently straightening her body to a more comfortable position against the thorn tree.

'It's OK, Rowenna,' he said.

She wondered again how he knew her name.

'You won't die yet. I promise you that. When we get back to the TARDIS I can give you something to rebalance your body chemistry. You'll live as long as you ever would have done. And Julie will too.'

He stood up, began pacing around the tree once more. Rowenna noticed that Julie's eyes had opened, and the colour on her skin was better. She tried to shuffle over towards her friend, using her arms as levers, but tipped sideways and lay helpless on the ground.

'Dammit!'

To her surprise, Julie stood up, swayed, stretched, and then walked over to her. 'Who's he?' she asked, indicating the Doctor. Her voice was rusty with the after-effects of fever.

Rowenna bit back her pain. 'Jo's friend. The one that

works miracles. You were *dying* a minute ago.'

'I don't feel too good now.' Julie brushed some of the flies away from her face, then knelt down and pulled Rowenna upright again.

'Where's Hynes?' she asked.

'Hynes? I –' Julie moved aside, and Rowenna realised that their captive wasn't where he should be.

'Doctor!' she called. 'Hynes has gone!'

The Doctor wandered round the tree, looked around for a moment. 'Oh, don't worry,' he said. 'I shouldn't think he's gone far. There aren't many places to go at the moment.' He frowned. 'A shame. I was going to ask him what he knew about this virus.'

Rowenna almost laughed. 'I think that might just be why he didn't want to talk to you, Doctor.'

The Doctor gave her a serious look. 'Oh, he wasn't responsible. He looked insane to me.'

'He had an alien friend.'

'Well, yes, I'd guessed as much. Big fellow, a bit like a horse with arms?'

Rowenna did laugh this time, so much that she almost fell over again. 'That's the one!'

'Not here, is he?'

'I don't think so.' Rowenna was still laughing. 'I guess we'd have noticed him.'

The Doctor leaned over her, extended a hand with two tiny pale blue tablets in it. 'Antiviral,' he explained. 'To keep you going until we get to the TARDIS.'

Rowenna took the tablets, and immediately began to feel better.

'Where is this... TARDIS?' asked Julie.

'Oh, not far.'

'What about Jo?' asked Rowenna. 'She went off to –'

'You mean she's *here*?' The expression on the Doctor's face changed to one of delight. 'Oh, how wonderful! I've been wondering how she was getting along! How old is Matthew now? Is he at university yet?'

'Whoa! Hold on!' Rowenna was giggling again, helplessly. 'I only met Jo for two minutes this morning. The last time I met her before that was nearly five years ago. As far as I know Matthew's just started high school – she says she hasn't seen you for twenty years.'

The Doctor rubbed his chin. 'More like three hundred. Where is Jo now, anyway?'

Julie was staring from one to the other of them. 'Hey! Let me in on this sometime, won't you?'

'Jo went looking for water,' Rowenna explained to the Doctor, ignoring her friend. 'We can't just pack up and leave.'

The Doctor sat down in the grass, drew his knees up to his chest and folded his arms over them. 'Then we'll wait for her,' he said. He looked down at his hands, saw the hypodermic, still with Julie's blood in it. He pulled a thing that looked like a green rubber tennis ball from his pocket and fitted the hypo to it. It started to expand and contract slowly, almost as if it were breathing.

'May as well start work on a proper antidote while we're waiting,' said the Doctor. 'Does anybody know any good African campfire songs?'

*The scents are changing.*

Kitig remembered Partil's warning, in the library at home. It seemed so long ago; hard to believe it was only yesterday. He tasted the air with his tongue, picking up the strange tones, the barely readable notes of this alternative reality.

He was fairly sure that he was still on Paratractis. The fundamental planet smell was the same, the deep rock, the salt oceans, the faint tang of polar ice. But the soft, pervasive scent of Tractite plants was gone. So was the sense of order, the visible glittering points of the orbital stations, the gentle touch of the pheromone relay net telling him where he was.

Here there was only emptiness. True wilderness.

A volcano towered in the distance, blue-tinted, shrouded in snow. There was a whiff of that snow in the dry wind, overlaid with the green things that lived on the slopes, and the hot acrid stench of a soda lake. Nearer, a series of rocky outcrops ended in a hill which tasted of slate, the hot dry rock baking in the sun.

And all around, the scent of the plains animals, their dung, their saliva, their exhalations, and the dry, crackling scent of the grass they ate.

Somewhere, water. Kitig realised that he was thirsty.

The Doctor's scent was strong, an alien track across the dry ground. It hovered in the air, visible, talking in alien voices.

Soothing voices. Kind voices.

*I can't kill this being. He smells of virtue.*

No. That had been a long time ago, on a different world, a world of libraries and ordered pheromones. The world that might have ceased to exist for ever, because of Kitig's own stupid indecision.

Narunil had been right. He was not suited for the trust he had been given. He had too many doubts, needed to think too much before acting.

But Kitig knew he had no choice now, whatever his reservations. He had his duty to his world, to his people, to his family. He had to carry out that duty whether he was suited to it or not. He would have to stop the Doctor, even if he did smell of virtue. And if that meant hurting him, Kitig knew he would have to do that, too.

He didn't want to think about what 'hurting' might mean in this context. He would do whatever it came to him to do. And live with the consequences.

He increased his pace to a canter, following the bright, easy scent across the grassland towards his target.

Jacob crouched down and watched the three of them singing under the time tree, hiding himself as well as he could in the tall grass.

He'd known it as soon as the Doctor had arrived. Despite his weird nineteenth-century costume, he had the air of a man from the Golden Age. The bright eyes, the brown-to-golden hair, the confidence. This was the future of humanity. And he had come to stop Jacob, to stop the Tractites.

I should have known it was too easy, he thought. I should have known it couldn't be possible that my dreams would really come true. Alien visitors who needed a helping hand to remove the human race from the face of the Earth. It's ridiculous. It couldn't possibly be that simple. Of course the human race is going to fight back. And here's this Doctor, making the first moves.

Jacob crouched down further into the grass, his whole body shaking.

He knew what the future humans were capable of. The death, the darkness, the destruction that came everywhere that Earth spread its empire. He knew that the Doctor's golden image was no more than an illusion: once the man found out what was happening, he would put a stop to it.

He would probably kill Jacob, too.

Alpha and Omega. The end of all things. But not for the whole human race; just for Jacob.

He closed his eyes.

*No*. He wasn't going to allow it to happen. He had planned this: and he was going to carry it through.

The original plan had been to use the whole UNIT platoon – infect them, spread them out among the habilines, let them die and spread the virus. Now he was going to have to do all the infecting on his own – and he was going to need a sample of the virus to do it.

He got up, ran crouching through the grass. On the other side of the time tree, antelope stirred nervously. But the Doctor and the two women were still singing, apparently oblivious of his presence.

I am the lion, he thought. I am the wolf. I am the sabre-toothed tiger. I can do this.

He slipped the knife out of his inside pocket, got up, pounced forward. He saw the Doctor's eyes, startled, then angry. Felt the force of the man's will.

*I am the predator –*

Jacob dived for the hypo of blood at the Doctor's feet. He lifted it and the tennis-ball-like object it was attached to, at the same time slashing one of the women with the knife. He heard a satisfying scream of pain, felt blood splash on his arm.

Then he was turning, running, running crouched through the long grass. Behind him there was a single gunshot, then a man's voice. 'No!'

Jacob just kept on running. He found a rough trail in the grass, recently beaten down, and followed it towards the mountain.

He could hide out there until the Doctor got tired of looking for him.

Then he would find his ancestors.

And kill them.

Kitig heard the percussive sound, the human shouts, and stopped at once. He stared around him in the rippling heat of the afternoon. He saw a thorn tree and two low bushes growing on the rim of a dry river bed. An outcrop of rocks. He could smell the Doctor's nearness.

He waited, heard more shouts, saw a bipedal form moving through the grass. He started towards it at a steady canter, feeling the loose ropes that had held the Doctor's basket dance against his flank.

As he got closer, he saw that the biped wasn't the Doctor, but another human. The human shouted at him: 'Gavril! Gavril! Stop him!'

Kitig stared, wondering who Gavril was, if there was another Tractite here, whom he was supposed to stop: then he saw the Doctor running through the grass, covering the ground at a truly fantastic speed for a biped, and gaining on the other human rapidly.

Kitig assessed the situation for a moment, judged the distance to the running figure, then he crouched down in the grass and waited.

The first human got the point. He changed course, led the Doctor along the dry river bed below Kitig.

Kitig watched him run past, watched the Doctor

approach.

At the right moment, he jumped. It was easy, like playing a game in the garden.

He landed on the Doctor.

The apelike being had tried to dodge sideways, had almost made it: but not quite. He was caught, lying flat in the belly of the dry river, his chest under one of Kitig's front hooves. A single stone rolled across the dusty ground, settled against the gnarled root of a long-dead tree.

Kitig leaned forward, felt the alien's ribcage bend under his weight. The Doctor's eyes bulged outward, his face flushed with blood.

'You – don't –' he gasped. 'Don't – want – to –'

'I don't want to, but I have to,' said Kitig.

But at the same time he lifted his leg slightly, easing the pressure on the Doctor's chest.

'There won't be anywhere to go back to, Kitig,' gabbled the Doctor. He took a heaving breath, went on, 'No home, no family, no nothing.' Another breath. 'Everything will cease to exist.' Another. 'You *have* to believe me.'

His eyes locked on to Kitig's. Kitig felt himself being persuaded. That was the danger of the Doctor, he thought: his ability to make you think he was *right*.

'No one can own the only road to virtue, or hold the only key to truth,' said Kitig, more to himself than to the alien.

'Bessarinil, from the *Vargukonon*,' commented the Doctor. He was breathing more easily now. '"Because there is more than one road, and more than one key". But that just isn't true this time. We're not talking about comparative philosophy: this is temporal physics, and you can't –'

Kitig lowered his hoof to the Doctor's chest again, then hesitated, trembling. He felt the heat of the sun branding the back of his neck.

*This is a sentient being.*

'We should be working together to solve this problem, Kitig. You're rational, merciful, civilised – surely you can see that there must be a way –'

He broke off, quite suddenly, his face darkening.

'Except that there isn't,' said Kitig, softly, a horrible certainty forming in his mind. 'There's no way out, is there, Doctor?'

He raised his free front hoof, ready to bring it down on the Doctor's head, and end his life with as much mercy as he could.

# CHAPTER 15

Julie was unconscious, the blood from the wound that Hynes had made in her arm pooling around her, soaking into the hard earth.

Rowenna had shuffled as close as she could, doing her best to ignore the blaze of agony from her back every time she moved. She'd found the cuff the Doctor had used and had applied it in an effort to stop the bleeding.

It wasn't a great success: the wound was too deep, she couldn't get the cuff tight enough.

She watched Julie's life seep out with a growing sense of panic.

*Doctor, where are you?*

Perhaps Jacob had got him. Perhaps the crazy son of a bitch would be back here in a minute...

She scrambled around under the time tree, cursing her useless legs, searching for the gun.

Then she saw the dog.

It was keeping its distance, watching her from the grass outside the shadow of the tree. It was lightly built, its coat almost the same pale brown as the baked earth.

'Shoo!' snapped Rowenna.

The dog growled.

Another dog appeared by its side.

Rowenna felt her heart rate increase. She looked around for something to throw, but there was only the grass and earth. She scrabbled around in the crushed grass, found a plastic strap.

It was attached to a bag: Julie's bag. She remembered

Jo taking the organiser from it, a half-hour ago.

A world away.

She picked the bag up, shook it, heard small change rattling inside.

Coins, she thought. I can throw them.

There were three dogs now, and they were advancing steadily, tails wagging. But Rowenna doubted they were about to become friendly. She poured out the contents of the bag. Two quarters, a couple of dimes, some Tanzanian small change. She flung one of the quarters.

It missed, but the dogs took a couple of steps back even so.

Then started forward again. There were four of them now – no, five, making a half-circle around Rowenna and Julie.

A growl behind her. She turned, and two more dogs skittered back, snarling.

Her hands shaking, she flung her remaining change after them.

The gun, she thought. The goddamn gun. Where is it?

She shifted her position, patting the grass frantically, looking for the dark shape of the weapon.

The dogs were advancing now, tails down, snouts low, ominously silent.

Rowenna felt herself beginning to panic. She found a deodorant spray in Julie's purse, an old lipstick, a computer disk.

She threw them, but the dogs only dodged the missiles. One lunged forward, bit Julie's sleeve, then danced back when Rowenna struck out at it.

Julie stirred, groaned, opened her eyes for a second.

'It's OK,' lied Rowenna.

She felt something pulling at her body, and with a sudden start of horror realised that one of the dogs was worrying her leg, far below the level where she had any feeling. She punched it, felt her fist connect with rough hot fur. The dog jumped up, caught her arm in its teeth.

Pain. Her arm was lifting up, with the dog still attached. Her body was tilting, she was losing her balance, and her arm hurt, it hurt, it was going to break, she was going to –

And then the dog had let go, retreated, but another had taken its place at her feet and this was going to go on, go on until she was exhausted and they killed her, and *another one had its teeth in her leg oh God it's eating me* and another dived for her throat –

'*No get back –*'

Her arm connected with something solid, and the dog was a snarling heap of fur on the ground, tangled up with the two that had been attacking her legs, the pile of them temporarily blocking the way for the others.

Rowenna knew she had only a couple of seconds. And there was one thing, one thing she hadn't tried…

She reached into Julie's bag, found a familiar flat plastic shape, pulled it out and pressed the button.

The air filled with the warbling, mechanical shriek of a rape alarm.

The dogs jumped back as if they'd been hit, vanished into the grass. The pile at Rowenna's feet disentangled themselves and ran. Only one remained, its teeth in Julie's arm, its ears flat against its skull.

Rowenna swung the hand with the alarm at it, and it too jumped back, its mouth full of cloth and flesh.

Rowenna saw the blood pooling around Julie and she

swallowed, hard. She felt sick.

But the dogs were *gone*.

She held the rape alarm tightly, trying to remember how long the batteries lasted.

It would have to be long enough for Jo or the Doctor to get back.

If either of them was still alive. If the dogs hadn't had them. Or the lions. Or the hyenas. Or the australos. Or Jacob Hynes.

She held the alarm above her head, hoping that it might make the sound audible a little further away.

Then she saw the dog.

It was looking at her from the grass, its eyes full of intelligent calculation. She waved the alarm at it, but it just took a step forward. Another was emerging from the grass, moving slowly, but advancing.

Rowenna's body began to shake. They had got used to the noise. They'd realised it wasn't going to hurt them. She saw the blood on the ground, the blood on her legs, *they could smell the blood –*

And they were coming back.

The shrieking electronic noise made Kitig pause, his hoof still raised above the Doctor's head.

'It'll be Rowenna,' gasped the Doctor. 'Rowenna and her friend. They're in trouble. Look, please, let me up. You have my word that I –' He hesitated. 'I'll let you do what you want, afterwards, but we must save them. We can't let them die; they're innocent bystanders.'

There was a faint, unmistakably human, shriek, blended with the continuing noise of the electronic alarm.

Pain, terror.

Kitig made his decision. He lifted the hoof that held the Doctor down and lifted the alien up in his arms and on to his back.

Then he started back along the river bed at a gallop.


Rowenna screamed again: 'Doctor!'

She saw that Julie's eyes were open, her lips moving.

'Dogs,' said Rowenna briskly.

She felt a sharp pain in her belly.

A dog. A dog clinging on. She slapped it, punched it, tried to pull it away. Felt the pain register as its grip on her flesh tightened.

Rough fur brushed her neck, and the rotted-meat smell of canine breath filled her nose and throat.

She rolled over, hoping to crush the dog underneath her. It wriggled, howled, slithered out.

Another dog landed on her back.

She heard Julie bawling for help.

*I'm not going to survive this – this time it's over – I'm going to die –*

And Julie was screaming and Rowenna was strangling the dog on her chest, her hands on its throat, but another one had her arm and it hurt and its jaws were on her throat and the blood –

The ground shook, and something knocked her body to one side. Colours flew overhead, scarlet and violet.

The ground shook again. A dog was flying though the air, contorted, howling.

The dog at her arm let go and fell back, limp. Everywhere, dogs were screaming, a wild, frightened keening totally unlike the professional yips and growls that had accompanied the battle up till now. Rowenna struggled to sit up, couldn't.

Her vision blurred for a moment, and then she was being lifted up by a knight on a huge white horse dressed in medieval finery –

No.

A horse on its own, with arms. Like the thing in Hynes's cave. And the Doctor was standing beside it, with an expression of desolation on his face.

Rowenna looked around, saw that one last dog was still worrying at Julie's body. The horselike creature stood on it, and there was a loud crack of bone.

'Oh God,' breathed Rowenna. The words bubbled in her throat. 'Is she…?'

But the Doctor wasn't looking at Julie. He was looking at Rowenna.

She tried to speak again, felt hot fluid running down her throat, on to her chest. She lifted her hands. They felt heavy, infinitely heavy, and they were covered in blood.

The Doctor was saying something, but for some reason Rowenna couldn't hear it. She tried to read his lips, but she was feeling tired, so tired, and it was complicated, too complicated, and the Doctor's hand reached out and touched her face, and then she heard the words –

– *innocent bystanders* –

And saw the tears in his all-too-human eyes.

And then she died.

# CHAPTER 16

Sam stared around at the shimmering yellow grass, twirling her backpack in her hands. The hot dry wind blew through the doors into her face, carrying a smell of dung and baked earth. The pack was heavy: the material cut into her fingers. In it were a book, a compass, a sketch pad and pencil, some pears, a celery sandwich and a bottle of water. Everything she needed for an afternoon picnic on the African plains.

Except that this was no picnic.

She squinted, pulled her sunglasses down over her eyes, then put the backpack on again, walked to the nearest rock, and scrambled up to take a look at the view. Tumbled rocks, bushes, and grasses were scattered across a vast plain dotted with small trees. A single, shambling mountain, about a kilometre away, perhaps five hundred metres high.

Nothing. The word 'trackless' must have been invented for this environment.

Sam had walked right around the TARDIS, a four-hundred-metre circuit. There was no trace of the Doctor anywhere. There was no mark that looked as if it might have been made by the Doctor's shoes, nothing that might have come from the Doctor's pockets.

She looked out at the plain again, felt the sweat start to trickle down her forehead.

Nothing for it: she would have to try to climb the mountain, and look from the top. She checked the position of the sun in the sky, began working her way towards the rocky outcrops that formed the base of the hill. As the rocks rose around her, she looked in the shadows where the earth might be softer, hoping for a clue.

More soft hoof marks. A pugmark – a big cat, she wasn't sure how big. She looked nervously towards the rocky slopes, wondering if any of the caves contained leopards.

Then, looking down again, she saw it.

A human footprint. A bare foot, and strangely shaped. It wasn't what she'd wanted to see, but nonetheless Sam felt a thrill, knowing that she was quite literally walking in the footsteps of her almost infinitely distant ancestors. Seeing what they saw. Hearing what they heard. Smelling what they could smell.

She took a gulp from her water bottle, listened to the sounds of the wilderness. Rustling grasses. A bird's call, raucous and repetitive. A distant roar that might be a lion or a leopard or –

Another sound. Closer.

A clatter of pebbles.

'Doctor?'

Probably not, she thought. Much more likely to be –

A grunt.

A movement.

Sam had a fleeting glimpse of a figure in the grass beyond the rocks, dark, apelike, moving fast.

Baboons? Some kind of primitive humans?

She stopped, waited, trying not to breathe too hard.

The movement again. A face. Deep, black eyes staring at her over the edge of a rock.

More movements, the patter of flesh on stone. She could make out a body now, crouching, no more than yards away: coarse, sparse hair, the skin underneath dark, but not quite black.

Shadows. Fingers, toes moving, flickers of grey-pink skin.

And then they were all around her. She could smell their breath, pungent and vegetal. They were shorter than she was, but not by as much as she would have expected. Big, more like gorillas than chimps. More like people than either. Their skulls were low, but their backs were straight. Their eyes were bright, intelligent, curious.

Almost human.

A hand reached out and pinched her sleeve. She jumped back, more afraid than she wanted to be. She felt the warmth of bodies behind her, cutting her off from the shelter of the rock.

They're just curious, she told herself. But she wasn't entirely convinced.

More touches. On her back, her arms, her legs, her bum. The back of her head, her throat.

'Leave me alone!' she snapped.

A chorus of grunts came in response. Then a tall male shouldered the others aside and faced her. He wasn't much shorter than Sam and must have been almost twice her weight.

He reached out, quite slowly, and took hold of her shoulders.

Sam tried to turn away, but the grip was solid. Other hands were touching her again, pulling at her clothes, pinching her skin. The lead male began to shake her. It wasn't gentle.

She felt a surge of panic, and kicked out. The male jumped backward, clutching his genitals in a gesture that might have been hugely amusing, in different circumstances. As it was, all Sam was interested in was the gap to his left. She dived for it, shaking off arms that tried to grab her. She thought she'd made it when a cuff to the head sent her spinning to the ground. A heavy body landed on top of her, cuffed her again.

Then froze.

The chorus of grunts was drowned out by a single terrifying, primal, scream. A scream that turned into words.

'I am the sabre-tooth! I am the leopard! I am all your nightmares come true, you overgrown baboons!' The words turned into laughter, helpless human laughter.

There were screams from the creatures, the thudding of feet. A heavy body leaping over hers.

Then, slowly, silence.

A face looked down at Sam, dark against the blazing noon sky. A human face, grinning broadly.

'You OK?'

Sam sat up slowly, looked around. The creatures were gone. The air smelled of their breath, of monkey sweat.

She closed her eyes for a moment, then opened them and looked at her rescuer. He was a young man, shabbily dressed, with dust on his clothes and a long-bladed knife in his hand.

The knife dripped blood.

Sam stood up, rather surprised that her head didn't hurt any more than it did. 'Thanks,' she said, extending a hand. 'I'm Sam.'

'I'm Jacob,' said the young man, shaking hands. 'Captain Jacob Hynes, of UNIT. I'm here on a special mission.' He stared at the rocks for a moment: Sam followed his gaze, saw a trail of blood on the rocks.

Jacob met her eyes, nodded grimly. 'You're with the Doctor, I suppose?'

Sam hesitated, thought about the Doctor's firm instructions to stay in the TARDIS, her disobedience. 'Sort of.'

Jacob nodded, grinned. 'We're "sort of" working with him, too.' He pulled an odd-looking object out of his pocket: a hypodermic syringe attached to a green sphere about the size of a tennis ball.

The sphere quivered.

'It's a blood sample,' said Jacob. 'We've got to inject it into one of these habilines. If we can catch one, that is.'

Sam frowned. 'Why? Did he say why?'

Jacob hesitated. 'It's sort of classified,' he said after a moment. 'What's your status, exactly?'

Sam grinned. 'I live in the TARDIS.'

A pause. 'Ah – right.' He looked away, a strange, tense expression on his face. 'Look,' he said at last. 'I need to follow the wounded one. I'll try and grab him, get this stuff into him like the Doctor said. I'd appreciate your help. So would the Doctor, I'm sure.'

Sam looked at her shoes. She wasn't sure about this man. He was trying a little bit too hard to convince her. But on the other hand, he probably wasn't sure if she was telling the truth, either. And she didn't know what he'd been through to get here.

'Are you coming with me?' Jacob had already started up the slope. The impatience was visible on his face.

Sam hesitated, then followed him. The Doctor had been right: she was going to have to decide. If this man was helping the Doctor to save these – what did he call them? – these habilines, then she could either let him do it, or prevent him.

And given that straight choice, between saving the human

race and not saving it, she knew what she was going to have to do.

She wondered for a moment if Kitig would feel it happen when his world was uncreated.

Jo ran, sweat streaming down her face and legs and sticking her clothes to her body.

She hadn't found any water, only a solitary patch of slightly softer earth and greener grass. She'd been heading for the mountain in search of something better when she'd heard the distant warble of what sounded like a rape alarm. She'd started running straight away, following the easy marker of the huge alien tree, but she'd been at least a mile from Rowenna and Julie. Now she was exhausted: her lungs heaving, her forehead burning. Sweat was dripping into her eyes, and she could barely see in front of her. Ahead, she could make out a big horselike shape that could only be one of Hynes's alien friends, and someone standing next to it – Hynes?

'Rowenna!' she yelled, then wondered if it wouldn't have been better to keep her head down.

The figure standing by the alien turned to look at her. It wasn't Hynes, but there was something familiar about him. The shoulder-length hair, the strange fancy-dress costume. She'd seen him before somewhere – somewhen –

'Jo!'

And she knew then.

'Doctor!'

He ran up to her, took her hands. 'Jo! I'm so glad to see you!'

Jo studied the young man. The unlined face, the bright young eyes, the untidy hair.

*Young again.*

Lucky Doctor.

'Where are Rowenna and –' she began.

Then she saw Julie's body on the grass. Saw the blood there.

She realised that there was blood on the Doctor's hands. Blood on her hands. Blood –

'What happened?' she said weakly, looking up at the alien creature. 'Did he –'

'No. He's harmless. They were attacked by dogs.' The Doctor turned away, and Jo could hear the pain in his voice. 'I was too late.'

Jo saw the crushed corpse of a dog on the grass, and another beside Julie's body. There was something bloody and dead and too big to be a dog somewhere beyond the alien, but Jo wasn't going to look, couldn't bring herself to look.

'The responsibility is mine.' An unfamiliar voice. The alien was speaking. 'I delayed the Doctor for reasons of my own.'

Jo sat down in the grass. 'I was going to find them water,' she said hollowly. 'I should have been here.'

'I *was* here.' The pain was still in the Doctor's voice, and he was looking away from her, hiding his face. Jo wondered if he was actually crying. He had never used to do that. 'I *promised* them.'

Jo stood up, walked up to the Doctor, put a hand on his shoulder. 'We've been here before, Doctor,' she reminded him.

He put a hand over hers. There was still blood on it. Jo closed her eyes for a moment. She'd often wondered what it would be like to meet the Doctor again. She'd never thought that it would be like this – in the middle of a hot, ancient plain, with two people dead beside them.

'What are the funeral customs of your people?'

Jo looked up, startled. The alien was looking down at Rowenna's body. The three-fingered hands were visibly shaking.

Not like the creature in Hynes's cave then. As the Doctor had said, harmless.

'I don't mean to be offensive,' the alien went on. 'But we should deal with the bodies or they will attract scavengers. There is no dignity in that.'

'Can you carry them?' asked the Doctor.

Kitig tossed his head slightly: a nod.

'We'll take them to the TARDIS then. When we get back –' He paused. 'If we get back, I can arrange for them to be buried at home. If not, at least...' He shrugged.

'If we get home?' asked Jo gently.

The Doctor turned to her, shook his head. 'There's a problem with the time stream. That thing –' he gestured at the time tree – 'and some rogue members of Kitig's species, Tractites, have tried to time-loop the human race. It couldn't possibly work – not with a one-way time-travel device – so all they've done is destabilise the vortex. Right now everything outside this area is just a quantum flux, a sort of fog of might-be-or-might-not-be. I have to sort it out or –' He swung round suddenly. 'Kitig, how did you get out of the TARDIS?'

'I followed Sam.'

'Sam! I should have known –' He whirled back to face Jo. 'Jo, you've got to find Sam for me. Jacob is still out there – you met Jacob Hynes?' Jo's face must have shown him the answer, because he went on without giving her a chance to speak. 'You've got to find her, and you've got to find Jacob, before it's too late.'

'Too late for what?'

'Jacob's trying to wipe out the human race, but that doesn't really matter – what matters is the stability of the vortex.'

Jo raised an eyebrow.

'Well, all right, both, then. In fact they're inextricably linked. The human race is simply so important to everything that happens in this sector for the next few thousand –' He broke off, seemed to sniff the air. 'Jo, *please*, you've got to help me. There's more going on than Jacob's little plans, and I've got to find out what it is.'

Jo shook her head. 'I'm not twenty any more, Doctor. I want explanations. Why do you think there's something else going on?'

The Doctor met her eyes for a moment, then nodded. 'All right. Kitig, how many mammal species are there on your alternative world?'

'On Paratractis? I'm not sure. Several thousand at least.'

'Jacob's virus, or more accurately, the prions that go with it, will kill *all mammal species* – or at least most of them. So something before this time wiped out humanity – if it was happening afterwards, there wouldn't be any mammal species on Paratractis. And I have to find out what it is, while the vortex is still stable enough to allow any sort of time travel.'

Jo shut her eyes for a moment, tried to think it through. It was as hard as ever to make sense of the Doctor's babble.

'Do you mean Jacob can't possibly succeed?' she asked at last.

'No. It's a neither-or-either loop. If I fail to stop whatever's happening *before* this time, then it won't matter what you do. If I succeed, then Jacob could still be responsible for destroying the human race in *this* time. Somebody was taking no chances.'

'So?'

'You've got to find Sam. And between you, you've got to stop Jacob.'

'And you're going to go off and do something else?'

The Doctor nodded. 'That's it!'

Jo shook her head. 'Nothing changes, does it?'

'I'm sorry, Jo. There isn't any choice.'

'Well, you said from the start that you needed my help. That's why I got mixed up in this.'

The Doctor frowned. 'From the start? Did I? When did I do that? I mean, perhaps I'm going to do that – I can never be sure.'

Jo shook her head again. 'Never mind.' She walked past him, towards the bloody mass on the ground under the shade of the alien tree. 'Now if you'll excuse me, I'm going to say goodbye to my friend.'


Sam and Jacob found the habiline not far up the slope, collapsed in the shade of a rock.

Jacob lifted the habiline's arm and put the needle against it. 'Here, can you hold this thing's fur out of the way?' he asked. 'It needs to be shaved off, but there's no time.'

Sam stepped forward.

And the habiline moved.

Jacob pitched forward, yelling. The habiline's dark hand clamped around his arm. Its other hand made a wavering arc towards his throat.

Jacob lowered the knife, but missed as the habiline rolled aside. The animal carried on rolling across the hard stone, almost knocking Sam off her feet. She jumped up, saw Jacob raising the knife to throw it – but it was too late: the habiline had vanished into the rocks.

A movement.

Something flew through the air, aimed at Jacob's head.

'Look out!' yelled Sam, but Jacob was already moving. The stone clattered past him. Sam saw black flint, a sharp edge.

Then there were habilines everywhere, screaming, waving their arms. Stones flew, clattering on the rocks. Sam felt one punch her side.

An ambush, she thought. Definitely almost human.

'Run!' she bawled at Jacob, but he was waving the syringe around, looking for a habiline to stab.

He looked over his shoulder, shouted something, pointing behind Sam. A rock hit her leg with bruising force. Another landed just ahead of her, clattered back on to her hand. She grabbed it, hurled it at the nearest habiline.

He caught it, advanced on her with the stone –

– *stone axe* –

– in his hand, sharp end forward.

'Wait!' If these things had any kind of language, there was a chance that the TARDIS translation system would work with them. 'Wait! I can help you!'

The habiline paused, and an expression appeared on its face that Sam could only characterise as puzzled.

Then something hit Sam on the head, and she felt her legs give way beneath her.

\* \* \*

Kitig watched as the Doctor finished shovelling earth over the bodies of the two women. He was still amazed by the room he was in: or rather, the *space*.

It was hard to believe that they were still inside the Doctor's time machine. There was a hillside. A distant horizon. And there were millions upon millions upon millions of butterflies, making clouds in the blue, sunlit sky. Some of them clung to the Doctor. Others drank greedily from the damp fresh earth of the graves.

'I don't think they'd mind, being buried here,' said the Doctor. 'And even if we take them home later, I'll always have a place to… remind me.'

Kitig looked at him, looked at the butterflies, the sorrow in his face, and could no longer believe even the possibility that he could be evil.

'Doctor,' he said aloud, as they returned through the incongruous panelled door to the console room. 'I think we should be truthful with one another.'

The Doctor looked up, met Kitig's eyes for a moment. 'You know who I am?' he asked after a while.

'Yes. But from what I've seen so far, I don't believe that you deliberately set out to destroy our people. It seems more that you are protecting your own.'

The Doctor made that strange bobbing motion of the head that Kitig knew meant he agreed. 'Not my own, exactly,' he said. 'But sort of. I've spent more time with them than I have with my own – and there are some people who say… Oh never mind. The point is, yes, your universe is the unstable one. It shouldn't exist. But I know I can't expect you to accept that.'

They'd reached the console now. The Doctor flicked a switch, set a dial, and the time rotor began to move.

'I believe it,' said Kitig quickly. 'It would explain many things. The whole existence of Paratractis, its history, is a paradox. A series of impossibilities. Nonetheless, I exist. My family exists. Or –' he hesitated – 'has the *potential* to exist. You can't deny that.'

The Doctor moved away and sat down, using a piece of furniture for support in the way bipeds often did. He was moving his head from side to side: the gesture obviously indicated discomfort. 'That's why I didn't want Sam to let you aboard the TARDIS,' he said. 'You see, you'll continue to exist now, even if we succeed and everything else you know is gone.' He looked up. 'You may never go home.'

Kitig remembered the distant horizon of the butterfly room. The blue sky. The sunlight. This machine was as huge as a planet, at least. It travelled in time and space as readily as Kitig could gallop down a street. The Doctor owned this machine, this power: if he said something about the status of time, of reality, then his judgement was likely to be correct.

'I should try to stop you,' he said at last. 'But I can't believe you to be evil. And if you aren't – if you're telling the truth –'

He broke off. *Was* the Doctor telling the truth?

'I know,' said the Doctor softly. 'I don't believe you to be evil, either, if it's any help. But I can't let that stop me from doing what I know to be absolutely necessary. I'm sorry.'

Kitig closed his eyes.

There was a thud. The ground shuddered. Kitig smelled burning insulation, opened his eyes, and saw smoke rising from the console, the Doctor dancing around, pulling at chains, pushing switches. One of the screens lit up, showing the African plain: golden grass, some animals, a stand of trees.

'Well,' the Doctor said, solemnly. 'This is it.'

Kitig took a couple of steps closer to the screen, saw that the aspect of the plain was very different. The volcano was different: smaller, more neatly conical. A trail of hazy smoke drifted through the sky from its summit. In the foreground there was a lake, only yards from the TARDIS, with a narrow white beach. When the Doctor turned the scanner around to look inland, there were stands of tall trees, separated by scrub and grass.

'We're in a different part of the continent,' suggested Kitig.

'No we're not,' said the Doctor, checking the reading from a brass dial on the console. 'This is the same place. We haven't moved at all in space, relative to Earth. But we've travelled back in time.'

Kitig peered at the console, but the figures were incomprehensible to him.

'How far?' he asked.

The Doctor flicked a switch on the console. 'Just over a million years.'

The TARDIS door opened, and the Doctor started towards it.

'I'm going to find out what's happening,' he said over his shoulder, baring his teeth in a brilliant smile. 'Aren't you going to join me?'

Kitig started after him, wondering why the Doctor was so keen that he should go with him this time, when he had been so anxious to avoid it on their last landing.

But as soon as he stepped out of the TARDIS doors, he

knew. He could smell them.

Tractites.

Was the Doctor wrong? Had they come back to Paratractis after everything that had happened? He looked around, sniffed, trying to find visual and olfactory evidence of his world.

Nothing. Just the grass, the animal dung, the distant snows of the volcano and the even more distant sea.

The same world as the one they had just left: pre-civilisation.

But he could smell his people.

And something else. Something alien – electrical –

*Dangerous*.

'Doctor,' he said.

The Doctor had walked down to the beach, was staring out over the lake at the volcano.

'Doctor, there are Tractites here. I can smell them.'

The Doctor nodded.

'Do you want me to try to find them?'

A pause. Then: 'There won't be any need, Kitig. If you have a look across to the other side of the lake, you'll see that they already know about us.'

Kitig followed the Doctor's gaze across the calm blue water, and saw something that frightened him more than anything that had happened so far.

There were Tractites, yes, but the tiny figures were dressed in some kind of body armour, black and gleaming like angry beetles. Kitig saw the glint of machinery, the long barrel of something that looked like an energy weapon.

The barrel tracked round until it was levelled at them, across the kilometre or so of water.

'No!' shouted Kitig.

Tractites didn't kill Tractites. Unless there was extreme provocation, Tractites didn't kill anyone. But –

The water of the lake boiled, and the world around Kitig exploded into fire and light.

# CHAPTER 17

'Living, not eating.'

Sam opened her eyes at the sound, saw a man standing over her.

Not a man.

Shaggy hair. A sloping forehead. Animal eyes.

A habiline.

'Waking.'

She heard the grunt, saw the hand gesture, a rapid twisting of fingers against the darkening sky. The TARDIS must be translating for her –

The TARDIS. The Doctor. The alternative universe. Paratractis. Jacob.

Sam sat up, felt a powerful hand push her back down again.

'Keep still. Danger. Other.' His hands moved in time with the words. In fact, there were no words, only undifferentiated grunts.

Sign language.

'What other?' she asked, whispering.

'Keep silent. Other.'

Sam swallowed. Was 'other' Jacob? What had happened?

She looked around, saw dark shapes crouching in the grass. The sun was low, and the slopes of the volcano were stained with a red evening light.

She became aware that she had a very bad headache, and that her neck was sore.

Movement. A crackle of grass, a thud. Grunts, bodies jumping.

Sam sat up again, and this time no one stopped her. Her

habiline was standing guard over her, a stone axe dark in his hand. She saw a white figure moving, heard a voice cry out.

'No! You can't –' Jacob's voice.

And Jacob was there in front of her, being held in place by two habilines. He struggled, then saw Sam. 'See? They try to kill you. Humans always try to kill you.'

Sam stared at him, bewildered. 'I think they just misunderstood what we were doing. We hurt one of them.'

Jacob giggled, an odd, undignified sound. It made Sam uneasy for some reason.

'Not kill,' said the habiline with the axe. 'Choose.'

Choose what? thought Sam.

He pointed at Jacob. 'Hurt people.' At Sam. 'Not hurt.' At Sam again, then at Jacob: then looking at Sam. 'Choose. Kill. Not kill.'

Sam felt the blood drain from her face as she realised.

They wanted her to tell them whether Jacob should be killed or not.

If she said 'kill', they would kill him. But if she said 'not kill'…

They might kill both of them.

Depending on what they thought was going on. Depending on their social rules, which she didn't know.

She hesitated, then pointed at Jacob. 'Mine.'

'What are you talking about?' said Jacob.

'Yes. Yours,' said the habiline. Sam decided to call him Axeman. 'Kill. Not kill.' He raised his axe, not far enough for a killing blow, but just far enough to be threatening.

Sam stood up, said slowly. 'Let him go.'

The habiline looked at her, then looked at the two

others holding Jacob. They let him go.

'Thanks,' he said, breathing fast, his eyes moving nervously. 'Look, I –'

'– was only returning the favour,' finished Sam for him. She smiled brightly. 'Don't worry, I guess I've just got more practice in this sort of thing than you have.'

Jacob grinned back. 'Well, thanks anyway,' he said. He lowered his voice. 'I still have the Doctor's syringe. We'll get another chance.' His face twisted for a moment, then straightened into a friendly grin. 'You don't know what you've done for the future of humanity.'

Steam. Smells of waterweed and of wet, warm grass.

Kitig was hungry. It had been a long time since breakfast, since Narunil's flowercakes served up on the wicker plates. He wondered where Mritig was. Perhaps he ought to check on him, the little beast often went wandering in the afternoons...

'A mirror. I always find them useful, with energy weapons about.'

The Doctor. The *Doctor* – the Uncreator –

'Get up, Kitig, you're still alive and we've got a visitor.'

Kitig opened his eyes, reluctantly allowing himself to remember where he was.

Africa. The volcano. The lake.

Three and a half million years back in time.

He was lying on his side in the long grass just above the beach. There was a Tractite standing over him: a Tractite in full body armour, with the glittering lights of machines in a collar around his neck. A Tractite who smelled wrong. Alien.

*The scents are changing.*

Oh, why didn't I listen to Partil? I could have arranged for the Doctor and Sam to be… removed. Then I wouldn't have had to think about it any more. I wouldn't be responsible.

'My name is Tvan Mauvril,' said the armoured Tractite. 'I command the Fifth Resistance Division. What's your name and area?'

'I'm Kitig. From Paratractis.'

'Paratractis? That doesn't –' A pause. A blink of night eyes. 'How did you get here?'

'Ah, only I can explain that properly.' The Doctor's voice again. 'There's a problem with the time lines, you see –'

'Shut up, human!' snapped Mauvril. 'You're not in the Empire now.'

'I'm not human and I don't approve of the Empire any more than you do.'

Kitig rolled upright: there was a rustle of metal as he moved, and he saw four more of the armoured Tractites, two with guns levelled at him. The other two were holding the Doctor, an arm each.

'You'd better explain who I am,' said the Doctor with a smile. 'And I think Mauvril here would like it to be the truth, or these two people are going to walk off in opposite directions, each of them taking half of me away.'

Kitig looked at the hard eyes of the two Tractites holding the Doctor, smelled the hard smells. He turned to Mauvril.

'This is uncivilised behaviour! How can you make threats like this? How can you use weapons on us?'

Mauvril blinked open her night eyes. 'You're here,' she pointed out. 'With a human. That's a serious threat to us.'

'He isn't human,' said Kitig. 'We're here because his time machine malfunctioned.'

'Are there any more of you?'

'No,' said Kitig.

'Yes,' said the Doctor. 'But they're in a different location in space-time. You haven't got a chance of finding them, and it's no good making threats because neither Kitig nor I know where they are at the moment.'

'Then it's clear enough that neither of you has any useful information,' said Mauvril. She turned to the Tractites holding the guns. 'Kill them both. Quickly, no torture.'

'Wait!' yelled the Doctor.

Mauvril turned to face him, her body exuding a faint smell of anticipation. 'Does that mean you do have something useful to say to us? Or is it just that you don't want to die?'

'There's more at stake than my life or yours.'

'That's true.'

'More even than all the lives of all the Tractites and humans that ever lived.'

'So you are human.'

'No, not exactly, but that doesn't matter. What does matter is the effect that your experiment in altering history is having on the structure of the multiverse. You have to realise that this little piece of Africa and another piece about a million years down the timeline are the only bits of reality left at the moment.'

Mauvril turned to Kitig. 'What is this nonsense?'

Kitig met the alien Tractite's eyes. 'There may be some truth in it, Tvan Mauvril,' he said carefully. 'It bears investigation. I swear on the honour of the Keeping.'

191

'The honour of what?' Mauvril's eyes swung from one to the other of them. 'Are you both insane?'

'No,' said the Doctor. 'It's just that the truth is a bit more complicated than you're prepared to accept at the moment.'

Mauvril pulled a long, black, ugly weapon from a holster strapped across her back.

'Tell me the truth, then,' she said, putting the barrel of the gun against Kitig's face. 'Tell me all of it. Then I'll decide what to do with you.'

Kitig swallowed. 'Very well. I come from a world called Paratractis. It's like Tractis. A peaceful place. But at the moment it's one of two alternative futures. In the other one, the humans survive and...' He hesitated, looked at the Doctor, who shook his head. Kitig took a breath, looked away from the Doctor and into Tvan Mauvril's eyes. 'The humans destroy Tractis in the other future. They destroy our people. And a small remnant go back into the past and make Paratractis happen by destroying the humans before they evolve. The Doctor is trying to prevent it, because he favours the humans. At least, this is what it says in the *Book of Keeping*. But the Doctor –'

'Good,' snapped Mauvril. 'That's all I need to know.' She turned to the Tractites holding the Doctor. 'Take him to the base.'

'Well done, Kitig,' said the Doctor, his voice heavy with irony. 'That should have just about made sure that none of us lives to see the morning.'

'I told the truth,' said Kitig.

'Yes, you told half the truth to an angry maniac who has the fate of everything that has ever existed or will ever exist straight in the sights of her blaster and her finger on the trigger. Next time, Kitig – if there is a next time, which I really don't think in these circumstances there will be – please do me a favour and try to tell a lie.'

The last word turned into a gasp of surprise as the armoured Tractites wrenched the Doctor off his feet. One flung him across her back, and both started out at a canter through the long grass around the shore of the lake.

Mauvril gestured with the gun. 'Kitig of Paratractis, you will come with us as well.'

Reluctantly, Kitig set off after the others, with Mauvril at his back. The grass whipped at his legs, and insects buzzed around him, disturbed by the movement. In the distance, he saw antelope galloping away, already taking fright at the approach of the huge, dark Tractites.

Were these armoured thugs really responsible for the creation of Paratractis? Was it right to let them destroy innocent primitives, just because they might one day evolve into humans?

Or was the Doctor right? Was 'everything that has ever existed or will ever exist' really under threat? Or was the Doctor lying, to protect his interests?

The questions hammered at the inside of his head, refusing easy answers. It was so hard to decide. If only he could decide, then surely everything would be all right.

Surely he would be able to go home.

The habiline settlement was in a narrow gorge cut into the base of the mountain. It was bigger, and better organised, than Sam had imagined: she quickly realised that Axeman's group of a dozen or so were no more than a hunting and foraging party. On the steep slopes of the gorge there were several dozen shelters made from sticks and crudely woven matting, built on ledges or at the entrances to small caves. The shelters looked too crude and temporary to be called houses, but they were certainly more than nests.

Inside the shelters, habilines lay on piles of dry grass and leaves. Most were already asleep, but they looked up sharply as Sam arrived, eyes glinting. Several got up and vaulted down the slopes towards her. Axeman and the others made signs which translated variously as 'our people' and 'others not dangerous'.

This didn't seem to have much effect. A habiline woman pointed at Sam, screaming. 'Dangerous!' came the rather unnecessary translation.

Other women started jumping up and down. 'Not our people! Dangerous! Children here! Take them away!'

Sam saw Axeman looking at her, frowning. She didn't for a moment believe that he or any of the males would defend her against their own people. She was going to have to act quickly or the tribe were going to rip her and Jacob apart. She clapped her hands together, looked around at the screaming habilines.

'I won't hurt you. I won't hurt your children. I'm here to help you.'

The screams subsided.

One of the women stepped forward until she was within spitting distance of Sam. 'You know our signs. You are kin of any here?'

Sam thought for a moment. 'I'm – umm – granddaughter.'

The habiline put her hands on her hips, a gesture so

startlingly human that it was almost funny coming from the naked, hairy, upright ape.

'Daughter of who?' She raised her hands in the air. 'Whose daughter is this?'

Again Sam had to think. Evidently the distinction between 'granddaughter' and 'daughter' had been lost in the translation. There was no telling how much of anything she said they were going to understand. And if she said the wrong thing...

The habiline woman was still staring at her.

'All of you,' said Sam at last. 'I'm the last daughter of all of you.'

'Liar!' snapped the habiline. 'Youngest daughter –' she gestured behind her, and Sam saw another habiline suckling a baby.

One of the crowd started jumping up and down and hooting. 'Danger! Danger! Kill! Kill! Kill!'

'Not daughter,' put in Axeman helpfully. 'Friend.'

'Not friend!' snapped the senior habiline woman, turning her gaze on the hunter. Sam decided to call her the Mother Superior. 'Not human.'

'I need your help to stay alive, so that I can help you,' said Sam, crossing her fingers and hoping that the Mother Superior could cope with a concept like that.

The habiline's eyes met hers, and the dark, semi-human face creased in a frown. 'Help people? What help people?'

'I have...' She gestured at Jacob. '*We* have – umm – healing stuff. Against disease. There was an accident. A mistake. One hunter got hurt.'

Sam realised she was babbling. Worse, she was babbling in pidgin English. The habiline watched her, with folded arms.

'We don't mean any harm,' concluded Sam desperately.

The habiline frowned, poked at the ground with a foot. 'You sleep in rocks,' she said finally, then turned her back.

And that seemed to be all there was to it. Sam heard a few echoes of the word 'rocks', then silence, apart from the muffled wailing of a baby.

'I keep watch,' said Axeman suddenly, and led the way back, beyond the shelters, to a place where the gorge ended in a dry, steep slope covered with pebbles. At the bottom of the slope, there was a jumble of broken rock.

'We're meant to sleep *here*?' asked Jacob indignantly.

'Not sleep yet,' said Axeman. 'Water.'

The mention of the word immediately made Sam realise how thirsty she was. There were still a few swallows of water in the bottle in her backpack, but if the habs had some here...

Axeman was leading the way across the rocks. Suddenly he stepped down, and seemed to vanish.

Following, Sam saw a crevice in the rock, and at the same moment heard splashing noises. She pushed her body through the crevice, found a cave – no, not quite a cave: she could see evening sunlight seeping in through cracks in the walls.

A glint of water.

A hand grasped hers: Axeman. He led her across what felt like pebbles, until she splashed into cold water.

Axeman let go, and she heard water moving, drinking noises. She bent down, cautiously cupped her hands and brought some water to her lips.

It smelled clean. It tasted clean. It obviously didn't do the habs any harm.

Sam took the risk and drank it.

She bent down, scooped up more water, drank again. Her eyes were beginning to adapt to the darkness: she could just make out the shadows of the habs crouched around the water, glints of moonlight on rock, dark blotches that might be moss.

A hand touched her left breast.

She jumped back, aware of a sudden silence in the cave.

The hand touched her again. Grasped.

Sam began to shake. How the hell do you tell a two-million-year-old apeman that he's really not your type?

Well, try the usual way.

'No,' she said firmly, pushing the hand away.

Silence. Then a flurry of movement, the sound of a fist hitting flesh, and a single, loud grunt: 'Leave!'

Habiline hoots and grunts filled the cave, turning into screams, splashes. Several heavy bodies pushed past her, heading towards the entrance.

Gradually things settled down again, but Sam's body was still shaking.

Cope with it, she told herself fiercely. Their manners might be two million years out of date, but they're still a human males, or nearly human anyway. And they're not all the same: at least one of the others – Axeman, probably – defended me.

Slowly, cautiously, she backed out of the cave.

She almost collided with Jacob at the entrance, and jumped with shock. 'What's going on in there?' he asked.

'One of the habs made a pass at me,' said Sam. She

grinned.

Jacob stared. 'Are you sure?'

Sam thought about it. Maybe the guy had just been curious, had wanted to know if she felt the same as his sort of woman.

'No,' she concluded. 'Anyway, it's nothing to worry about,' she said. 'Come on, let's find somewhere to sleep.'

The Tractite base was big, but, worse than that, it was ugly. It smelled bad.

Kitig was afraid of it.

Most of it was hidden in a narrow valley where the river that fed the lake had cut through the land. Kitig saw black domes flickering with red and amber lights. Ramps, tunnels vanishing into the grey rock, and felled trees around them. Crude drilling and earth-moving machinery. Gleaming vehicles, the painful semi-audible whine of antigravs. The polished barrels of the guns. In the middle of it all, strung out along the riverside, were about a dozen Tractis-native trees, their orange leaves rippling in the breeze.

As he got closer Kitig could smell the metallic pheromonal buzz of alien nanomachines: they tickled his skin, invaded his nostrils. Complex subliminal patterns of light flickered against his eyes, superimposing right-angled geometries on the landscape.

'You're wasting your time,' commented the Doctor from his undignified position slung over the back of one of the leading Tractites. 'My retinal patterns won't make any sense to you at all.'

Kitig noticed that not one but two of the big guns

were tracking them as they entered the settlement.

There were *roads* here. Black, heavy, smelling of new tar and alien plastic.

The party marched along one of the new roads to the largest of the black domes. The gates smelled of metal: the air inside smelled of disinfectant, as if it had been scrubbed clean before anybody was allowed to breathe it.

There were illuminated pictures on the walls, stylised bas-reliefs of armoured Tractites in battle with armoured bipeds, of spaceships falling from the sky, of cities in flames. Metallic colours crawled across their surfaces: flames flickered, blood flowed.

'This is more than a military base,' said the Doctor, as the Tractite carrying him set him down on the polished plastic blocks of the floor.

'Yes,' said Mauvril. 'We're planning to live here for the rest of our lives. We've sacrificed our own futures to the cause of Tractite freedom.'

'You've sacrificed everybody else's future, too,' said the Doctor gloomily. 'And the Tractite freedom you're talking about is very much an illusion, I'm afraid.'

'So you say,' said Mauvril. 'I want to find out more about this. I hope you will help me willingly – you don't sound unreasonable. But I warn you, I have no liking for humans or –' she turned to Kitig – 'human sympathisers. If I decide that you're lying, your lives will be short.'

Kitig felt a sudden glimmer of hope. For all the armour, all the weaponry, all the horror stories on the walls, Mauvril was still a Tractite. Now that she had calmed down, there was still a possibility that she could be reached by reason.

The Doctor had evidently come to a similar conclusion,

and was already talking. 'Let me show you the future you've created. I can use my ship, the TARDIS, to –'

Mauvril shook her head. 'We're not letting you near your machine, you can forget that. And at the moment I want to speak to Kitig in private.' She gestured at the guards, who started to hustle the Doctor away along the passageway.

'You can't stop all this,' said the Doctor, pointing at the bas-reliefs on the walls. 'Whatever you do, you can't *stop* anything!'

'We'll see about that,' said Mauvril. She turned to Kitig. 'Were you a farmer?'

Kitig shook his head. 'I was brought up in sub-arctic swampland. I'm a museum curator.'

Mauvril started walking along the passageway. Kitig noticed that the Doctor's scent had already dispersed in the scrubbed-clean air.

'I was brought up on Tractis,' the armoured Tractite began. 'Not the Tractis you know, of course. A backward, horsy little world in a human universe.' A pause. 'I don't suppose you can imagine that. I don't suppose you can imagine what it was like –' She broke off. They had reached an open space in what Kitig felt was the centre of the dome. This was more like home: the lights were diffuse, and soft organics wafted soothing scents into the air.

But in the middle of the space, under a harsh electric light, was a three-dimensional image of a Tractite, so sharp and clear that for one horrified moment Kitig thought it was real.

He was on one knee, blood frothing from his nostrils, more blood streaming down his sides. Excrement, mixed with more blood, dribbled down his back legs. All four eyes were open, full of terror, and slowly clouding with death.

Mauvril turned to Kitig. 'This is what it was like – *will* be like if you don't help me, and the Doctor succeeds in whatever it is he's trying to do. This isn't a sculpture: it's a hologram. A human technique. We stole this from their files.'

'I've heard of holograms,' said Kitig, still staring at the image. 'And there were stories of things like this in the *Book of Keeping*. I know about this.'

'Yes, but you haven't lived through it. You haven't stood on the road, helpless, while Imperial troops – humans, like your friend the Doctor – disembowel your friends.

'I wish I hadn't, Kitig. I wish I'd been killed back there, so that it was all over. I wish I'd died on the farm – did you know they burnt all the farms? They were trying to starve us out. Because we didn't agree with the might of the Empire. Because we wanted to live our own life on our own planet. But no, they had mineral rights to worry about. Xantium. Cardinium. We'd have let them mine the stuff for nothing – it was useless to us – but they wanted our farmlands, our race parks, everything. They wanted to grow their drugs – coffee, pixirin, opium. Then they sold them back to us, at prices three hundred times what they paid us for the raw crop. Our people became weak, addicted, exploited, *slaves*. And this –' she gestured at the hologram – 'this was the end of it. Death. Death for every Tractite. Because a few of us stood up and said no.'

Kitig became aware that there was a line of foam

around Mauvril's lips. The room was full of the stink of her fear and pain. Kitig's own heart was thudding.

Perhaps they were all the same. Violent apes. Perhaps Mauvril was right to try to kill them all.

No, not kill. *Prevent.* There was a difference.

After a while, Mauvril seemed to calm down, and the scrubbed air took over, wafting back the soothing smells of Tractite plants. The armoured Tractite opened her eyes again and looked at Kitig.

'Now,' she said. 'I want you to tell me about the *Book of Keeping* you refer to. It had occurred to me to prepare a record of what we have done, so that our...' She hesitated. 'So that when Tractites come to Earth, they will find out what happened. You said that the Doctor is mentioned in this book?'

'He is referred to as the Uncreator,' said Kitig carefully. 'But yes, I believe the Uncreator and the Doctor to be the same person.'

Mauvril blinked her night eyes. 'Good. I want you to tell me exactly what the book says about the Uncreator, so that we can ensure that the correct situation arises in your time and the Doctor does not succeed.'

Kitig remembered swearing his oath, that bizarre ceremony in the gold-and-red Chamber of Keeping, with the book open in front of him: 'I will defend the right of the Tractites over the Uncreator and the aliens who would destroy us...'

He hadn't taken it seriously then. Now, he realised that it was serious.

Deadly serious.

He could keep his oath and save his species. Save Narunil. Critil. Jontil and Mritig. The vast, peaceful,

Tractite-run galaxy that he knew.

Or he could lie to Mauvril, as the Doctor had told him to, and perhaps save the humans.

Kitig looked into the eyes of his fellow Tractite, saw and smelled the suffering there, the pain under the hard eyes, and knew that he had only one choice.

Sam felt the hand on her shoulder and practically jumped out of her skin.

A giggle. Jacob.

Why did he giggle? she wondered. It didn't seem very military.

'Sorry to wake you. But I think we ought to give it another go. While they're asleep.'

'What, injecting them with that stuff? It won't work.' She gestured at Axeman, sitting upright only a few feet away, wide awake. She was sure he was watching them as they talked.

'Perhaps if you tell them it will do some good…'

'Me?'

'You're with the Doctor. They might believe you more.'

Sam frowned. 'What exactly did the Doctor say about this stuff?'

'I don't know. My CO was the one with the detailed instructions. He…' A pause. 'He didn't make it over.'

Sam felt a faint breath of wind. Somewhere below them in the settlement a habiline grunted. She looked up at the moon, wondered if there would ever be any human bases on it in this universe, any wide, green, terraformed forests under the lunar seas. If the Doctor was right there would be no humans to –

'We've got to save them!'

Jacob's excitable voice woke Sam from her thoughts. She sat up, extended a hand. 'Give me the hypo,' she said. 'I'll see what I can do.'

With the syringe, she walked up to Axeman.

'Danger,' she told him. 'Disease.'

The shadowy form of the habiline moved slightly. Hands touched hers.

Of course. Sign language in the dark.

Axeman's fingers moved. 'No disease.'

'There will be,' said Sam. 'I need to protect you. That's why we're here.'

'I protect you,' Axeman informed her stoutly.

'Yes. But if you're ill, you can't protect anyone, can you?'

'Not ill.'

'You will be ill tomorrow.'

'After sunrise? Ill?' She could feel the tension, the confusion, in the habiline's hands. The future was obviously a difficult concept for him, unless a specific event was involved.

'You'll be ill after sunrise unless I protect you.' She raised the syringe, tapped it. 'Protect.'

'No.' Axeman pushed her away. 'Not protect. Dangerous.'

Sam sighed with exasperation. She heard Jacob walking up behind her –

And then something cannoned into her body, and for a moment she thought Axeman had attacked her. Then she saw Jacob snatch the syringe and plunge it into Axeman's arm.

The habiline screamed aloud and cuffed Jacob.

Jacob yelled, then danced back. The habiline was standing now, making warning grunts which were being echoed around the settlement.

'Push the plunger in!' he yelled at Sam. 'We've got to get him!'

Sam caught hold of Axeman's arm.

'It was an accident,' she said, trying to calm the habiline down, trying to *keep him still*. 'He wasn't attacking you.'

Axeman hurled her back. She could still see the syringe, attached to his arm. She reached out, grabbed it, pushed in the plunger, then pulled it out.

'Got him!'

Axeman whirled on her, roaring. 'It's OK,' said Sam, her voice shaking. 'Jacob. Tell him it's OK. Tell him we've protected him.'

But Jacob only laughed.

Axeman roared again. Terrible, strong hands grabbed her shoulders, pushed her down against the rock.

'Jacob!' yelled Sam.

But there was only laughter, and retreating footsteps.

Jacob was running away.

Sam felt her head banged against the rock, and screamed with pain and fear and fury, *'I haven't hurt you!'*

But Axeman didn't believe her.

# CHAPTER 18

The air was acrid with sulphur, so much so that Kitig was sure that even the Doctor would have been able to smell it, if Mauvril hadn't been keeping him locked up in the air-scrubbed dome.

'Is this the best place to build your base?' asked Kitig, indicating the column of ash and smoke rising from the dark cone of the volcano.

'Definitely. The mountain isn't that near. And the regular ash fall keeps the soil fertile. We'll be able to grow crops. We can survive for decades here.'

'Do you want to? After what you've done to the humans?'

Mauvril stopped walking, looked out over the rippling surface of the lake. The ash cloud was making the sunlight hazy, and a hot wind was blowing across the plain.

'Yes,' she said at last. 'I'm surprised, but I do. I never imagined that I'd want to be at peace, if we won. That I'd want to do anything but fight, and fight, and fight, but...' She hesitated. 'Perhaps I just want to be a farmer again.'

Kitig kicked up the ash-white sand of the beach, watched the dust scatter in the wind. He thought carefully for a moment, then said it. 'And your children?'

Mauvril looked up sharply, and her night eyes opened for a full second, glaring with blood. 'You smelled it?' she snapped.

'I have a wife and children,' said Kitig. 'And I had younger brothers and sisters. I know the scent of a pregnancy. And I would guess that you aren't the only one.'

Mauvril turned back to the lake, said nothing.

'It's a colony, isn't it? You're building Paratractis, aren't you?'

Mauvril tossed her head. 'I didn't want to tell you,' she said after a while. 'I wasn't sure I could trust you. I'm still not sure. But I suppose you were bound to work it out eventually.'

'The Doctor will work it out too. He is very perceptive.'

'Yes. I know.' She turned back to him. 'Is he an Imperial agent?'

'I really don't know. I don't know much about the Empire. But I think…' Kitig hesitated, looking for the right words. 'Even if that's part of it, he's more than that.'

'But he favours the humans?'

'He has to. He says it's to do with the nature of time.'

'Yes, I spoke to him.' A pause. 'I could have him tortured, you know, until we get the truth.' A longer pause. 'I could have *you* tortured, until we get the truth from him.'

Kitig's throat constricted. The smell of ash and sulphur in the air seemed to get stronger. 'You'd do that to me? To him?'

'You saw what they did to us.' Mauvril swung round, rose on her hind legs and kicked at the air, disturbing a cloud of insects. She turned as she fell back, so that she was facing Kitig. Took hold of his hands. 'Do you know why I don't think you're an Imperial agent? Why I didn't just kill the pair of you?'

'No. In your position – taking everything into account

– I would probably have felt that I had no choice but to –'

Mauvril laughed. 'That's it! "In your position – taking everything into account –"!' Her hands gripped harder. 'You're a child, Kitig of Paratractis. You're innocent and naive and beautiful and you're everything we're fighting to make happen. And I don't think that even the Empire would be clever enough to make you that way just to fool us into giving up our dreams.' She let go. 'But you do realise that the Doctor might be deceiving you?'

Kitig took a few steps back from the beach, felt the first stems of grass prickle against his back legs. 'I think that he's telling some of the truth,' he told Mauvril. 'You know I'd do anything to make the future I lived in real. My wife – my children – everything I knew is there. I want to go back, and even if I can't go back I'd like to know that I've done everything I can to make it happen. But if the Doctor is telling the truth, then all of us will lose everything. Or perhaps we already have.'

Mauvril stood for a long time, staring out at the volcano. Kitig could hear a faint, almost subsonic, vibration in the wind.

'I should have you tortured,' said Mauvril after a while. 'I'm sure it's the only way of getting the truth out of the Doctor. I know the type of person he is. He won't crack under anything else we can do to him. But, you see, I can't do it to you. I can't take away your innocence like that.'

Kitig kicked at the sand with his forefeet. He felt more irritated with Mauvril than afraid of her. 'I'm not innocent,' he said. 'Torture me if you have to.'

'You are innocent. You've never been tortured, you've never seen anyone tortured. If you had, you wouldn't make stupid remarks like that.'

There was a silence. The wind grew stronger, throwing up whitecaps on the lake. The volcano still grumbled in the distance.

'I can try to get the truth out of him myself,' said Kitig. 'I could pretend that you had threatened me. That might be enough to persuade him –'

'I was hoping you'd suggest that,' said Mauvril, glancing over her shoulder at him, her eyes cold. 'I didn't want to have to make you do it.'

*Click*.

There was light in Sam's eyes. Torchlight. *Human* light.

'Jacob?'

'He's been here?'

A woman's voice. A dim face behind the light.

Sam realised that only a minute or so had passed. Her head hurt, and her arms hurt. Axeman and several of the other habs were bounding up the slope, scattering pebbles.

In a minute they would start throwing rocks.

'Whoever you are, we've got to go after Jacob, now!' snapped Sam.

'What's he done?'

Sam felt a nudge of fear. Whose side was this woman on?

It might be better to run for it, find Jacob, work out some kind of strategy – but Jacob had already abandoned her once.

A hand grabbed hers. 'Can you get up?'

Sam got up, felt a stabbing pain in her neck and almost vomited.

The other woman held on to her.

A rock clattered past them.

'We've got to go!' urged Sam.

'No. Wait. They won't hurt us if we – ow!'

Sam almost laughed.

They both started running, Sam clumsily: her neck was still hurting and her head buzzed. She saw habiline shadows around them, but none approached, though there was quite a lot of hooting and grunting.

Finally, they seemed to be clear of them. The woman peered uncertainly at Sam in the weak moonlight. 'I – umm,' she began. 'You *are* Sam, aren't you?'

Sam nodded. 'Who are you? Why don't you like Jacob?'

The woman must have heard the suspicion in Sam's voice. She said quietly. 'I'm Jo Grant. The Doctor's mentioned me, I expect.'

Sam remembered a name like that from somewhere. She looked at the woman, taking in the floppy Indiana Jones hat and the purple striped pullover that looked ten years out of date, even for someone of Jo's advanced age. She looked a good deal more incongruous than Jacob, and a good deal more –

*Genuine.*

Sam suddenly began to feel sick.

'He made me inject one of the habs with something,' she told Jo.

'*What?*'

'He said he was from the Doctor. That's what all the fuss was about back there: the habs thought we were attacking them.'

There was a moment's silence.

Jo took Sam's hands in hers. 'Sam. The Doctor said that

Jacob had –'

'Let me guess. A virus. In a syringe. Attached to a green thing about the size of a tennis ball.'

'He didn't mention that, but –'

'What have I injected them with? What are we going to do about it?'

Jo didn't answer.

'What have I done?' wailed Sam.

But she knew.

*I've just injected them with the virus I let Jacob fool me how could I have been so stupid?*

'I've just wiped out the human race,' whispered Sam. She heard Jo swallow in the darkness. 'Tell me I haven't.'

Jo didn't tell her that. Instead, she said, 'The Doctor will turn up. He had to go somewhere else in the TARDIS, but he'll be back. Everything will be all right then.'

But she didn't sound entirely convinced.

The room was small, and smelled of blood and pain.

It was almost dark: Kitig had to open his night eyes before he could see clearly. The Doctor was hunched in the corner, his face white, dried blood staining the front of his shirt. His jacket and shoes had been removed, and there were red welts on his face.

Kitig stopped in the doorway, shocked despite everything that Mauvril had told him. He hadn't expected them to have tortured the Doctor *already*.

The Doctor looked at him and smiled. His upper lip was cut wide open, and there was a gap in the row of teeth. 'Hello Kitig,' he said in a muffled voice. 'I wondered when you'd turn up.'

Kitig shuffled forward into the cell. A guard closed the door behind him.

There was an ominous clicking of locks.

'Mauvril –' he began. But he couldn't just launch into his prepared lie. 'Why did they do this?' he asked, surprised at the anger in his own voice.

'Do what?' The Doctor saw Kitig's stare, looked down at himself. 'Yes, sorry, I do look a bit of a wreck. Don't worry, I can control the pain. Old Gallifreyan technique.'

'Yes, but why?'

The Doctor frowned. 'I'm not sure, but I think some of Mauvril's thugs had got a bit bored, without any humans to beat up, and I look human, don't I?' He shrugged. 'Well, there you are.'

'Doctor, Mauvril has asked me to find out the truth. She says...' He hesitated, swallowed. 'She'll torture me if you don't confess.'

'Yes, that's usually the next step,' said the Doctor. 'And you don't want to be tortured, I suppose?'

Kitig swallowed again, looking at the Doctor, feeling the locked door behind him. It was no use fooling himself: it was obvious that Mauvril might well carry out her threat, for all her talk of Kitig's beauty and innocence. He wondered how he would feel, after living the life that Mauvril had led.

'I don't know,' he said. 'She's unstable. She changes her mind constantly.' He sat down on his haunches. His folded legs almost touched the Doctor in the confined space. '*Is* there anything more to be told?' he asked quietly.

'Not really,' said the Doctor. 'I suppose I could tell them my life story – that might keep them busy for a while.' He smiled again. It was probably supposed to be reassuring, but his lip dripped blood. 'Don't worry, I'll think of something.'

Kitig shook his head. 'It's not enough, Doctor. We have to tell a story that will convince Mauvril she's heard the whole truth.'

The Doctor's smile broadened. 'Ah, Kitig. I see you're learning the arts of diplomacy at last.'

Kitig stared at him.

The Doctor leaned forward, wincing. Kitig wondered just how much pain he was in, and how well he could really control it.

'They're not going to let me out of here,' he said quietly. 'Not ever. So you need to do something for me, or, rather, arrange for something to happen. I'm not sure it will work, but if it doesn't I suspect we'll all cease to exist after a little while, so I think you'd better give it a try. What I need you to do is –'

'Before you tell me,' said Kitig quickly. 'I should tell you something.'

The Doctor looked at him, looked directly into his eyes. Kitig could feel the biped's will, like a monstrous hand, pushing him towards making a promise he couldn't keep.

'I can't guarantee that I'll help you,' said Kitig, speaking with slow determination. 'If you tell me about your plan, I may decide to sabotage it. I must put my own people first.' A pause. The Doctor didn't look away. 'I'm sorry.'

The Doctor looked down at last. 'I understand,' he said. Then, quite suddenly, he grinned. 'But you're my only hope, so I'm going to tell you anyway.'

'I understand. Go on.'

'I need you to bring the TARDIS to me.'

Kitig closed his eyes in sadness. Because, before the Doctor had even finished his sentence, before he even began the technical explanations of how Kitig should move the space-time machine, Kitig knew that he was going to have to refuse him.

Tvan Mauvril was glad to be back in charge of an operation. A genuine operation, with a target, with an enemy, with dangers. She'd hated the war, but she'd got used to it: managing a colony, even one under the possible threat of discovery by Imperial agents, was dull by comparison.

She trimmed the steering of the flitter cautiously, minimising the load on the irreplaceable power cell. The volcano was quite close now; the plains below were coated in white ash that had fallen from yesterday's eruption. It reminded her of snow, the snow that had fallen on the fields of her home town on Tractis, many years ago in another, more innocent life.

She looked over her shoulder at the Doctor's space-time machine, the thing he called the TARDIS, strapped down in the bomb bay of the flitter. She remembered Kitig's warning: the TARDIS is very powerful. The Doctor can call the machine to him at any time. If you try to kill him, it will come to his rescue. You can't destroy it with guns, you can't destroy it at all, unless you drop it into the sun. You have to seal it off from him, put it somewhere he can't ever find it.

Well, she couldn't drop it into the sun. Not without a spaceship. But the volcano was the next best thing, and there was just enough flitter power left to get her there – though she was probably going to have to walk part of the way back. The heat of the magma would be enough to destroy the machine, surely.

The ground beneath vanished for a moment, replaced by grey-blue water, streaked with golden sunlight. The alkaline lake. After a moment the water filled with flame-red bacteria, blooming where nothing else could grow.

That's us, she thought. Our colony. Blooming in the heart of the wilderness, safe from the Empire.

And, incidentally, robbing the humans of their planet. Or at least that had been the idea.

Until the Doctor came along.

The flitter's autopilot beeped, warning her that the volcano's slopes were dangerously near: she gained height quickly, following the contour of surface. Beneath her, the ground changed from pure white to a mixture of dark lava flows and small, ash-covered trees.

Then, suddenly, it was all gone, and she was flying over the vast, grey landscape of the crater. Disappointingly, there was no huge bubbling lava pool.

Still, there had to be a main vent. It was simply a matter of finding it.

She switched the flitter's display to a thermal-imaging system, and was rewarded with a rainbow of hot spots and a screaming blue-white disc that was the throat of the volcano. She locked her 'weapon' on to the disc, then let the flitter fly itself and returned the display to a natural-light view.

She watched as the bomb bay ejected its load, and the TARDIS fell in a smooth predetermined arc into the smoky darkness of the vent.

Then she swung the flitter round, and set a heading for home.

# BOOK FOUR

*Mauvril looked at the Doctor's face. It was pale, and the eyes were closed, but there was a tension in the eyelids, in the muscles of the face, which told her that he was conscious.*

*She had toyed with his death, testing him, watching him fail to retrieve his time machine time after time, until she was quite sure that he could not retrieve it. That it was destroyed.*

*So she had told him her story, not just because she needed to tell it, not just because he deserved to hear it, but also to keep him alive long enough for her to be satisfied.*

*Now, she was satisfied. He couldn't bring back the TARDIS.*

*It was dead.*

*Soon, the Doctor would be dead too.*

*As soon as she'd finished her story.*

*'When I woke up, after killing the alien, it was dark. After a moment I realised that this was because there was a spaceship moving across the sky. Vast, sharp-edged, dark as the night sky and outlined by the stars around it.*

*'I'd worked out a few things while I slept. I suppose you do, even when the sleep is a preparation for death. Perhaps especially then. Anyway, I knew that this immense machine in the sky had come to destroy me, because I had destroyed one of its people. I'd realised that the alien I'd killed was a human, despite the body armour: I think I'd worked out that the armour, like the glittering fibre optics around her eye, was a machine. And I knew that this was an invasion, that*

*the humans wanted to destroy us. I'd remembered the
Earth Reptile's warning, and worked out what it had
meant.*

'*Poor Pakip, I thought. He should have listened to his
friend.*

'*I was quite calm. I didn't care, you see. I knew now
that the humans had decided to destroy us, as they
had destroyed others before. If that was the case, then
everyone – every Tractite, of every land – was going to
die. My death, at least, would be a deserved one. I even
thought that it was possible that all of Tractis deserved
to die: for surely, if the Earth Empire with all its
glittering power had decided we weren't fit to exist, it
must be true. So I lay there, a tiny, half-dead horsy
quadruped, and I waited for the explosion of light
which would kill me and absolve me of my crime.*

'*It didn't happen, of course. Perhaps if I'd been
moving around, and anyone on the ship had noticed
I was alive, they might have taken the trouble to kill
me. But more probably not. They had other business.
So the ship crawled overhead, an inverted landscape
of dead, jagged metal, and it didn't even notice me. An
hour after it was gone, I was still waiting for death,
only half conscious, when there was a false sunrise on
the northern horizon.*

'*I stood up, on shaky legs, and took my bearings.
There was only one city in that direction: Noctutis, the
capital of our land, the city of my dreams, the city of
all that spice and perfume and dancing and gold and
beauty, the city I had never actually seen, but
dreamed of so much and one day hoped to see.*

'*And now that city was dead.*

'I think it was the death of my dream, rather than the deaths of the two million or so of my people living in the city, that affected me then. It made me angry. Angry enough to want to live – at least, to live long enough to find out what had happened, whether we really deserved this and, if so, why.

'So I took the weapon from the thing that I had killed and started to try to understand the function of the switches and levers attached to it. I don't think I was consciously planning to kill any more invaders, not as such. That was still a taboo. I was just trying to find a way to survive – for a few days, at least. I think I somehow imagined I would hijack one of their flitters and get off the planet. I thought about trying to find the Earth Reptile, Menarc, and asking him to intercede with the Empress for us.

'But as the days passed, and the refugees came out from the cities, thousands of them, starving, terrified, I began to realise what the invasion really meant. It wasn't just the end of my dreams, but the end of a whole world. Our world was being picked apart, a whole, complex web of culture and civilisation, a worthy civilisation, was being reduced to nothing more than a few random glimmerings, like the movement of light along those fibre-optic cables in the dead human's eye. I realised the value of the peaceful, dull, Tractite culture I had been brought up in only as it was being destroyed. I could tell you many stories: deaths, nightmares. But this is my story, and I dare say you've heard – and seen – more than enough stories like that on your travels.

'What's more important is the effect that it all had on

221

me. Slowly, I became a killer. Killing in self-defence became killing in the defence of others, became killing in anticipation of attack, became killing for the sake of killing. I don't know when I actually started to enjoy it. When I discovered I could have blood lust, just as if I were a carnivore. When I started torturing the humans, just as they had tortured us. When I started drinking their blood, for the salt, for the hatred. But I know that it silted up my mind – thickened it. I had nightmares in which I killed my brother, and his wife, and their child, in which I pulled the trigger on a vast blaster weapon and burnt out Tafalis and Noctutis and all those people and all my dreams.

'I had become my enemy.

'Can you understand that?'

The Doctor's eyes opened, but he said nothing.

After a while, Mauvril went on.

'Can you understand, then, how we felt when we found the time tree? Can you understand how we realised that this strange alien plant with its orange leaves and its appetite for heavy metals could actually turn back time, and knew that we had to do it?

'At first we were going to sabotage the invasion – but how? We would have to smuggle a six-metre tree into orbit – position it exactly – and make it travel back an exact number of years! No, it was too difficult. The nature of the plant made precise settings impossible. We needed a broad, easy target – and I thought of it.

'I thought of it.

'You can understand it, can't you? The temptation? It would all just go away. The invasion would simply never have been. All of our terrible crimes would vanish. Our lust, our hatred, would be gone. We would never have to drink blood. We would be clean again.

'And the human race would never have existed.

'Of course it wasn't easy. Our first jump only took us back a thousand years, for some reason. One of my people was left behind in the confusion that followed, with a seedling from the tree – I don't know what he did, he may have tried to continue the mission. Some of the things that Kitig has said make me think this could be the case.

'The second jump was better. We arrived in a primitive human village. But one of the humans got into the tree, and one of my soldiers panicked and shot it. The tree jumped out of control; we ended up here. There were no humans, and astronomical evidence suggests we have arrived before the human race evolved.

'What else is there to do but survive? And, in surviving, replace our enemies?

'Doctor, do you understand what we have done? There has been no killing – only one small village of humans has died – and yet we have destroyed the human race. Kitig has told me the story of his people, the mystery of their origin. The fact that they are peaceful.

'Doctor, I want to believe that you will accept that what we have done – what we have achieved – is the best future for the universe. I want you to believe that. I want you to forgive me before you die.

'Please, Doctor.'

The Doctor stirred at last. The blue-green eyes

*opened, turned to meet Mauvril's.*

*After a long while, he spoke.*

*'If you want me to forgive you –' A rattling breath, a silence.*

*'Yes?' Mauvril wondered if he would beg for mercy.*

*'Fetch Kitig.'*

# CHAPTER 19

The place where the TARDIS had materialised was still marked by a faint depression in the short grass, and by a right-angled bite taken out of the hard soil.

'That's what's different,' Sam said over her shoulder to Jo. 'Corners.'

Jo looked down at her, squinting in the bright, low morning sunlight. 'You mean that's the difference between natural landscape and cities?'

They'd been talking about it on the way across from the gorge. Both of them needed distraction from the one big fact of their lives, the fact that the Doctor had been gone six days.

*Six days.*

Sam hadn't asked whether Jo had ever been abandoned by the Doctor for that long. Jo hadn't asked Sam about it, either. Both of them avoided talking about it as far as possible.

'Yup, I think so,' she said, in reply to Jo's question. 'In cities, everything's designed. Even if it's curved, even if it's a mess, it's still got corners. Corners from up here.' Sam tapped her head. 'But all this…' She waved her arm around at the enormous landscape.

Every hummock, every ridge, every thorn tree cast a long, rough shadow in the grass. The irregular cone of the volcano seemed to be floating on a shimmering something that might be a lake, or might be an illusion. In the other direction, a low ridge of hills retreated towards the horizon, each distinct peak higher than the last, jumbled green and buff and ochre rock streaked with shadows. The first outcrops of the hill were only yards away, low, random rocks, subtly uneven.

'Not a corner in sight,' Sam concluded.

'Not everything man-made has corners. There are trees and parks.'

'Trimmed trees. Planted-out, well-watered, looked-after parks. Even if you go for a walk in the woods, they've been "managed". This hasn't been managed.' She paused. 'That was the difference with the Tractite world – with Paratractis. It was still Earth, really, but it was still wild too – can you understand that?'

'Maybe you just didn't recognise the alien corners.'

Sam looked up. She'd begun to realise that Jo was a good deal brighter than she seemed. With her striped sweater and floppy hat she seemed so… daffy. So English and old-fashioned.

But she knew how to survive in this environment. She was the one who had picked their campsite, she was the one who had found fresh water, she was the one who had managed to light a fire.

The fire had at least kept the habs away.

'Maybe not,' she admitted. 'But I wish there was more of this on our Earth.'

Jo squatted down, brushed the hair away from her eyes. 'You sound as if you think Jacob was doing the right thing.'

Sam looked away, swallowed. *She* had pushed the plunger. *She* had infected the habilines. *She* was responsible.

Jo put a hand on her arm. 'Sorry. That was tactless.'

'No. It's OK. I… sort of thought he was, for a while.

When we went to Paratractis, it was so beautiful. And what the humans had done to the Tractites in the alternative reality – in *our* reality – was so horrible. But –'

She broke off. Jo's hand on her arm had tightened, and she was staring into the long grass.

A shadow.

No.

A habiline.

'Sam, I think we're in trouble.'

Sam turned, saw that the habs were standing in a ring around them. The males, and some of the females, were swinging the heavy stone axes in their hands.

Axeman stepped forward.

'Death,' he said, pointing towards the nearest hill, where the habiline settlement was. 'Death. Death.'

He pointed at Jo and Sam, each in turn.

Sam felt her stomach heave in panic.

Jo grabbed her arm. 'Run!'

Sam hesitated for a second, staring into Axeman's eyes. Was there any hope of making him understand?

'Jacob did this,' she said 'Not us.'

Which isn't entirely true, she thought, with a sick feeling.

'Stranger,' said Axeman, pointing at them again. 'Stranger. Stranger. *Enemy*.' He raised the axe.

Sam ran.

Jo was ahead of her, waving her arms back and forth. After a moment, Sam saw the stone axe held double-handed. Brown habiline bodies moved in front of them, dancing, screaming, teeth bared. Drool and sweat flew. Jo became aware of a rhythmic shout, almost like a football chant, a *ceremony*. This was a *ritual killing* and then there was only rock in front of her, a bare reddish wall of rock, and they were going to be pinned against the hillside, pinned against the rock and –

*Killed –*

The rains had come. The air on the lake shore was clear and fresh, the grass on the plain high and green and glittering with new flowers.

Kitig trotted along the narrow beach, as he did twice every day, morning and evening. Quite a lot of Mauvril's troopers did the same. He could see them, bunches of jogging figures moving clockwise around the shore, some of them casting up spray as they cut across the shallow water of seasonal streams.

Kitig jogged anticlockwise.

He'd come to enjoy dodging them, making them steer into the water or into the long, cutting grass. They cursed him, but they knew he had Mauvril's protection, and he'd received nothing worse than a few painful 'accidental' kicks.

A drifting cumulus cloud obscured the sun for a moment, and Kitig realised that one of the jogging figures was Mauvril.

He stopped, waited, watching her come closer. He wasn't sure how he knew that there was something wrong, but he knew.

Their eyes met as she came closer.

'The Doctor,' he said, feeling an icy chill touch his heart. Surely, after all he'd said to her, after all her talk of forgiveness and peace, she hadn't let him die. 'Is he dead, then?'

'No,' said Mauvril. 'He isn't dead. But he wants to see

you.'

Kitig walked up to Mauvril, touched the side of her neck gently. 'Then do you believe me now?'

' "Evil can only foster evil"?' Mauvril hesitated. 'Yes. But that doesn't mean I can trust the Doctor.' A pause. To Kitig's surprise, she took hold of his hand. 'But I do trust you. I'll take you to him now.'

She let go of his hand, led the way along the foreshore and up the newly greened slope to the settlement.

'Quán-Nafarnis is almost a town now,' she commented.

There were fourteen confirmed pregnancies among the soldiers: marriages were being arranged for the raising of children, the shapes of households and clans to come forming in the air like the great white clouds of the rains.

The future, thought Kitig. *My* future. Do I really want to risk it all?

But Kitig knew that he couldn't abandon the Doctor. His conscience demanded that this essentially *good* being should be allowed to live. Surely the Doctor could be persuaded, somehow, to serve the cause of the Tractite future? Couldn't he *see* that it was better?

The fresh scents of flowers had penetrated even into the scrubbed air of the command dome. In fact, to his amazement, Kitig saw a low bowl filled with water lilies in the main corridors, new curtains over the images of death on the walls.

'I didn't realise –' He stopped, not quite sure what to say.

'Realise what?' asked Mauvril sharply.

'That you – umm – were redecorating.'

'It seemed appropriate.' A pause. 'After all, we're not at war any more.'

'Except with the Doctor.'

Mauvril didn't reply, just led the way to the Doctor's cell, told the guards to move aside.

Inside, Kitig was shocked by what he saw. The Doctor's form was skeletal, a broken puppet inside the loose shell of his clothing. He smelled of weakness, of death. There was a glucose drip attached to his arm.

Kitig turned to Mauvril, furious. He didn't know what he'd been expecting, but he hadn't been expecting this. 'Is this your idea of mercy?' he accused her.

Mauvril looked away, then began to back out of the cell. 'I'll leave you with him,' she said.

'I want to know why you've done this! You obviously weren't giving him any food – why not? Why –'

'Food was short before the rains. I didn't see why we should make a special effort for an Empire agent when the rest of us were rationed. Anyway, he has to die in the end. Why waste good food keeping him alive?'

'That's a ridiculous excuse. There are a hundred Tractites here. The amount of food needed for the Doctor would have been tiny.'

'Nonetheless, we felt we couldn't spare it.'

'I would have spared some from my own rations if –'

'And it was decided that –'

' "It was decided"? "We felt"? Are you claiming you weren't responsible for these decisions? What kind of –'

'Please.' The Doctor. His voice was little more than a whisper, but it cut across all their shouting. 'Please stop arguing. I need to speak to Kitig alone.'

Mauvril's eyes met Kitig's for a moment. 'Tell me

what he says.'

She backed out of the cell and closed the door.

Kitig leaned over the Doctor, looked at the sunken face, the bruises where the circulation had failed under the stress of hunger.

'I'm sorry. My people – I apologise –' He couldn't find the words, not even the most simple, elementary phrase. His mind was numb with shock and anger.

'You didn't know.' It was a statement, not a question. 'Her way of killing me, without killing me. A sloppy decision. Not very military. But –' the ghost of a smile – 'I'm still alive. Perhaps you can change her mind.'

'Perhaps,' said Kitig. 'I'll try. I'm certainly going to tell her that she must give you food. Fresh clothing. Larger quarters. It's obscene to keep you like this.'

The blue-green eyes fixed on Kitig's, and suddenly there was no trace of weakness there, no trace of the weeks of privation and near-starvation. 'You'll have to do better than that. My survival isn't all there is to it, you know.'

Kitig felt his body tense. He knew what the Doctor was going to say next. But he didn't know how he was going to answer.

The Doctor's dry lips opened again, and the expected words came out. 'You'll have to help me, Kitig.'

Rocks pitched against the cliff wall, bounced back. Jo felt habiline hands grabbing at her arms, her legs.

'No!' she shouted. 'We can help you!'

Ahead of her, Sam was climbing the cliff wall, as agile as any of the habs.

Then she was at the top, reaching down.

Jo grabbed the arm, half jumped up, got a grip on the top of the rock wall and hauled herself the rest of the way.

The habilines screamed at them from below.

'Come *on*,' said Sam.

Another stone hit Jo's stomach. She almost lost her balance, had a brief teetering sight of the bottom of the rock wall, a furious habiline face staring up at her, then Sam was dragging her away again, up the rough slope of the hill.

The first habs appeared behind them, and another stone clattered past.

Jo ran, ran wildly in a way she hadn't done since she'd last been with the Doctor, panic making her legs go on long after they should have stopped working. Sam kept ahead of her, stopping occasionally to let her catch up.

Gradually, the habilines fell behind, the pursuing screams and stones less frequent. Finally they faded away, and all Jo could hear was her own gasping breath and the pounding of blood in her ears.

'OK, stop,' she called to Sam.

The younger woman kept running.

'Sam, *please*.'

Sam looked over her shoulder. 'They might ambush us again. We need to be out on the plain. Well clear of this'

They followed the trail down through the rocks to the plain. Sam slowed up a little, but Jo could hardly keep pace. Her ears were ringing, her legs felt as if they'd turned to jelly.

Must spend some more time in the gym, she thought, then almost giggled at the ludicrousness of the thought.

At last Sam stopped. Jo slowed to a walk, gradually

caught up. Sam was leaning forward, her hands on her thighs, breathing in great gulps like an athlete after a marathon.

Jo settled for sitting down.

'What now?' asked Sam after a while.

Jo looked around. They were out on the open grassland. The grassland where Rowenna and Julie had died. Where there was no water. Where there were dogs, hyenas, lions, all on the look-out for an easy meal.

'I don't know,' she said. 'I'm sorry, Sam, but I simply don't know.'

Jacob had always been different, but until he'd exiled himself to ancient Africa he hadn't known how different.

He pushed the knife into the throat of the terrified antelope and watched as the blood spurted out. He waited for the pressure to drop, for the dying animal's struggles to weaken, then he knelt down and began to drink.

Rich. Salty. Delicious.

He was living as people were meant to live: by the destruction of other life. He understood now why it had been so essential to destroy humankind. If they were all like him, it was no wonder the planet was falling apart all around them.

He remembered the environmental group he'd tried to join. He could still remember the forest clearing, the idiots with their poems and their paper bags and their lunatic idealism. And he – he had been prepared to do something. To really make a difference.

To *destroy*.

That was why destiny had chosen him.

And Jacob knew that he was still different now. While the two women had lived like the apemen, had made themselves less than human and waited to share a messy and uncomfortable death, he had stayed away. Here on the plain, with his knife.

There was plenty of food and drink, if you were prepared to kill for it. And the more you killed, the more fun it was.

He began to cut open the antelope's chest, searching for its heart, but was distracted by a sound.

A voice.

*People*. Here on the plains.

For a heartbeat Jacob was afraid. Was it the Doctor, back again?

Then he realised that the voice was female.

Jo. Or Sam. Probably both.

Jacob crouched down, scurried into the long grass, trying to wipe the blood from the rags of his clothes.

Then he realised what he was doing. Running away. Hiding. He was *afraid* of them, as if they were the murder squad.

Well, they weren't.

He was.

He could murder them. Easy.

He pulled the knife from the crude sheath he had made for it, then listened.

The voices blew in the wind, snatches of a discussion. '… have to go… lions… water hole…'

Jacob crept towards the voices, knife at the ready. The last voices on Earth, except mine, he thought.

And I'm going to shut them up.

\* \* \*

Kitig stood on the rocky crest of the hill, on the far side of the lake, looking down at the shore, smelling the wind.

*Follow the scent of the humans.*

Kitig could still hear the Doctor's voice, echoing in his skull. The alien had refused to explain the message, simply tapping his ear until Kitig understood: there were listening devices in the cell.

He'd repeated the message to Mauvril, certain that the Doctor had expected him to do this. Mauvril had said that the Doctor was 'obviously delirious', as if that explained everything. But she had looked and smelled unmistakably guilty.

Kitig had realised, then.

There was something that Mauvril was trying to hide. Something she had told the Doctor, or something he had guessed.

Kitig sniffed the air again, trying to take in every nuance. Flowers, fresh grass, the faint tang of ice, of distant water, of the soda lake, of ash –

No. Not ash. Something burning –

*Screaming and burning –*

Yes. The smell of pain.

Kitig started to pick his way down the rocky slope, tracking the smell. It was mixed with the smell of deep soil, the smell of the earth uncovered when he had helped Mauvril and the others dig out the foundations of the new houses at the top of the settlement.

So. A place where the soil had been broken, then. And not far from the settlement.

Kitig tracked the scent through the long green meadows and their flowers, losing it often, but always finding it again, hovering over the new life like an angry ghost.

At last he found the source. A place where the grass was

higher, the flowers were brighter, the colours of life more wonderful.

And there were bones sticking out of the earth.

The bones were charred, often ending in sharp spikes of charcoal, the ends broken away by scavengers. But they were recognisable: the femurs and ribs and skulls of apelike bipeds.

Humans.

*Follow the scent of the humans.*

He saw the burnt-out husk of a tree in the middle of the bonefield, and guessed what had happened.

The human village. A fire, or a weapon discharged accidentally, perhaps when one of the humans tried to get away. The time tree jolted into action by damage, sending humans and Tractites into the deep past.

*Humans and Tractites.*

But only the Tractites had survived.

Not because they were better, Kitig realised. But because they had the guns, and the ruthlessness necessary to kill the defenceless bipeds.

Kitig knelt down in the long grass among the bones, and thought about that. After a while, he could no longer think: he could only feel.

Feel what the humans had felt.

Terror. Anger. Madness.

He took the nearest, sharpest, spike of bone in his hand, closed his three fingers over it until the pain stopped him.

He watched the blood flowing for a while.

I will never go home, he decided. Home is built on these bones. These deaths. These burnings. It should never have existed, and neither should I.

Then, very slowly, he began to walk back to the settlement.

He had a duty to follow, and at last that duty was clear.


Sam felt rather than saw the man-ape rising out of the grass. She felt the threat, heard the roar, and was running, dragging Jo with her until the older woman too became aware of it, a rust-red demon rising from the grass with a knife in its hand –

*A knife in its hand* –

And it wasn't a man-ape, it wasn't *Homo habilis* or *australopithecus*, it was *Homo sapiens*, it was *Jacob*, Jacob, running at them with the knife, screaming like an animal, and they were running again across the dry grass, and Jo must have realised because she was yelling –

'Jacob! Jacob! Stop this!'

But Sam knew there was no chance he would stop. He was the predator now and they were the prey and –

Jo screamed.

Jo was falling, sinking into – no *over* – the cliff and Sam was stopping, digging her heels and her hands into the ground and tumbling and she could hear Jo calling from below, shouting with pain, and the animal Jacob was standing over her with the knife and Jo was still screaming and Sam was fighting, a rabbit punch towards Jacob's crotch, but he'd dodged it, dodged back and the knife was coming down –

# CHAPTER 20

Sam stared at the blood pooling on the grass for a full minute before she realised that it wasn't hers.

Jacob was lying there, his body twitching.

Axeman stood over him.

The habiline was staring at the body with an expression that Sam took a moment to recognise.

Horror. Regret.

She made herself sit up, made her mouth work. 'It's OK. You had to do it.'

Axeman touched the body, shuddered.

Sam realised that Jacob's eyes were open, frosted windows staring at nothing. Her hand shaking, she reached down, awkwardly tried to close them.

It didn't work. They stayed open.

A cuff. Axeman had hit her.

She looked at him. 'Dead. Don't touch.'

Sam nodded, stood up, saw the blood splashed on her battered clothes. The air smelled of it.

Axeman pointed at himself. 'Dead.'

Sam shook her head. 'You're not dead! You – oh.'

He had a fever, perhaps. One of the symptoms of the virus. He had come after her, hoping for something – a cure? And he had found Jacob, and –

'Thank you for saving my life,' she said.

Axeman said nothing, just pointed into the ravine.

Sam frowned.

And then she remembered, and peered over the edge, and shouted.

'Jo! Jo!'
There was no reply.

Jo ran, cursing the thickets and creepers that crowded around the muddy remains of what was probably a major river in the rainy season. She'd tried walking on the river bed, but the mud that had cushioned her fall – and probably saved her life – had clung on to her bruised and aching legs, refusing to let her make any progress.

Yet she had to get back somehow, she had to get back up to Sam before Jacob –

Try not to think about that. Probably too late anyway.

Ahead, a tree. A scrambling, deep-rooted, many-branched snake of a tree. Jo didn't recognise the species – perhaps it was extinct in the modern world – but it should be possible to climb.

She tried to follow the maze of branches, to plot out a route that would take her to the top of the cliff.

Then she saw something impossible.

At first she thought it was carved into the tree, perhaps by Jacob; then she realised that it was in the rock behind the tree.

Letters. *Words*. Each one must be six feet high.


SAM – THE TA


The rest was hidden.

No. Not hidden. *Lost*. Cut off by a dark spur of rock. A basaltic intrusion: millennia-old magma, breaking open the fossil.

*Fossil. Fossilised words*.

I must have hit my head when I fell, thought Jo. I simply have to be seeing things.

A voice.

Faint, echoing, but unmistakably female.

Sam's voice.

Jo shouted back, but kept staring at the fossil. Somewhere behind her, there was a splash, a curse, and a habiline grunt. Jo frowned, turned, saw Sam and Axeman up to their knees in one of the muddy pools.

She started to smile, then saw the blood.

'Sam – are you –'

'I'm fine.' The younger woman was staring beyond Jo.

At the rock wall. At the words. Her name. SAM.

'Uhh – I think somebody wanted to leave a message for you,' said Jo.

Their eyes met, and they both started to laugh. Axeman looked at them in amazement.


As soon as Mauvril saw the blood on Kitig's hands, she knew. She had watched him come down from the hilltop, had watched the way he was walking, the way his head hung as if it had become too heavy, and she had suspected.

But the blood told her for certain.

'You found them,' she said.

Kitig looked up, stopped his slow, funereal walk a few yards from Mauvril. His night eyes flickered: even in the tropical daylight, she could glimpse the anger there.

Mauvril faced those eyes. 'We could have hidden them better, I suppose.'

Kitig pushed past her. Mauvril could smell the anger now, the fear and the despair.

'You knew we'd killed humans. I told you. You knew why.'

There was no reply. Mauvril turned and followed him down the paved road towards the command dome. Their hooves clicked on the coloured stone. She felt it slipping away from her: the future, the innocence and beauty she had tried to create from the fire.

'Kitig!'

He was at the door of the dome now, trying to get past the guards. They looked up at Mauvril, uncertain.

'Let him through!' she ordered. She increased her speed to a trot, caught up with Kitig in the entrance hall with its curtained-over pictures of death.

He was drawing back the curtains.

When he shouted at her, the sound was so loud that it echoed.

'*This* is your civilisation!' he roared. 'This is what you tried to hide from me!'

'I didn't try –'

Kitig ripped back another curtain. The city glowed, Tractites died.

'You hid it from our whole civilisation. You have made it unreal.'

Another curtain. Blood, death, misery.

'You can't blame me for –' She heard the guards trotting up, waved them back.

'The *Book of Keeping*. The Watchers. You're already doing it, aren't you? You're already writing the lies. "Just one threat. There's only one evil, one person who brings it. Everything else is dealt with by sweet reason."'

'You're not making sense. Would you rather have been fighting endless wars? Like all the other races, the Zygons and the Daleks and the Draconians and the Chelonians and the humans – is that what you want now? This way, we've got a head start on everybody else in this sector – practically every other species in the galaxy is still learning how to make fire. We can make all that space ours, and live in peace. For ever.' She curled the long fingers of her hands. 'Kitig, you've lived in that world. You *are* that world. Surely you understand?'

Kitig tore back the last curtain, stared at the images of death for a while. 'My world is based on a lie.' His voice was quieter.

'A small lie.'

'And death.'

'A few deaths.'

Kitig turned his head, and their eyes met.

'Let the Doctor go,' he said.

Mauvril closed her eyes. 'I can't,' she moaned. 'You know I can't.'

'Then I will leave your community. I will not live among murderers.' He walked past her, his body almost touching hers in the narrow passageway between the bas-reliefs of death.

Mauvril stopped him with a touch of her hand on the bare skin of his flank.

'You're my future. The future I want to build. Please don't leave me.' Her voice choked on the last word, became an incoherent sound, a child's terror at being left alone.

She felt him trembling. 'I'm sorry.'

Then he was gone.

Mauvril looked at the bas-reliefs on the wall. She looked at the Tractites in agony, the blaze of power from human weapons.

Then she made her decision.

* * *

They found another part of the message further down the ravine. Sam spotted it first. It was engraved on a different kind of rock, inverted, and weirdly distorted, the letters almost unrecognisable as such: but, now they knew what they were looking for, it was easy enough to work out what it said. There were two pieces, separated by a fault line:

ATED 1.07 MILLION YEARS BEFORE Y

and

ED INTO THE VOLCANO JUST BEFOR

'A million years before?' asked Jo. 'Before what?'

'Before now, I suppose. I reckon the TARDIS materialised in the volcano – no, that can't be right, they'd never have got it out. On the slopes?

A grunt from Axeman. 'There!'

He was pointing at the opposite wall of the ravine, at something that glinted in the sunlight.

More letters, smaller, made of patterned quartz set into the rock. Jo looked at Axeman, who was staring at the pattern with a curious expression on his face. He'd obviously realised what sort of shapes they were looking for. She wondered if the TARDIS had translated the words.

HE WILL FIND YOU. BEWARE ARMED
TRACTITES. I AM IN THE MAIN D

'Armed Tractites?' Sam seemed bewildered.

'I told you,' said Jo. 'They always turn out bad in the end. I'm more worried about who's going to find us.'

'There!' said Axeman again.

Sure enough, there were more letters, in the same quartz pattern:

BASALT

If only Rowenna were here, thought Jo. If only Rowenna were *alive*. She would know how to find more of the message. It must all be about the same age, from whenever the Doctor got stranded. He must have carved it lots of times.

'I've got it,' said Sam suddenly. 'The TARDIS is here! That's what he's trying to tell us!'

Jo turned, stared into the younger woman's eyes. Sam was actually jumping up and down, her face flushed, running her hands through her hair in excitement.

'It has to be here!' she said. 'It's obvious! Otherwise we'd never have been able to understand Axeman! And "volcano" and "basalt" – he must have landed it in the middle of an eruption, the dozy idiot.'

'"Beware armed Tractites"?' asked Jo.

Sam stopped jumping up and down, looked down at her muddy and battered trainers. 'Umm.'

'I think he got himself captured. "I am in the main d"? Is that "dome"? "Dormitory"? "Destructor unit"? And there's probably any amount of volcanic basalt round here and no way of telling how old it is. Even assuming it isn't buried under a thousand feet of more recent sediments. We've got to find more of the message, something more specific.'

'And we'll have to find it quickly,' said Sam. Her voice was strangely thick.

Jo looked at her, saw that her face was still red. So it wasn't excitement. 'Are you –' she began.

Sam nodded. 'I've got a fever.'

# CHAPTER 21

The air was drier here, on the slopes of the volcano. The land fell away to the west, showing Kitig a wide variety of landscapes: scarps, soda lakes, green swathes of forest on the rainward flanks of the hills, drier grasslands on the flats, all of them fading away into the hot glow of the afternoon.

He raised the crude chisel he had made from metal scavenged around the settlement, and resumed his work, hammering at the hard basalt, copying the square, awkward lettering the Doctor had palmed to him in the cell, all those months ago. He didn't know what the message meant – whatever translation system allowed him to talk to the Doctor didn't work for this script – but it didn't matter. The Doctor's instructions had been explicit.

Carve the message as many times as you can. In letters as big as you can make them. In as many different places as you can.

Kitig meant to do just that.

He meant to keep carving the message for the rest of his life.

Sam was struggling to think, but her hands were shaking.

No, she thought. I am *not* dying. I *haven't* caught one of Jacob's viruses. It's just a tropical fever – nothing serious – I'll shake it off and we'll go and look for the TARDIS and everything will be fine.

The ravine had widened out, the walls sunk down, the half-dry river come to an end in a muddy water hole. Sam was in the shade of a solitary tree. Jo was looking under a rock overhang on the other side of the water hole, where Axeman, eager to please, had found some new words.

'L, then another L, then "find her", then an O,' Jo reported. 'It's no good Sam, we could go on for ever like this. The message could be quite complicated.'

*I'll* find her? thought Sam. *You'll* find her? The Doctor sometimes called the TARDIS 'old girl'. Maybe he'd just said 'You'll find her' in an effort to reassure them. Or maybe O was the beginning of 'on', directing them to some specific place.

If only there were more *time*.

Sam closed her eyes, felt her bones ache. She felt more ill than she had at any time since a bad dose of flu at fourteen. Her thoughts were beginning to cloud up, get confused. If only she could get to some water – not the tepid, muddy, infected-looking water in front of her, but the cool, clear water of the cave in the habiline's settlement –

A hand, shaking her shoulder. 'Sam? Does the TARDIS still look like a police box?'

Sam looked blearily at Jo, nodded. 'Circuit stuck, or something.' She struggled to raise a smile. 'Least, that's what he says.'

Jo smiled back. 'I've thought of something.'

Sam sat up, swallowed a thick gob of saliva. Her throat hurt.

Perhaps it was just flu, or malaria, or something.

Jo was drawing with a stick in the mud at the edge of the water hole. Axeman crouched nearby, water dripping from his chin where he'd been drinking. He watched.

'Words,' said Jo, pointing at part of the picture. 'Like

those.' She pointed at the rock overhang.

Axeman nodded, then, chimplike, turned his head one way and then the other, scampered round the diagram. Suddenly he leapt up and shouted – an almost human sound.

'Home!' he said. 'Water home!'

Jo looked up at Sam and grinned. 'Let's just hope it's not a square rock.'

Sam stood up, then felt a sharp pain in her stomach. The world wobbled around her.

'Sam?'

'Just going to – sit –' muttered Sam.

Then her legs gave way underneath her.

Mauvril watched as the honour guards burnt the curtains on the cairn of stones by the river. They were in full armour, lights glittering, polish gleaming, their eyes respectfully turned away from their commander. These were the curtains that had hidden the pictures of death.

No. The pictures of *Tractite history*.

Oily smoke rose from the curtains: she remembered that they were made from some unnatural plastic fibre of human manufacture. Well, there would be no more of that. No more humans.

Kitig was a fool, thought Mauvril. A product of his culture. He'd never known anything but peace, civilisation, easy living. He couldn't accept his past, couldn't accept that all living was based on the blood of the dying. She ought to have him hunted down and shot – but she knew she couldn't bring herself to do that.

Which meant she had no alternative. She couldn't have Kitig wandering around loose and the Doctor alive. One day, somehow, Kitig might contrive to get the Doctor out. It was improbable, but not impossible. It was too much of a risk.

Whatever she felt about the matter, it was a military necessity now.

She was going to have to kill the Doctor.

Now.

She saluted the guards, turned away and trotted towards the main dome.

'Wake up! Sam! You've got to wake up!'

*OK, Doctor.*

'Come on! I can't leave you! They'll kill you!'

*Vampires, Zygons, hyenas, wolves…*

Water. Warm, weedy-smelling water, running down her face.

'Sam!'

Jo's voice. Sam wiped the water from her face, felt precious drops trickle down her throat.

Hands touched her face. Cool hands, bristly, smelling of water and earth. Sam drank. When the water was gone she sucked greedily at the wet fingers, searching for more.

The hands were gently removed.

She opened her eyes, saw Axeman knuckle-walking away, chimp style, to scoop more water from the muddy pool. Jo was looking down at her.

'Can you stand up?'

Sam frowned. Her body felt as if it was separate from her, somewhere below her perhaps. She was aware that it ached, that it was hot and shivering and seared with cramp.

She put a hand on the ground, felt cool grainy earth. Pushed, and found herself standing.

'I can stand. I can walk. How far do we have to go?'

'Back to the gorge I think.'

Axeman had returned with more water. Sam sucked it out of his cupped hands, still greedy for more.

'I'm not sure you should be drinking that stuff. You could catch typhoid.'

'The TARDIS has antibiotics. If we don't get to the TARDIS fairly soon I'm dead anyway.'

That sounds suitably cool, thought Sam distantly: 'I'm dead anyway.' It's probably better not to think about what it means, any more than I'm going to think about –

'If I fall over again, leave me. All right?'

Jo stared at her. 'No, as a matter of fact it's not all right. You're not –'

What would the Doctor say? mused Sam, blearily.

Try this: 'It isn't just you and me. It's the whole future of the human race. The future of everything. You *have* to get to the TARDIS and find the Doctor. You can't let me slow you down.'

Axeman was gesturing out across the yellow plain, towards the russet-coloured hill that was his home. Sam didn't need a translation: she started walking.

She felt as if she were pulling her own legs up and down with long strings, but the mechanism of her body worked. She moved forward, into the sun.

After a moment, she heard Jo start to follow her.

The eyes were just the same, staring at her from the same sunken sockets.

'You're here to kill me,' said the Doctor conversationally.

Mauvril said nothing. She could feel the weight of the human-made blaster she always carried, just as if it were the first time she had ever worn it.

'Kitig didn't like what he saw,' the Doctor went on. 'So he's gone and left you, so now you're going to finish me off, because you loved Kitig and you don't want to believe you aren't good enough to be his friend.'

Mauvril reached for the blaster. 'You're a danger to my species. To Kitig, to everyone.'

The Doctor closed his eyes. 'No I'm not,' he said. 'Just the opposite.' He sighed. 'You know, the real reason Kitig left isn't because you killed people, but because you're capable of killing people for stupid reasons like this. That's what he realised when he saw all those bones. Those people couldn't have hurt you –'

Mauvril pulled out the blaster, levelled it at the Doctor.

'You are very persuasive, Doctor. But I've met a lot of persuasive humans. It isn't going to work this time.'

'You're killing me because you're afraid.'

'I'm not killing you. I'm going to have you executed.'

'It's the same thing. It only means you're afraid of pulling the trigger yourself.'

Mauvril let her finger tighten on the trigger, then blinked her night eyes to show him the furious blood there.

'Only because I don't want to start a fire,' she hissed.

The Doctor's eyes met hers, and his mind seemed to bore into hers, digging out all the ash, the blood, the charred bones.

'The fire started a long time ago,' he said quietly. 'Don't you think it's time to put it out?'

Then he was moving, too quickly, the drip was wrenched from his arm, the blaster was out of her hand, skidding across the floor, and he was past her –

*But he was too weak for this he seemed too weak he must have planned it all – Kitig, the accusations, all of it – and he almost had me fooled there I was almost going to let him live again –*

And Mauvril was backing out of the cell, and the door was banging against her flank, trapping her for a second until she could fling it back open and then she was in the corridor and he was *gone gone gone where could he have gone?*

Mauvril felt the old, familiar fury building within her. The human had tricked her. He couldn't be trusted. So when she found him she was going to kill him.

Without hesitation.

Without giving him a chance.

The habs were lined up across the front of the gorge, hooting, grunting, screaming. Leaping up and down. Making gestures with their fists.

Scattered words of translation bloomed in Jo's brain: 'go', 'kill', 'evil' and 'death'.

Sam saw stone axes in some of the hands. She looked at Axeman, saw him waving his own axe high over his head. Jo stood behind them.

Sam turned back to the row of habilines, trying to ignore the sweat dripping from her face, rolling down her body. With difficulty she suppressed a violent shivering.

'Go!' 'Sick!' 'Kill!' 'Death!'

What would the Doctor do?

Yes. That was it.

'Life,' said Sam, pointing forward into the gorge. 'Life. In there. For all of you.'

Fifty pairs of habiline eyes stared at her. Gradually the crowd noises subsided. The habs began discussing among themselves, signing frantically. Some began grooming each other. Cuffs and barks were exchanged.

'Life,' repeated Sam, suppressing another violent shudder.

Axeman stepped forward. 'Life.' He too was pointing into the gorge.

Sam smiled. He trusts us, she thought. That's why he saved my life. She began to walk forward.

'Wait a minute –' began Jo.

But Sam didn't stop, just walked towards the habs, swaying a little.

They parted and let her through.

The rocks seemed to waver and shimmer ahead of her. Behind her, feet shuffled on stone. Sam looked round, saw Jo, Axeman. All the habs, slowly shuffling forward.

Jo caught up with Sam, said, 'Do you know where it is?'

Sam shrugged. 'Water. Home. Where do you think?' She pointed at the jumbled rocks that roofed the water cave.

The dark rock.

Basalt.

She began climbing the slope, flanked by several of the habs. Jo followed. The sun was still finding its way to the rocks around the cave, and they were almost too hot to touch.

Inside the cave, it was still cool and quiet.

Sam knelt at the water's edge, cupped water in her hands and drank greedily. Almost immediately she felt faint.

'No!' she muttered aloud.

She felt a hand on her arm: Axeman, pulling her up.

Jo giggled. 'It's ridiculous. For the last six days we've been stranded half an hour's walk from the lifeboat and we never even knew it was here.'

Sam smiled. Slowly she walked around the edge of the water, to the crevice at the back of the chamber.

Inside the crevice was a surface with a familiar texture. Wood. Paint. Then metal: the rounded metal of the lock.

Sam took the spare TARDIS key from her pocket, opened the door, and stepped forward. The door swung open ahead of her, and she almost fell –

Into a small, claustrophobic, wooden box.

For a moment she couldn't believe it. She pushed at the wood, felt the bare, smooth substance under her fingers.

'No!' Her voice. She hadn't been aware of speaking.

She turned, saw Jo, a faint silhouette against the light creeping in from the entrance to the cave.

'We're too late,' she said. 'Something must have happened to the Doctor. The TARDIS is dead.'

Then her legs gave way beneath her.

# CHAPTER 22

Jo hammered on the TARDIS, on the blank dead walls.

'You asked me to help you!' she bawled. 'You got me into this – you can't give up on me now! Let me in!'

None of it made much sense. The Doctor was a million years away, by his own account. The TARDIS was just dead wood, fossilised into the rock.

Behind her, Sam moaned.

'She's *dying*!' bawled Jo. 'You've got to do something!'

The Doctor could see the daylight streaming in from the entrance to the dome. There was only one guard, and he was talking anxiously into a communications device of some sort.

Good.

Keeping low, the Doctor moved towards the guard.

And stopped.

*Sam – dying –*

No! thought the Doctor. This shouldn't happen. *Couldn't* happen. He couldn't allow it.

He put all his energy, all his power, into feeding the telepathic link to the TARDIS.

*Magma moved, roared up from the throat of the volcano. Flowed down the slopes –*

Changed direction –

*Ash fell. Rock solidified, the pattern changing – changing – changing to allow a different future –*

And the TARDIS came to life.

The Doctor felt a cold circle of metal against the skin of his face. He opened his eyes, saw the Tractite guard standing over him. She was still speaking into the communications device.

'He's here. Shall I bring him to you?'

The Doctor couldn't hear Mauvril's response, but he didn't need to. He could hear her hoof beats approaching down the long passageway.

The light from the TARDIS dazzled Jo for a moment. Axeman jumped back, with a violent hoot of dismay.

Sam sat up, then fainted.

Jo leaned over her, slapped her face gently. 'We need you to operate the TARDIS,' she said.

Sam's eyelids twitched, but her eyes didn't open. Her breathing was fast, ragged.

Jo looked up at Axeman, who was cowering in the entrance of the cave, afraid of the light.

Fire. Of course. He thought it was fire.

'Nothing's on fire,' she told him. 'I need you to help me with Sam.'

The habiline moved forward, a foot at a time, watching the light. He sniffed the air, felt it with his hands.

At last he bounded down and picked up Sam's feet.

Jo lifted her shoulders, and together they bundled her through the door into the huge brassy light of the console room.

Once they had lowered Sam on to the floor, Jo looked around, trying to get her bearings.

It was hopeless. The TARDIS had completely changed. The time rotor was recognisable, but the rest was a jumble of dark rugs, brass surfaces, and an incongruous VW Beetle parked by the edge of a dark Persian carpet.

There were brass gods, ranks and ranks of clocks, shelves of books disappearing upward into infinity...

'I need medicine for Sam,' she said aloud.

The TARDIS didn't reply, but behind her a weak voice said, 'Try under the harpsichord.'

Jo had to grin. Trust the Doctor to put something as important as the medical chest in such a stupid place. She couldn't even see the –

Ah, there it was, almost drowned in a sea of a hundred clocks. Beyond the time rotor, across a rug littered with a model train set, several sorts of gramophone, and a chair with a crown on it.

She threaded her way across the floor, looked underneath the polished wood of the musical instrument.

A phonograph, a ticker-tape machine... Ah.

A green box with a red crescent on it.

She dragged it out and opened it, getting her hands covered with white dust in the process. The box had clearly been in the wars.

Inside were bandages, a hypodermic, some tablets, several bottles of tablets.

She read the labels. 'Paracetamol', 'Antibiotic (pre-resistant)', 'Antibiotic (post-resistant)', 'Antiviral (human, chimpanzee)'.

Well. Here's hoping. She opened the last bottle, read the instructions (the entire label was handwritten), and shook a couple of the tablets into her palm. They were pale-blue, like tiny duck eggs.

She crawled out from under the harpsichord, clutching the tablets. She was rather shocked to see Sam standing up, leaning on the console. She jumped over the train set, almost ran to the younger woman.

She held out the tablets. 'Take these.'

Sam looked round. 'Never mind me,' she said. Her teeth were chattering. 'We need to move the TARDIS. Now.'

She pressed a lever on the console, and the time rotor heaved.

Once.

Then it stopped.

Sam hit the console. 'No! You've got to go! You've got to get there!'

The time rotor remained ominously silent.

Jo stared at it, looked frantically around the console for anything familiar.

Switches, levers, buttons, pull-chains. A calendar display, currently showing:

HUMANIAN ERA: 2,569,878 BC

She thumped the nearest row of switches with her free hand.

Nothing happened.

And then the cloister bell began to ring.

Somehow he had got away again. One minute he had been on the floor, inside the doorway, and the guard behind him; then he had been underneath the guard's legs; then he had gone.

Mauvril charged out through the door, screaming abuse at the useless soldier.

The Doctor was running up the hillside.

She took aim.

'No! Mauvril! You don't –'

She fired.

A chunk of hillside vaporised, but the Doctor had moved, was moving crabwise towards the big gun that guarded the settlement from possible Earth Empire interference.

Mauvril muttered an instruction into her communicator, saw the gunner draw his hand weapon and take aim at the approaching figure.

'Only my personal timeline –'

Mauvril fired again, and the Doctor was rolling down the slope, away from the gun, towards her.

'– is holding all this together.'

Mauvril took aim again. The blaster issued a faint beep: it was out of charge.

The Doctor scrambled to his feet. 'You can't win, Mauvril. It can't work. Your beautiful future simply isn't real. It isn't stable. *It can't happen.*'

Mauvril took no notice. She clamped a new power pack on, then levelled the blaster.

The Doctor dived out of the way, but she'd worked out the answer to that trick now. She followed his movements for a moment until she was satisfied that she knew what his next dodge was going to be.

Then she pulled the trigger.

Axeman watched the two stranger-women hitting the breaking stone.

He knew it was a breaking stone, a thing to make stone tools with, just as he knew that this place around it, with its vastness and strange colours, was nonetheless a sort of nest. The place itself was telling him, even though he couldn't hear its voice. It was telling him not be afraid, constantly telling him that.

But he didn't need to be told. It was as if he had made a journey inside himself, had travelled beyond fear, beyond wonder.

He looked at his hands. So many strange things. Sounds, lights, deaths.

But this at least was familiar.

These women could not make the stones ring. He didn't know why, but it had always been the way. Only some people could make the stones ring, could break them in the way they must be broken to make tools.

He advanced towards the toolmaker and raised the stone axe in his hands.

The older woman turned to him, screamed, 'No!'

But Axeman knew what he was doing.

He angled the axe against the light from the central column of the strange breaking stone, and then brought it down with all his strength.

The beam from the blaster became visible about halfway to the Doctor. Then it spread out, shimmered – and Mauvril cursed. Where had the alien managed to find an energy shield?

But no.

The air was thickening, becoming opaque. A wheezing, groaning sound filled Mauvril's ears, confusing her.

Then the blaster cut out, and an all-too-familiar blue box materialised in the air in front of her.

Mauvril felt her heart stop for a moment. The time machine hadn't been destroyed after all. The Doctor had only been waiting for the appropriate moment to recall it.

Everything had been a sham. And now the Doctor was

taking away everything she'd worked for, everything she'd lived for.

'You can't do this to me!' she yelled.

She realised that the Tractite who had been guarding the dome was standing by her side, staring at her. She looked over her shoulder, saw the gunner trotting down the slope. 'Get back to the main gun!' she yelled. 'Cover that machine!'

The soldier scurried back up towards the huge black shape of the gun.

The *human-made* gun, thought Mauvril, with a sudden shock. Perhaps he can override it... She was already at full gallop, struggling to get another sight on the Doctor.

She saw him, running down the slope towards his machine.

'Doctor!'

He looked up, flashed her a smile. 'Sorry, can't stop, people to see, things to –'

Mauvril shot at him, but he dodged. She shot again, gaining on him all the time.

He had almost made it when she caught up with him and put the blaster against his head.

He struggled.

'Not this time, Doctor,' she said.

The door of the space-time machine opened.

'Take the tablets.'

Jo's voice was fuzzy, surrounded by a bell-like echoing. Her face seemed huge, and at the same time very far away.

Sam took the tablets in her hand. They felt tiny, and

cold. She put them in her mouth, swallowed –

Instantly she began to feel better. Jo's face became normal, human, smiling.

'Are we there?'

Jo nodded, gestured at the scanner screen. Outside, the Doctor was running down a grassy slope, fire exploding to the left and right of him.

'Usual situation,' said Jo wryly, running for the door.

Sam ran after her.


Axeman saw the two stranger-women running towards the door.

He smelled the fire outside, the danger.

This wasn't right. They would be hurt.

He started after them, pushed them aside as they reached the door.

Outside he saw the rainy-season grass, and a jumbled creature, half human, half animal: a dream thing, a spirit.

Had he entered the world of spirits?


Mauvril saw the figure emerging from the door, saw the dark fibrous body armour, and without pausing for thought turned the blaster on it and fired.

It exploded into flames, screaming.

'No!' bawled the Doctor, struggling to get free.

'Too late,' muttered Mauvril, watching the charge light of the blaster, waiting for it to be ready for the next shot.


Sam saw Axeman's burning body fall, saw Jo with her hand against her mouth, white with shock, saw the Doctor outside, struggling in the grip of an armoured Tractite.

Have to act. Have to act *now*.

She crouched down, burst out of the door at a run, zigzagging wildly. She could see more Tractites charging up the slope, one heading for a sleek black object which could only be some kind of field gun.

If they get to that, we're finished, she thought.

She started through the long grass, ignoring the Doctor's shouts, ignoring the thought of *Axeman in flames and this is dangerous* –

The gun getting closer, the *gun*, she was going to have to do something with the *gun* because the galloping Tractite was almost there, almost on top of her –

She dived on to a curved surface, made of a white substance curiously like polystyrene foam, saw a wheel and a large green button in front of her.

*Wheel for steering. Button for* –

It was obvious enough. She rolled the wheel, saw the barrel of the gun pan towards the galloping Tractite.

It didn't stop.

Sam put her thumb over the button, and was going to shout a warning, a threat, the simple word 'Halt' – but there was *no time* to shout, *no time* to give the alien fair warning, she just had to –

*Fire* –

The Tractite exploded.

A leg clattered down on the metal shield between Sam and the barrel of the gun. A solitary leg. There wasn't even any blood, just a seared lump of meat with a piece of charred bone sticking out.

*The smell of burnt flesh and the humans are coming, they're coming to kill us all* –

She heard the Doctor's voice. 'Sam! Try not to use –'

Sam couldn't take her eyes off the leg. The hairs were standing on end, the muscles were still twitching.

A Tractite spoke. 'This is Commander Mauvril. Whoever you are behind that gun, I've got your spy here. If you value his life, you'll get out from behind the gun now.'

'Don't take any notice!' The Doctor. 'Mauvril, I can take your people to Tractis. In any time you like. But you can't alter the whole universe just to get revenge on –'

Sam could hear the footsteps approaching. She had to do something now.

But all she could do was stare at the dead meat she had just killed.

'I can't kill anyone.'

It was her own voice, she realised after a moment.

'I won't kill anyone.'

That was better. At least it sounded as if she was making a decision, instead of –

*I – have – just – killed – someone.*

The Tractite spoke again. 'Good. Then come out from behind the gun.'

She could see two more Tractites approaching through the grass.

A hand touched her shoulder. She jumped, almost fired the gun by mistake.

Then saw that it was Jo.

'You might not want to kill anyone,' said Jo quietly, 'but I want to go home.'

She aimed the gun at the advancing Tractites, and pressed the firing button.

The ground exploded. The Tractites jumped back. Pieces of steaming soil spattered down around them.

Gradually, there was silence.

'Right!' bawled Jo, the shout almost making Sam jump out of her skin. 'Everyone into the TARDIS. Now. And leave your weapons outside.'

The silence continued.

Sam saw that Mauvril was talking into a communicator. The Doctor was underneath her, one huge hoof pinning him to the ground.

'Jo –' she began.

Jo turned her head, and at that moment the metal shield of the gun blazed with light.

Someone had fired at them with a hand weapon.

Sam saw Jo's hand hit the firing button, saw the leg of the Tractite she'd killed vanish into a ball of fire.

In front of them, the Tractite dome crumpled, like a building being demolished. Flames shot out of the falling wreckage, and pieces of debris began to tumble through the sky with all the crazy slow motion of a large explosion. Then Jo was turning the gun, and a searing column of fire was moving along the river valley, destroying everything it touched.

Sam felt Jo pulling her down behind the gun shield, but all she could look at was the Doctor. The Tractite holding him was balanced on her back legs, her front legs pawing the air, her arms holding the Doctor against her body.

A wall of dust and flame hit them, and an instant later slammed Sam against the ground.

After a few seconds she realised that she was alive, unhurt, and the dust was settling. But this time there was no silence, only a ringing in Sam's ears.

She scrambled up, ran across the grass towards the

Doctor. The grass had been knocked flat, and was full of small pieces of smoking wreckage. The big Tractite was lying by the TARDIS, her body still, apart from a few flickers of light from her armour.

The Doctor was kneeling beside her, his hand touching her neck.

'Oh, Mauvril,' he said sadly. 'You should have changed your mind sooner.'

# CHAPTER 23

Sam watched Jo and the Doctor arguing.

'It was an accident! They were firing at us! I was just trying to stop them –'

'You were trying to kill them!'

'I didn't have any choice!'

'Yes you did. I had the situation under control –'

'You were about to be killed and we were about to be killed! You think that's under control?'

'Mauvril was ordering them to stop firing! She was listening to me at last! She was talking to them when she – when you –' He shook his head. 'Jo, Jo, Jo, Jo, Jo! I thought you knew better than this!'

There was a silence. Suddenly the Doctor swayed, almost fell. Sam darted forward, but Jo had already caught the Doctor's arm. Staring, Sam became aware of how terribly thin the Doctor was. His face, under the battered sun hat, was so gaunt as to be hardly recognisable. Had the Tractites been starving him?

'I wanted to go home, Doctor,' said Jo at last. 'I wanted to be certain that home was still going to be there.'

Then she walked away into the TARDIS.

After a moment, the Doctor went after her.

Sam looked around at the smoking chaos that had been the Tractite settlement, smelled the reek of burnt flesh. She began to feel sick. Had Jo really intended to cause this much destruction? Or had she just panicked and fired the gun in the wrong direction? Sam remembered the gun turning, the column of fire moving across the Tractite settlement. What had Jo said? 'I wanted to be certain that home was still going to be there'? Had she *deliberately* destroyed the entire settlement?

Sam realised that she could never know for sure. All she was sure of was that the magic had failed this time. The Doctor hadn't intended the Tractites to die. He'd tried to prevent it, even at the risk of his own life and hers. But they'd died anyway.

The sound of hoofbeats startled Sam out of her thoughts. She looked around, saw a Tractite galloping down the hillside.

*A Tractite –*

She scrabbled around in the flattened grass by the gun for a weapon, any weapon, anything she could get hold of that could kill the alien before it could kill her.

She found a handgun, perhaps the Tractite commander's. She aimed it at the galloping creature.

'*No!*'

The Doctor's voice.

Sam hesitated, realised that the Tractite wasn't wearing any kind of armour, that he looked very familiar –

'Sam! I'm not armed! Please, whatever has happened here, let us talk –'

Cautiously, Sam lowered the gun.

Kitig addressed the Doctor, who was standing in the doorway of the TARDIS. 'I carved the messages. I caused –' He gestured at the carnage, then shook his head.

'You didn't cause anything. No one did. It was an accident.'

Sam frowned at the Doctor, then realised: he was covering up for Jo.

For her, too.

She wondered if he knew that she'd fired that first shot. That she'd *killed* –

She shook her head. No time to think now. Later, it would have to be later.

'I can take you anywhere,' the Doctor was saying to Kitig. 'Except –'

'Except home. I know.'

There was a silence. Sam became aware that the smoke and dust had cleared, that the sun was shining again on the flattened grass. Flies were settling on Mauvril's body. Soon it would be vultures, hyenas.

'I think I will need to stay here. The messages –'

'There aren't enough of them. I know.'

Sam stared at the Doctor. Surely he wasn't going to let Kitig stay *here*? Here, all on his own?

'I didn't want to make you do it,' said the Doctor in a low voice.

'Doctor, you can't!' protested Sam. 'You're sentencing Kitig to –'

The Tractite stepped forward towards her. 'To what I would prefer to do, Sam,' he said gently. 'I don't want to go to some other Tractis. I don't want to live in a world dominated by humans.'

'No Tractite would,' said the Doctor.

The Tractite swung his head around, away from Sam, and she saw his night eyes flicker open.

'Can you –' He broke off, perhaps afraid to continue.

Sam wasn't sure what he was asking, but the Doctor knew.

'I can't prevent the invasion of Tractis,' he said. 'That would just set up another paradox. But I'll do what I can to clear up the mess afterwards.'

Kitig lowered his head. 'Thank you.'

'No, no, thank *you*,' said the Doctor. 'Thank you for saving my life. And Sam's. And Jo's.'

There was a moment's silence, then Kitig said, 'Will you help me bury them?'

The Doctor looked around the remains of the Tractite settlement, then looked at Sam.

She nodded. Knowing that she was going to have to face what she'd done, the stranger she'd killed.

'Of course we'll help,' said the Doctor.

# CHAPTER 24

The Imperial Throne was vast. The Imperial Throne was gold, it was diamond, it was spun pearl; it was viridian, opal, agate, majolica; it was carved fake ebony, it was spun Draconian galaxite, it was rainbows of stars and the plasma of nebulae imaged in spheres of perfect crystal. The canopy of the Imperial Throne was as high as the great rainforest trees that no longer grew on Earth; the pillars that supported the Imperial Throne were as huge as those of the long-eroded Parthenon; and the air in and around the Imperial Throne was filtered and scrubbed until it was as clear as the air of mountain valleys had once been, before they had been filled with the detritus of centuries of industry and war.

In the middle of the Imperial Throne, on cushions of velvet and satin and force and air, sat the tiny, wrinkled husk of a woman.

The Empress.

Her hand still rested on the controls of the gold-and-obsidian magnaflux drive which had brought her instantaneously from Earth to Tractis: the single most powerful machine in human history, controlled by the single most powerful human ever to breathe the air of Earth.

Sam stood, refusing to kneel.

She wasn't a subject of this woman. She didn't care what everyone else was doing. The humans, the Earth Reptiles, Draconians, Ice Warriors, Zygons, GórEntelech, even the Tractites, all knelt around her, thousands of them in every kind of regalia under the almost infinite marble-and-gold ceiling.

But the Doctor had remained standing, despite the weakness of his still-emaciated body. So Sam was standing too.

She felt the Empress's eyes on her, felt the power for a moment.

At last the shrivelled woman spoke.

'It pleases us to allow the request of the Protectorate of Eta Centauri 6 to assume the status of a Duchy Royal, with the name of Tractis. It further pleases us to appoint as our personal representative to the Duchy the Earth Reptile Ambassador-General Menarc.' A pause. The eyes in the shrivelled face blinked. 'So *decreed*, by authority of the Voice of the People of the Empire, on this day –'

'You know who she reminds me of?' whispered the Doctor. Sam shrugged. 'Old friend of mine. Name of Davros. He used to make decrees as well, and it didn't do him much good either.'

'Never met him,' said Sam.

'I hope you don't.'

Sam glanced up at him, frowning. There had been a definite undertone to those words, as if –

Well, think about that tomorrow.

The cheering had started around them. The Empress's decree didn't sound like much, but in practice, the Doctor assured her, it amounted to independence.

In here, the Baron's Residence, the cheering was muted, but outside, Sam knew, it would be like thunder, the joyful braying of a thousand million horses.

But when Sam looked up at the Doctor's face, there were tears on his cheeks. Amazed, she put a hand on his arm.

'What's the matter?'

'Mauvril,' said the Doctor. 'Kitig. All the others. I wish –'

Sam bit her lip. 'So do I.' She still hadn't told him about that first shot, about the Tractite she'd killed. Somehow she couldn't quite bring herself to do it.

She tried a smile. 'At least we could save the habilines.'

It had almost been worth it, seeing the smiles on those nearly-human faces when the Doctor had walked among them, feeding them with vaccine-filled jelly babies.

The Doctor jogged her arm and Sam realised that the Earth Reptile Ambassador-General had begun to speak, announcing free elections and the formation of a planet-wide council.

'Will it work?' muttered Sam as he droned on.

The Doctor shook his head. 'The Earth emigrants will form a separatist party and assassinate council members. The Empire will be falling apart by then, but it will try to restore order. Unfortunately, it will make a mess of it. Hundreds of thousands of people will be dead at the end of the war. But after that, it will get better. It *will*.' A pause. 'Anyway, it's the best I could do.'

Sam looked down at the jewel-studded floor, then took a grip on the Doctor's arm and began to steer him towards the exit.

'What's the matter?' he asked. 'Where do you want to go?'

She flashed him a grin. 'Come on,' she said. 'There's a world to explore. And whatever's *going* to happen, they're happy today.'

The Doctor looked at her for a moment, then smiled back.

It was like a moment of sunrise.

She led him outside, beyond the marble gardens and sterile air that blew from the palace, under a blue sky and along the coloured streets of a vast and happy city, where the billion inhabitants of a small, grassy planet were celebrating their freedom and their victory.

# EPILOGUE

His arms aching, Kitig lowered the chisel and surveyed his final work.

Yes. It was good enough. The letters gleamed in the quartzite, catching the low-angled light of the early-morning sun. They were perfect, each shape clear, glass-edged, defined by the sparkling mineral; yet, despite the simple blocky shapes imposed on him by the necessity of keeping the message clear, they were somehow also infinitely complex. Individual crystals were like stars, forming and re-forming geometric patterns as Kitig moved his head from side to side.

He had often wondered which one of the messages they would read. Or which *ones*, if Sam was right. But lately he had come to realise that it didn't matter. They were only looking for the message, the crude words. The subtle differences of texture in the stone, the fine variations in the way it cleaved to the different chisels he had used, the different effects obtained by striking the stone in different ways – all these would be lost on them.

It didn't matter. Kitig knew the truth.

He looked up at the time tree, towering over the block of quartzite. Most of his later messages had been inspired by the tree, by the flowing colours of its branches, by the tiny, glittering, clusters of its seeds. Lately it had become the base of his operations: he had ventured out on to the plain less and less, remaining here by the lake shore where the tree had appeared, as the Doctor had promised it would, a few days after the TARDIS had left.

'Take care of it,' he'd said, 'but don't let it outlive you. It's too dangerous.'

Kitig had promised that he wouldn't fail the Doctor, that he would ensure the Time Tree died: and now he knew the time had come to redeem that promise. He could feel the cancerous mass inside him, growing, pressing on his heart. He could feel the blood leaking from his veins, oozing through the spaces between organs. And, too often now, he felt the deep, hard, idiot bite of pain.

He walked up to the tree. It was huge now, and crowned with feathery orange leaves. The light from its branches was visible even in the day, and at night it blazed like a beacon, keeping all but the bravest animals at bay.

He reached up to the lowest branch. The seeds had been building up for decades now, a dark encrustation, covered with the poisonous slime that kept the birds and insects at bay.

Kitig gripped them firmly, and pulled.

The sky changed to night. Kitig opened his night eyes, saw a pine forest in faint moonlight, a huge shaggy beast watching him with glowing, terrified eyes.

It roared at him. Birds clattered out of the trees.

Kitig reached up and scraped away more seeds.

Further back. More light. Low, heavy, clouds. A barren plain.

More seeds, and he was under water, in darkness, his body shouting with pain at the sudden pressure of the ocean above him. He scrabbled at the branch, and the pressure was gone, replaced by a clear blue sky, sand, and a sail-backed reptile about half his size, scuttling away with a hissing sound.

He rested for a while, enjoying the silence, the clear dry air.

Back again: barren land, an ashy taste in the air.

He took a deep breath, knowing that the air was going to be unbreathable soon.

The next two moves took him under water, then to a lake shore. The lake was scummy with life, and bubbled. The ground trembled constantly.

The time tree was changing, Kitig noticed. The light in its branches had dimmed, concentrated itself in knots around the seeds he was pulling away.

He saw the exposed roots beneath his hooves, tendrils of light.

No time for curiosity now.

He scraped more seeds off, felt heat on his skin. His lungs were bursting for air.

*Now*! he thought. And: this is for you, Doctor. For all that you gave me.

And for all that you took away.

He pulled away the last of the seeds on the branch he had chosen, and the sky blazed with light.

Just for an instant, the bulk of the time tree protected him from the direct light of the newborn sun, and Kitig could see the vast plane of glowing rock and dust that was slowly making Earth and the other worlds of the solar system.

Pain blossomed as the burning, dying tree drifted away and the raw sunlight hit him.

I wish I could make worlds, thought Kitig. I would make each one a new shape, a new beauty, a new chemistry and colour.

*Endless variation…*

*The alien figure on the low bed was asleep. The skin was softly lit by the TARDIS nightlights, but the eyes seemed welded shut.*

*Recuperation, he'd called it: the Doctor had been asleep for nearly twelve hours.*

*Sam watched the sleeping figure for a long time, wondering how she could tell him. Finally she spoke.*

*'I know you wouldn't forgive me if I told you. I don't expect it. And I know you're right not to forgive me. I could have shouted a warning. I could have fired in front of him.*

*'But I want you to understand.*

*'We've both got to live here, so it really makes a difference, what I do, what you think about it. Whether we can forgive each other.*

*'I need to know. I need to know if it was possible to have acted in a different way.*

*'The way you would have acted. That's the way I want to act.*

*'Doctor? Can you understand me?*

*'Are you still asleep?'*

*The figure on the bed didn't move, barely even seemed to breathe.*

*Sam turned and silently walked away, back to her own room and the guilt and the bad dreams.*

*Perhaps she would tell him about it in the morning.*

Also available from BBC Books:

# DOCTOR WHO
# THE EIGHT DOCTORS
By Terrance Dicks

Booby-trapped by the Master, the Eighth Doctor finds himself suffering
from amnesia. He embarks on a dangerous quest to regain his lost
memory by meeting all his past selves...

ISBN 0 563 40563 5

# VAMPIRE SCIENCE
by Jonathan Blum and Kate Orman

The Doctor and Sam come up against a vampire sect in present-day
San Francisco. Some want to coexist with humans, but some want to go
out fighting. Can the Doctor defuse the situation without bloodshed?

ISBN 0 563 40566 X

# THE BODYSNATCHERS
by Mark Morris

The deadly Zygons are menacing Victorian London, and only the
Doctor's old friend Professor Litefoot can assist the time travellers in
defeating them. But why are the Zygons stealing the bodies of the dead?

ISBN 0 563 40568 6

Other *Doctor Who* adventures featuring past incarnations of
the Doctor:

# THE DEVIL GOBLINS FROM NEPTUNE
by Keith Topping and Martin Day
(Featuring the Third Doctor, Liz Shaw and UNIT)

Hideous creatures from the fringes of the solar system, the deadly Waro,
have established a bridgehead on Earth. But what are the Waro actually
after – and can there really be traitors in UNIT?

ISBN 0 563 40565 1

# THE MURDER GAME

by Steve Lyons
(Featuring the Second Doctor, Ben and Polly)

Landing in a decrepit hotel in space, the time travellers are soon
embroiled in a deadly game of murder and intrigue – all the
while monitored by the occupants of a sinister alien craft…

ISBN 0 563 40565 1

# THE ULTIMATE TREASURE

by Christopher Bulis
(Featuring the Fifth Doctor and Peri)

The Doctor and Peri become involved in a deadly tresure hunt
on the planet Gelsandor.

ISBN 0 563 40571 6

# BUSINESS UNUSUAL

by Gary Russell
(Featuring the Sixth Doctor, Mel and the Brigadier)

SenéNet is no ordinary company: its managing director deals in
death through alien technology, and the Brigadier is his captive…

ISBN 0 563 40575 9

_Doctor Who_ adventures out on BBC Video:

# THE WAR MACHINES

An exciting adventure featuring the First Doctor pitting his wits
against super-computer WOTAN – with newly restored footage.
BBCV 6183

# THE HAPPINESS PATROL

The Seventh Doctor battles for the freedom of an oppressed
colony where misery is a sin.
BBCV 5803